RA

Your Link To The Streets

©2012 by Ra Jones
Library of Congress

Edited 12/2012
First print 2/2013

BOOKSTORE DISTRIBUTION

ISBN 978-0-9889623-0-9

StreetLink Publishing
PO Box 24270
Belleville, Il. 62223

Printed in the United States of America

Acknowledgements

I never thought that I would write a book. I guess the talents that I possess have been given to me by the, "Most High" and it is limitless when you put your mind to doing something. I greatly appreciate my God and all that he has blessed me with.

I would also like to thank my family and friends who helped to make this possible. Everyone involved is considered family, whether immediate or not. You're family and I thank you and love you for all the time and effort you put into this project.

I greatly appreciate Crystell Publications for their work and care in helping those in need turn over a new leaf. You have helped them to find a different way other than the deadly grips of the street life. You are appreciated and will reap many blessings for your work and unselfish contributions.

To my Mother, Father, Sister, Brothers; Huti, "Thank you." Trell, Tez, Timeka, Cristobal Guiterrez, Amerson-Bey, Derkky, Geno, Q-dog, Coop, Beymo, TRB,and Dirt "Thank you." To my DC crew: B, Pat, Rick, Jack, "What up." NY: Box, Cess, Meat, "What up. Mexico the Valley: Sanchez, Juan Sanchez, Hernandez, Herrera, and my partner Hector, "What up."

I have to thank and cannot forget the one who helped the most, Dynell at Shelton Graphics. You have many blessings coming man, straight up. Thanks to Marion designs for helping design the cover, I appreciate it. Special tribute to my boys, Richard Prude Jr. and Jermaine Lockridge (RIP), I miss you guys.

To all of those I did not mention, you know who you are, love, peace, and keep it 100. Everyone enjoy!

Ra Tem Jones Sr.
Trell is Sadik.

Prologue
East St. Louis, IL.

"Somebody's at the door," I told my boy Rell.

As I got up to walk in the kitchen, he eased over to the counter and grabbed his P-89 Ruger. Rell was the type that was always trigger happy and ready to blow. We'd been grinding out of houses on the Eastside of St. Louis for years, so we knew the East was real grimey. Like with a lot of the surrounding projects, the East was infested with niggas that just didn't give a fuck. And although we hustled on both side of the bridge, the East was the best. It was an area where you could get money and not have to worry about cops that often.

We were raised on both sides of the Mississippi River, so when we met, we clicked almost right away. During our time as homies, we'd ducked a few police raids, and also opened new spots just as soon as one got raided. Usually if we were anywhere else, we'd only get 2 to 4 weeks of work out of a house, but on the East, you got 2 to 4 months.

The local police just didn't care. So when MEGSI raided your house, which was a local task force, you didn't have to worry. But, if the U.S. Marshals ran in on a nigga, you better be concerned.

We were down to our last and had been hitting the highway lately, looking for a connect. The nigga we were copping from, SL, named after the Benz, because he coped one every year, had been taxing our asses. We were paying anywhere from 24 to 26 a brick, and my nigga Mike, kept telling me to go out West, but I was leery about fucking with muthafuckas I didn't know.

It had been like that for awhile. Well, until I ran into Jessica and found out that she worked for Southwest Airlines. She was a flight attendant, and an old friend of mine from High School. She said she had a friend named Heather that may be able to help me out. See, Heather flew often, actually a little too often, and one day she end up conversating with her on a flight. She found out she was from Phoenix, and it had been plenty of times when Heather invited Jessica to come there with her to get some real money. That had my attention; but I was really listening when Jessica said she knew Heather had some form of connections with the streets down there. Then she said she may be able to talk her friend into putting something together for me.

I took advantage of the opportunity and asked Jessica would she be cool with bringing something back for me every now and then. I watched as she paused to think about it for a few minutes, then agreed.

I was in the back, when Rell opened the door. Through the dark of night, he tried to make out a face. All he could see was someone standing with his hands in the front pocket of a hoodie. He seemed to be tugging at the pockets, trying to pull something out. Rell lifted his P-89, sensing the intruder was pulling for his gun.

He wasted no time, BONG—BONG-BONG. I heard the shots and quickly grabbed my gun from my shoulder holster and ran into the room. As I approached the porch, Rell was standing over someone.

BONG—BONG BONG.

"Motherfucka!" he yelled shooting at another person who was running away from the scene. I looked at the guy running. He was holding his arm. '*Rell must've hit him*', I thought, taking off after him.

"Wipe everything down and roll out!" I yelled back at Rell.

While in pursuit, I cut through the houses, trying to cut the guy off at the corner. I could hear his footsteps coming up the side of the house. I peeked around to see him. He was looking behind him to see if anyone, gave chase. I stepped from behind the house, waiting on him

to turn around. He was stumbling, trying to keep his balance as he wobbled from side to side, holding his wound. With his gun hanging loosely in his other hand, I lifted my weapon and aimed it at his head. When he turned around, I fired.

BONG!

Seconds later, Rell pulled up. "Nigga, let's roll," he yelled.

We had to get out of there before the neighbors called the cops. I hopped in the car and we quickly sped off.

"Who the fuck was that?" I asked, tucking the gun into a bag. I was preparing to toss it out of the car and into the river, once we crossed the bridge.

"It was one of them niggas from the hood, I don't know his name though, but I recognize him from hanging around." Rell answered.

That was the first robbery we had ever dealt with. All the other spots were either shut down by the cops or we either got tired of the traffic and moved before the cops ever came. I knew one day we would have to face the black mask. I'm just glad we were prepared for it.

"Yo, before we cross the water, swing by the store," I said. "I needed something to drink. Something to take the edge off of what just occurred."

Rell quickly pulled over at a One Stop and I jumped out.

"What up nigga, where you been. We ain't seen ya," Mike said.

Mike was one of the owner of the One Stop liquor store on 25th and St. Clair, which was on the Eastside. He ran it with his brother Mamun. They were real cool and two of my closest friends. "I thought you were dead or something," he jokingly interjected.

He always joked like that, so I wasn't offended. Besides, I fucked with him and his brother tough, because they kept it real and didn't take no shit from no one. They weren't the type to hide behind the glass and talk shit. As a matter a fact, the store had an open counter, and they didn't mind coming across it to get it on with anyone.

"N'all, nigga you know I been on the grind." I said, grabbing a bottle of Patron off the shelf. Rell took out some money to pay Mike.

"That's what I've wanted to talk to you about," Mike said, looking at the money in Rell's hand. "Ballas, ya'll need to quit fucking with that dude, SL, or whatever that niggas name is. He came in here the other day all on the phone. He was talking reckless as a muthafucka, too.

I think he might be them boys dog, straight up. Ya'll need to quit fucking with him and get your own shit." Mike insisted, appearing paranoid, which was good sometimes. He didn't trust anyone at all, and for that reason, I trusted his judgment about others. Also, not to mention that over the years, neither Mike nor Mamun had ever steered me wrong.

"Don't trip my nigga, I will." I poured the Patron in the cup, mixing it with a Monster energy drink, then took a sip. "We gon get our own shit soon."

Chapter 1
Phoenix, AZ.

'It's hot as hell', I thought to myself, getting out of the rental car to stroll into Houston's. Houston's is an upscale restaurant in Scottsdale, AZ. I was told to sit there until Heather arrived with the connect. I didn't even know what she looked like, so I glanced around the restaurant, and then took a seat at the bar to order a drink. This was my first time in Phoenix, and my first time trying to shop a real connect. I wanted Rell to come, but while I was gone, he wanted to maintain the streets. I didn't know how long this would take, so I told him, I wasn't coming back until we got on. I had been waiting for a while, so I ordered something to eat. I kept looking around the restaurant, occasionally wondering to myself if my behavior seemed suspicious. It looked like all the people in the restaurant were citizens with good jobs. Actually to be honest, they all looked like they had nothing to do with my line of work at all. As I sipped my Mojito. I saw a group emerge from the back of the restaurant. They had already been in here for just as long as I had and was switching seats. They were all Mexican, well dressed, not like the type with the big belt buckles. They had style. Two of the men had on jeans, with Gucci loafers and button up shirts. The other men who were dressed in black jeans and t—shirts sat around them as if they were guards. There was a female with them who got up to approach the bar. She headed right in my direction. I watched as she made her way through the aisle. Her jeans complimented every curve of her body, and she looked like one of those models out of a magazine.

'Damn.' I thought to myself, watching her smile, as she motioned for the bartender. I glanced back at the others; they were all sitting out of earshot, so I figured I would holla at her. I tapped her elbow softly, waiting for her to look up. When she turned around and faced me, I spoke.

"Como se llama?"

She smiled, looking surprise at that fact that I could speak Spanish.

"Heather," she answered. "my name is Heather."

Her response brought a quick expression of surprise to my face; especially once I realized that was the chick I was here to meet. I extended a hand.

"Tyrek, but you can call me Ty," I introduced myself. She was bad, and the group she was with looked like they had exactly what I was looking for.

"O.k. Ty, nice to meet you. Jessica said that you were handsome," she smiled.

"Am I handsome enough to take you out?" I asked, looking back at the table to see if she was being closely watched. I didn't know if she was fucking with one of the men or what, but her beauty had me not wanting to pass up that statement. "Now if you're fucking with one of them, we ain't gotta kick it here. Maybe I can fly you to St. Louis and we can play there." I added.

She walked up close to me and placed her hand on my chess. Slowly she rubbed from my pecks down to my stomach.

"Ooh, you got a private jet you wanna fly me to Saint Louis on?" she reached up to pop my collar. I felt like she was mocking me. "Look Papi," she continued, flipping my collar back. "To answer your question, I am not fucking one of those dudes, but they do have private jets, and I have already been to Saint Louis before, so I don't think you are reppin the "Show —Me" right, because you have not shown me anything thus far," she smiled, glancing over at the table where her group sat. Out of nowhere she winked. I caught it, but paid it no mind. I just figured she was only being sassy. I smirked a cheap grin and chuckled at her comment.

Heather had more going on than just a body and a pretty face, she also had an accent that was sexy as hell to me. I wanted her, but I had to keep in mind that I was there on business and not pleasure. Once more, she looked me up and down, and then informed me that I needed to wait at the bar. I sat back down and took another sip of my drink. I was trying not to finish it, because one thing for certain, I didn't want to get tipsy in unfamiliar territory. I had to stay as clear minded as possible. I watched her pretty ass walk all the way back to her seat, until she sat down. Once she got back with her group, I noticed as she leaned over to whispered in one of the guys ears, one of the guys look my way.

Realizing he'd focused in on me, I lifted my glass in harmony and turned back around.

After a few minutes of sitting, I asked the bartender for the check. I was so engaged in what I was doing, I didn't notice one of the guys from the group as he walked up and took a seat next to me. When the bartender brought the bill, he waved it off. The bartender quickly took the bill back.

"Como te Va?" he asked, which meant how is it going. I turned and looked at him then looked behind me to see if there were any of the guys in the t-shirts standing behind me.

"What's up, I'm cool." I said, relaxing myself to give him complete eye contact, which would assure him that I was serious.

"Just wanting to talk, dat's all." he said.

"Talk! I don't do too much talking unless it's something to talk about," I hinted, not wanting to just come out with questions about work. Hell, this was our initial meeting, so I didn't trust him, and I'm sure he didn't trust me.

He chuckled.

"You see her Senor?" he asked, looking at Heather, " I say to her look, there goes the man you say is looking for something," he took a sip of his drink. "Something that may be worth talking about." When he put his drink down, I noticed the watch he was wearing. It was a Audemar Piguet. He noticed me looking and smiled. "You like?"

"It cost five hundred grand, it's one of two like this one."

"Yeah, that's tight." Right then I knew he was serious business. A business that I wanted in on.

"Yen conmigo, come with me." He ordered, getting up from the stool,~the men in the back got up also. They hurried over to the door and we walked outside. Heather stayed in the restaurant. As I hit the remote for my car, he looked at the rental I was in. "Leave your car." he ordered.

'Damn', I never got a chance to ask if he wanted me to follow, I thought to myself.

One of the men opened the back door to a Navy blue S55 Mercedes Benz and looked at me. I got in and was offered a cigar.

"Naw, I'm straight," I said. "What they call you?" I asked.

"Why, I didn't ask your name." he said.

"I'm sure she gave you my name."

"Your name was of no importance to me. What was of some importance was if you were wired or was a cop."

Yeah, she was sure to pop my collar and rub down my shirt for a reason. I guess she was checking me for a wire tap….I thought. Okay, now that makes since. – so that's why she winked.

For the rest of the trip we didn't say much. As we road, I couldn't help but wonder where we were headed. I glanced out the window at the scenery. It had already taken us over 30 minutes to arrive at the destination. And since the trip was so long, I couldn't help but think, *it better be gold on the other side of this trip.*

Finally, we pulled up to a 3-story home. You could see the chandelier that hung in the foyer in front of the spiral staircase. At the entrance of the home were marble floors with paintings all on the walls. As we entered a room with a bar and two sofas, I noticed there were several guards inside of the house. The man I'd been interacting with most of the trip offered me a seat and a drink.

"Have a Tequila, Cabo Wabo." His words seemed more like an order than a question to me. "So what's your profession?" he asked.

"I thought you knew," I said not wanting to blatantly admit to dealing drugs.

"I know you have the aura of a dealer, but I see something more to you." He eased his glass on a table and fixed his cufflinks. "So where are you from?" he queried.

"St. Louis."

"Saint Lou-es," he said, dragging his accent. "I have a friend in Saint Lou-es, we do business there. It may not be good to mix business in the same area."

"Yeah, well we may never bump heads, St. Louis is pretty big - ya know. Besides, whoever this friend is, he ain't reaching too far around town, cause it's hard to get something good now and days." I was starting to get impatient and uncomfortable. I didn't know where I was, I was in a house with all these strangers, and was talking to a motherfucker that thought he was Pablo. "So what's up, you wasting my time or what?" I added.

"Calm down my friend, impatience is no good. Although for one, I am very impatient when it comes to my money. I don't like talking on the phone at all, prefer in person. And never bring no one here to meet me. If you don't see me, then it's no deal; understand. And let this one sit well with you," he paused then leaned in closer to my face. "Never rat, that would not do anything but get your family killed," he insisted, staring at me. I knew he was looking for a sign of weakness, but I didn't flinch.

"Good! Now that we're on the same page, where's the work at." I said, staring back, as I sat my drink down. He chuckled.

"I like dis one," he said to the other men in the room. "What hotel are you staying at?"

I looked at him a little suspect, then I gave him the room number and the extra keycard. After explaining to him my plans for getting the work back to St. Louis, he gave me a better deal. The best part of it was that I didn't even need money up front. I was warned not to be in the hotel room between 10 and 11pm.

"It's best you no see," he said, as we arranged for me to get 20 kilos for 12 thousand each. We also negotiated that they'd get 2 grand for transporting the work to the U.S. "Also, only contact me by Instant Message or text, whenever I flew into Phoenix. Other than that, no contact," he cautioned me, and then ended with these last words, "One of the perks of Mafia Mexicana is that I will and always can find you."

I didn't let him know this, but in my mind, I couldn't believe that I had just landed a deal with the Mexican Mafia. I was just looking for a connect, but it turned out to really be gold on the other end of the trip.

"Take Senor Ty back to his car," he ordered one of the guards.

I got up out the chair. We shook hands and I walked out front with a big balled Mexican to the Benz.

"I thought names weren't important?" I asked, realizing he had just said my name.

"No my name is of no importance." He said, "Now have a good time and I will send you over a gift tonight," he added right before he stepped back into the house.

Once we arrive at the restaurant, I got into the car and sat there for a moment. I was tired as hell. That Cabo Wabo was wearing down on my ass. I didn't want to turn it in though, so I drove the city route back to the Hotel. Phoenix was pretty big. There was the main street between the numbers and avenues. Both where on different sides of town, and I was staying at the Marriot Residence Inn, in downtown Scottsdale. I was riding up Indian School Blvd., when I noticed a car tailing me closely. I turned down another street at the spur of the moment to see if the car would follow. When it did, I had to think quickly.

Because I was in an unknown area, I didn't know what to do without a burna, and the fact that I didn't know anybody didn't help. I quickly busted a U-turn and pulled up alongside the car.

'Fuck it,' I thought wondering if I was being set up. I had no way out, and I couldn't see shit through the tint of the other cars windows. Right when I was about to floor it, Heather appeared.

She was laughing at me.

"Bitch, You could've got fucked up!" I yelled, wondering why the fuck she was following me.

"By what Papi. You don't even have a weapon. We searched your car," she giggled. "You don't like your present or something?" Once I sat back to calmed down, I began to notice the cars slowly passing and honking, due to me blocking the left lane. Heather looked around at the cars also. "Papi, you no like?" she asked again.

"Yeah, follow me." I responded, looking at her pretty ass.

We made it back to the hotel, and I copped another suite so that I wouldn't be in the way while they made the drop. Soon as we got in the room, she went into the bathroom and came out in a thong.

"Damn," I said out loud. Her curves were amazing. I tried to maintain my composure, but she was tempting.

"Now let's see if the "Show-Me," can show me a good time," she said, unbuttoning my jeans. "Mmin," she moaned. My dick didn't even hit the air, it went straight out of my boxers and into her mouth.

"Shit!" I moaned, quietly trying to last. She was choking and gagging like a porn star.

I knew if I didn't pull out, I was going to explode. I can't even count the number of times I wished I had a pill, or some X to fuck her like I wanted to. Her looks alone were enough to make any man cum. And though I wasn't cut up, just more like alright, I still took my shirt off. Without pause, she rubbed her fingers up my abs to my chess. Then she took my hand and placed it behind her head, urging me to force my dick further into her mouth. I pushed as hard as I could, forcing her to gag, cough loudly, and then she placed both of her hands on my thighs, trying to pull back.

Tears came to her eyes from the gagging. When she pulled back, I shot warm protein all up in her mouth. She swallowed, then wiped away the little that ran down her lip.

"Damn, Papi that was a lot, you no fuck often." she laughed.

She thought I was dead after I shot off, but she had me back hard soon as she touched me. I bent her over and began pounding her from the back like I was trying to kill her ass. The more she yelled out in that sexy accent, the harder I tried to hit. She came so hard, she started shaking and trying to get away from me. She was putting her hands behind her, trying to stop me from digging deeper into her, but I kept going until I shot all over her ass. I could tell she was ready for me to bust again too, cause as soon as I did, she fell over on her side on my king sized bed.

"Fuck Papi, Damn! I never came like dat!" she held her stomach. "You are a winner."

I went to the bathroom to wipe off, and put my pants back on. When I came out, she was on the phone ordering room service. I couldn't help but stare at how fine she was. I mean, I knew she was really off limits and that we could never have more than this; because though I didn't say, I knew she was only here to keep a eye on me, and I was cool with that.

"Order me the Tilapia," I said, lying next to her on the bed.

Once our food arrived, we ate and fell asleep. About three hours later, I awoke to the sound of my phone buzzing on the dresser. I looked over to see Heather still asleep. She was sleep naked with her ass in the air and legs spread open, almost like and invite. I shook my head and looked at the phone. It was Rell.

"What's up, my nigga." I answered with excitement in my tone, because I realized I hadn't told him about anything yet.

"Shit, what up with you. You al-ight?" he asked. I could hear females in the background, so I knew he must have been out in the clubs.

"Yeah, I'm good, everything's cool-" I replied thinking about the drop. "Hold on nigga, Imma hit you back!" I whispered, not wanting to awaken Heather.

"What up, you straight?" I could hear him yelling into the phone, as I hung up. I was already in motion to discontinue our call, so I didn't respond. I slid out of the bedroom, put on my pants, crept to the other suite, and slowly opened the door. I entered then looked around for the work. Instantly, I checked the closet, noticing a suitcase. I slung it on the bed, opened it up and looked inside. I felt around the edges in the bottom of the compartment, and I felt something hard. I pulled it up and there it was; 20 kilos, tightly wrapped. I was excited, so I hit Rell back right quick to tell him about our deal.

"Yo, we straight nigga!"

Chapter 2

Early that morning. I had to get the work to Jessica before she boarded for work. I was worried about Customs at first, until she inform me that she had a brief relationship with the supervisor over that department. She assured me that she had everything under control as long as the number of carryons didn't get out of hand.

During her training, she got real familiar with the entire staff. She new police security, customs agents, and air marshals. Just to be frank, if you asked me, she'd probably already fucked them all. I didn't care, she could fuck the world as long as the work was safe.

After a few successful trips, the connect took the product up to 50 kilos. Heather would fly in to St. Louis occasionally for her own personal needs with me. I just figured she was keeping a close eye on the operation, not catching feelings. She had all the bitches jealous, and niggas frequently watched us whenever we stepped out. But no matter how envious anyone was, I still couldn't see myself with her, because she was too damn demanding at times.

"Papi don't do this, Papi, don't do that!" Damn her!

Real talk, she was only good for fucking and showing off. Tonight we were planning to show off at the Loft nightclub. This was an upscale spot in downtown St. Louis, off Olive Blvd. I threw on a fresh pair of Ed Hardy's, along with a pair of Gucci sneakers, a jacket and a t-shirt. I didn't like necklaces that much, so I went with the 2.2 carat trillion cut earring and a diamond Franck Muller watch. I had just coped a Maserati Quattroporte from my man TQ, so I pulled up in front of the club and got out.

TQ owned a nice dealership out in Baden, so he could get you anything you wanted. As we walked away from my whip, everyone just kept looking at my ride that was sitting on 24-inch black floaters. I had all eyes on me. Feeling like that man, I walked around and tossed my keys to one of the Valet guys at the door. At 5'll, 175lbs, my dark skin with my low wave cut gave me extra confidence. I ain't gon' even lie, I stepped inside straight feeling myself. Immediately, I looked around to find my crew.

Rell was already in the club. He noticed me entering and waved his hands in the air to get my attention. As I made my way over to Rell,

I noticed this chick with her friends in the corner. She was nice looking; actually one of the baddest I'd seen in St. Louis. By the way her hair was cut, she reminded me of Halle Berry, with a Serena frame on her. I had never seen her around before, and that was the type I liked. She stared me down as I walked by. I made a mental note to go over and introduce myself, once I finished talking to Rell, and we got settled in.

"What up nigga," Rell yelled over the music. He stood to hug me and was about 5'l0, 170lbs. Rell was light skinned with braids, and was an O-Dawg looking as nigga. "What you looking at?" he asked.

I knew not to tell Rell about the chick in the corner. He would have only tried to bag her first.

"Nothing; what's up with yall? Why y'all over here with no hoes." I asked, making my way around to shake hands with the rest of the click.

Although me and Rell hung close, we still had a crew that we were loyal to as well. Most of our guys were from Mont, Edgemont. We were also the youngest out of a well respected click of older hustlers. The guys that were with us tonight, all hustled for us.

"Nigga wave some of that cash and pop some of these bottles, get some hoes over here!" I said excited. Man, this was a long time coming. We were finally out of spots and into major distribution. So, it was a celebration for me.

We started offering drinks to every chick that walked by and before you knew it, the entire club was over our way. It was trick shit, but I wanted to politic and kick it. I didn't know I was being watched by Easy and T—Mac, who had been keeping a close eye on me since I'd entered the club. T—Mac was the friend my connect spoke about.

"A, I heard that nigga and Heather been kicking it a little too tight." Easy said to T—Mac. Little did I know, Heather was a regular for everyone that copped from my connect. T-Mac even dealt with her at one point. And just by me being seen with her, he knew just how deep in the game I was. Easy continued, "Yeah I've seen them out at Bristols and shit, too."

T-Mac was from an area called the Mac, on the Southside of St. Louis. The set started from a street called Accomac. The set was called

2-7 Mac. He had been in the game for a long time and was paid. Very popular and very feared. Easy, his right hand, was one of the reasons T—Mac was a feared man.

To stay on my toes, I was glancing around like I normally did in the clubs. I saw T—Mac looking at me with a firm stare. When I looked again, he raised his glass to me, as if to tell me to come over. I didn't think nothing of it, the game was all about rubbing elbows every now and then. With no sense of urgency to speak with him, I waited until the club was near closing before I made it over to his area. If it was something other than business, I wasn't worried, because I stayed strapped. T—Mac saw me approaching and walked away from his crew to talk with me in private.

"New money," he said, shaking my hand. I had been touching some guy's hands on the Southside, off Magnolia. So, I already knew where our conversation was about to go.

"What up?" I asked, looking him in the eyes,.

"Shit, I see you doing good for yourself. You could be doing better if you were fucking with the right mafuckas." He leaned against the bar and stared off at some chick. She stopped in front of us to pull her skirt down; apparently it was too short to cover all of her ass, or she was desperately trying to get some attention. I was focused, so she got nothing from me, and T-Mac just shook his head and chuckled.

"Who is the right people, and how you know I ain't fucking with them already." I looked off, noticing Rell. He was locked in on our conversation just waiting for anything to jump off. I could also see T—Mac guys watching us. Tonight we were outnumbered, but it didn't matter to me. If anything popped off, T-Mac was getting it first.

"You know who the right people are," T—Mac gave me a serious look. "Let's say we have lunch tomorrow, we can meet at Friday's, downtown." While he talked, I signaled for the valet to get my car.

"Yeah, Friday's downtown, tomorrow, I got you." The valet pulled up with my car. As T—Mac and I made our exit, a crowd of niggas followed. The valet came around and tossed me the keys.

"That's you?" He questioned, looking at the Maserati. I tipped the valet and got in the car. T-Mac nodded his head in approval.

"Yeah, this me," I boastfully replied, and then sped off, hitting the sunroof to throw up the dueces.

Through the rearview, I could see T-Mac leaning over to say something to Easy. I didn't know what he said, but I knew I had to stay alert.

My phone started buzzing in the console. I picked it up, and it was Rell.

"You straight nigga? What the fuck was that all about?"

"Shit, we'll rap about it later. What you about to do?" I asked.

"I'm bout to shoot over to the Eastside, you know what's up," he said. He was on his way to pick up some late doe. You had to catch these niggas on club nights sometimes just to get what was owed to you. Especially before they started tricking that shit off.

"Yeah, I'm bout to shoot through the Mag after I switch whips," I said, popping open the glove box to slide the gun on my lap. "Don't go in before I get a chance to holla at you." I added. Now I knew Rell, so I knew he would get into the clubs and lose track of time; especially since the clubs on the East didn't close until six in the morning. "Make sure you answer the phone nigga."

"I got you nig, Imma pick up."

I hit Highway 70 to 270, on my way out to Sheryl house. She stayed in Chesterfield. Once I got there, I called up the lil homies from Magnolia. They were trying to cop, they had a twenty four—seven spot and would be out all through the night. They wanted to get at me before I went to the club, but I promised I would holla at them once I left.

"Lil Derrty, what's good," I answered in the phone, pulling into Sheryl driveway. "Imma be there in a few," I said, getting out of my ride.

I switched Sheryl's whip with mine. And because she stayed in a very upscale community, it was common to see nice cars riding through the area. As I hit the garage door, I saw the bedroom light come on soon.

"Damn." I didn't want to wake her ass up.

She was cool, but she nagged too much. But because she was independent with her own shit and good looking, I fucked with her. She even had a banging body, and I liked that in a woman. Sheryl opened the garage door with her hair pulled back in a ponytail. She was in her nightgown that slightly opened and revealed her shaved pussy.

"Why didn't you call first, Tyrek. You can't be poppin up over here." She cautioned.

"What! Girl take yo ass back to bed. I'm bout to switch cars real quick." Sheryl had a black Infiniti FX35 with tinted windows, which was far more low-key than the Maserati.

"Then what am I supposed to drive, Tyrek?" She questioned, walking out into the garage to grab her keys.

"What the fuck you think you gon' drive," I snatched away from her.

"Oh, you gon' let me drive your car?" she asked, smiling and holding her hand out for the keys.

"Yeah, and don't be in the city in my shit. Straight up,"

I warned her, giving her the keys. I wasn't worried about her driving the car. She was a county chick who hardly ever went into the city. I got in the car and started it, and then she came around to the driver's side to give orders.

"Don't bring my car back empty like you always do," she fussed, walking back into the house. I waited until she closed the door, then pressed the button to open it. Then I hit the trunk three times, popping open the secret compartment. Rell and I had secret compartments stashed in everybody's car we used. Any giving day, they could be riding around with bricks and don't even know it.

The dashboard passenger airbag popped open, revealing a brick and a semi-automatic 45. I closed it back and pulled out the garage.

Chapter 3

Tre stood peering down the block. He was waiting on the big homie to come through so they could get back on with their product. Most of the homies were out clubbing. Bella and Him were the only two out on 3100 Mag that night getting money. They stayed on the hustle, that's why I liked them niggas.

"Nigga you get that change together, the big homie said he'll be through in a minute." Tre said to Bella.

Bella shot back into the house to get the money ready. He seen some cars coming up the street, one of the cars past, honking the horn. It was some niggas from around the hood. They were probably riding by in a stolo, which was a stolen car. The other car pulled up and asked for some pills. Tre placed one hand on the gun that was hidden inside the pocket of his jacket, and another on the pill bottle. He ran down to serve them. He knew walking up to the car was a mistake, but he wanted to clear the block before I pulled up. He noticed it was one of the homies from the Mac.

"Oh, what up homie, what's good." Tre said, taking his hands out of his pocket. "I ain't know who you was. What you trying to get?" Tre asked. He was talking about jars, 100 pills in each bottle at 500 a pop, because he didn't sell singles.

"Let me get two." The driver said.

They were in a blue Impala
with dark tinted windows. It was hard to see through the tint just how many others were in the car. Tre reached in to grab the money, and was blind to the AK-47 pointed at his chess from the backseat. The rear window came half way down as Tre yelled to Bella.

"Yo! Bring me two jars!"

When he turned back around, the first thing he saw was the fire bursting out of the barrel.

BONG-BONG-BONG.

Bella quickly spun around from the sound of the shots. As soon as he was facing Tre, he witnessed Tre's lifeless body drop to the street. He tried to jump off the porch, but couldn't get down in time.

BONG-BONG-BONG-BONG-BONG_BONG_BONG.

Bella fell from a slug to the back. As he heard the door opening, he was nervously trying to reach for his gun. He heard the footsteps approaching, and before he could get a shot off, the AK hit him seven more times. Afterwards, one of the guys bent down to grab the bag of money that was in Bella's pocket.

"Leave it," Easy said, wanting to send a message to the new breed flunky, whom he was testing.

"Nigga this money," the youngster said, reaching down to pick up the bag.

He felt the barrel press to his neck, as he retrieved the money. Before he could say anything, BONG. His head blew in the wind. I kept calling Tre's phone, but he wasn't answering. When I got to their block it was swarming with police cars, officers and yellow tape. I saw a addict standing nearby watching the scene. I motioned for him to come over, and then asked him what happened.

"Somebody came through and killed Tre and Bella. Man, they're dead - they dead," he kept repeating.

He also kept repeating the cars that came through the hood that day, and who they might have had beef with. I knew he was probably pointing me in the wrong direction, because he mentioned some dudes that wouldn't hook him up for five dollars one day. I reached in my pocket and gave him ten dollars then I pulled off. It was hard to figure out where that could have come from. The set they were on was gang related, and so it could have been a hit done for a number of reasons.

I took the dope out of my lap and stashed it back in the compartment. Right after closing the lid, I phoned Rell.

"Meet me on the Landing in 20 minutes."

***

" Sup, the new breed ain't work out, huh?" T-Mac asked as Easy walked thru the door alone.

"I knocked that nigga. He was hard-headed."

"Where Shai at?" T-Mac questioned, peeling back the curtain.

T-Mac was about 6ft, 230lbs. He was a light-skin, clean cut guy. Shai, the woman he was inquiring about was a very close business associate, or at least that's what she called them. She helped T-Mac out by keeping his business afloat thru her connection with the Cartels.

"I dropped her off, she's deadly with that choppa Fam. She cut that nigga down like a tree," Easy said.

Easy was short, about 5'8, with a stocky build. His hair was twisted and he was dark-skinned. Most didn't know that Shai and Easy had a brief affair some time ago. But, it didn't last long, as with any relationship Easy had ever had, which was because he didn't trust anyone.

"Yeah, that bitch is deadly," T-Mac added and took a seat. "A, I need you to be up early at the Airport."

"Airport?" Easy wondered.

"Yeah, I need you to pick up Heather."

***

Rell leaned up against the car with his hand rubbing his chin. I walked over to him and informed him about what happened to Tre and Bella. We were now both in deep thought, because it could have been over some gang related shit, but after that run in with T-Mac, I couldn't take anything likely. Tre and Bella, were bangers, but they also were getting money, and they wasn't copping their product from T-Mac. By Magnolia being so close to Accomac, T-Mac had to know they were moving good over there, and probably wondered where the dope was coming from. Finally, after almost wrecking my brain, I broke the silence.

"Nigga, we also got Jessica flying in tomorrow, so we don't need no beef right now," I said. "Shit, I'm trying to get this money," I briefly paused to hear how Rell felt about the situation, but he didn't say anything. "Let's move this shit, and at the same time stay on point," I insisted, opening my car door to get in. It was almost dawn, and I needed to get some rest. "Imma holla later." We shook up and I drove off.

It was almost 5 in the morning. I was tired and didn't feel like driving out to the county. I had recently purchased a Loft, downtown above the Kitchen K Restaurant, on 10th and Washington. I loved staying downtown; due to it being so many women staying in the lofts now and days. When I parked, I walked across the street to the back entrance. While walking up on my building, I saw a black Mercedes Benz ML500 parked with a slim chick bent over in the window, talking with someone. The windows were tinted so dark, I couldn't make out the person.

I looked on and then strolled pass, not knowing if she was talking to some dude or not. Before I could get in the building, the female leaning in the window said something.

"Excuse me," I didn't think she was talking to me, so I didn't pay her any mind. Then she called my name, "Tyrek." I turned around with a puzzled look.

"Who is you?" I asked.

"My friend wanna holla at you." she said, stepping aside.

"A-ight girl, Imma holla at you," she said to the female sitting in the Truck.

She looked at her then walked back into the building. She was fine. I don't like skinny chicks, but she was beautiful enough to make an exception for. Her long wavy hair and light complexion had me assuming she was mixed. She was dressed in a tight pair of sweat pants with a shirt that hugged her breast. For her frame to be so small she had very nice curves that defined her shape, she was bad. She gave me a quick glance as she walked pass, but it wasn't one of interest, it was different. I looked back at the truck, but I still couldn't make out the female inside, and I wasn't about to walk up on the ride, so I asked her to step out.

The door opened and I quickly noticed it was the same chick from the club that I saw the other night. She walked around the truck, and up close I noticed she was thick, had a big ass, huge firm titties, and was beautiful. She was wifey material. She leaned against the truck, and flirtatiously smirked at me.

"How you doing?" she asked. I couldn't get pass how sexy she was, she was far more sexier than any woman I've ever known.

"I'm good, you the one that was at the Loft last night?" I asked.

"Damn," she looked off, giggling to herself. "You had that many bitches getting' at you that you had to refer to me as the One."

"N'all, I was just making sure it was you that's all, because you're the one I was looking for. So you wasn't just the one, you was the only One." I stepped a little closer.

"I saw you, you were talking with someone, so I ain't say nothin," She stepped closer . "So when you saw me, why you ain't say nothin' to me," She licked her lips. "I know.... you shy?"

She had something about her that was unique. She was very intimidating and game conscious.

"I ain't never shy, just cautious."

"Why you gotta be cautious, you a wanted man or something?" she backed away, looking at me up and down to study me.

"Yeah, all the women want me, so I gotta be cautious not to let the wrong one get me." I gave her the same stare up and down. "You might be the wrong one." I added with a smile.

"Okay Papi," she smiled.

"Papi? You Spanish, Latino?" I asked curiously.

"Yeah, my father was Mexican and my mother Black. Why?"

"I just asked - that's all; just curious."

"Mmm, it's all good." she said, reaching in her purse to pull out her phone. "So when are you gone take my number, so you can call me and ask me about taking me out?" she handed me the phone. I grabbed it from her and logged my number in her phone book.

"How you know I wanted to take you out?"

She laughed at my question.

"Cuz you want a shot at this ass, but from the looks of it, yo game might not be tight enough for me," she teased.

"Shit, what you doing tomorrow night?"

"Nothing so far."

"Call me around 6 tomorrow evening and we'll see how tight my game is," I suggested, giving her the phone back. "What's ya name?" I asked walking behind her to the other side of her truck. She turned around to catch my eyes fixed on her ass.

"That's all you want?" she asked, getting in the truck.

"Unless you want to give me something else."

"Well for now, I'll give you my name," she winked. "Hi, - I'm Shai," she closed her door. "Imma call you soon."

Without another word, she pulled off.

Chapter 4

Rell was out and rolling by the afternoon. He mainly hustled over on the Eastside, while I hustled in the Lou. He fucked with some cats in Edgemont, but I didn't fuck with Edgemont or Charlie Park period. The niggas over that way were too grimey for me. While out that day, he pulled up to one of the homies spot over on 84th Street, and placed a call.

"I'm outside," He said, then hung up. A few seconds later, Los came running down the stairs and hopped in the car.

"I only got 20-," he said, and immediately, Rell cut him off.

"Shh," Rell whispered, pointing to the On-Star device in the car. That's one thing I liked about Rell, he didn't trust a motherfucker. And that's how he kept me on my toes. Rell started throwing numbers up with his fingers, as a form of speaking in kind of like a sign language.

"Nigga, you too paranoid. Man what I owe you, Cuz-."

This time Los was cut off with the barrel of a lemon squeeze Parabellum. Rell placed the barrel to his head, then reached over to lift up his shirt, checking him for a wire. While looking him over, he noticed and grabbed the phone from his waist. Quickly, he looked at it, and discovered it was off.

Afterwards, he threw the brick at him and held a three up signaling to Los his tab. Rell then waved his hands, motioning for him to get out. Los grabbed the brick, tucked it in his pants and held up the peace sign. As he walked away, he hoped Rell forgot about the incident. He got out of the car and watched as Rell left.

I was just getting out of bed around one o'clock. I had forgotten all about Sheryl. I knew she was probably everywhere in my car, and considering that half the day was gone and she still hadn't called about her car confirmed that she was content. Realizing that I still had to get my car and go to a meeting with T-Mac, I got dressed and headed out.

I drove past Friday's to see if he was there, and once I saw his Bentley GT, I pulled up behind it, and walked inside. He was sitting at the bar with a female, who had her back to me. When I walked up, I noticed she looked familiar. T-Mac saw me, so he swung around.

"What up big—time," he smiled sarcastically. "I know you met this bitch Heather already." He glanced over at Heather, who held her head down to avoid making eye contact with me. I couldn't hold my expression, I was mad as fuck. *I just wonder what this bitch done told him up to this point.* And the fact that she couldn't even look at me, assured me that she told him something. "So you ready to fuck with the right people or what?" he asked, offering me a stool. "Have a seat, we need to holla."

"About what?" I questioned.

"I gotta deal foe ya."

"A deal! Man, you ain't got it like that," I expressed, but since Heather was here, and I felt like she probably told him everything, I had no need to hold back. "I'm straight where I'm at." I added.

"Oh, I doubt that. Nigga, you still small time. You ain't been in this long enough, ya line been cut. I'm ya new line now," he raised his glass. "..Big Homie." he added with a grin.

I knew then he had everything to do with what happen to Tre and Bella the night before. He was playing hard, and it was starting to piss me off, so I got up.

"Whateva Nigga! I don't know what the fuck you talking about, so we'll see." I started to walk away, but he said something that grabbed my attention.

"Mafia Mexicana." I turned around. "See the Mafia Mexicana have ladders, and you ain't even on the first step yet," he added, "Me, I been in this shit for years. I ain't too far from the roof. This ain't just St. Louis, Nigga, this is My St. Louis. I love it when niggas think the Southside is all I got. So when I say to my people, run this lil nigga's line through me, they ain't got no problem." He leaned in a little closer to my face to put emphasis on his point. "The deal is the same, just a little side fee.. say 'bout a hundred stacks."

I sat back down, and looked him in his eyes. I was being extorted and black balled. *This nigga is asking for it.* And I knew I couldn't do anything in a downtown restaurant, but if I was anywhere else, I would have blew that niggas top back. I had to stall him to try to confirm this shit.

"Yeah, well I ain't gon' be able to do that one right now." I said, getting up from the table.

"Right now, huh. Well soon you'll find out that you ain't gotta choice," T-Mac added while I was walking off.

I knew this nigga was gone be a problem, but I didn't think this much of a problem. Stepping on my toes was definitely crossing the line. He should have at least known that much.

"Why did you call Tyrek here?" Heather angrily asked, spinning around in her stool to face T—Mac.

"Stipud Bitch, shut the fuck up foe I knock yo ass back around in that stool," T—Mac gritted. "You just better be lucky I ain't let Elan know that you've been flying out here, falling for this nigga."

"I'm no falling for no one!" she hissed. She knew falling for anyone was a big mistake. Especially with those that are in business with the Cartels. It could have gotten her killed. Her only job was to watch and seek out the weak links.

This was what she attempted to do with me, but she knew deep down inside that she had fallen in love with em. She dreamed about me and her running away from this lifestyle and starting a family together. But in her mind, she could never allow me to know her feelings, because she feared I would not feel the same way. So she kept her feelings to herself and flew in as often as possible to be by my side.

Now all her dreams were catching up with her.

Chapter 5

Downtown back at the Loft apartment, I went over the details of my meeting with T-Mac.

"Fuck dat shit nigga, dude got to go!" Rell was pacing back and forth.

"Imma fly out there tonight on the Red Eye to see what's going on with this shit. Did Jessica get up with you on the last demo?" I asked, hoping that T-Mac wasn't informed about Jessica also.

"N'all, I took care of that, but right now everything cool." Rell sat down on the couch and grabbed the remote.

My phone started buzzing on the counter. It was a text coming in from Shai. I picked it up and started smiling as I read it.

I see your ride downstairs, you up there at the apartment? I'm in the building. Is it cool for me and my girl to come thru.
I texted back: Yeah it's cool.
I put the phone back down and took a seat on the couch.

"Nigga watch these chicks that's about to come through here," I said, tapping him on the leg. "They bad as a motherfucker, and I'm already on the thick one."

Five minutes passed, and then they knocked on the door. I opened it and Shai was smiling from ear to ear. *'Damn'*, I thought to myself, watching Shai walk into my apartment. She turned around and pointed towards the female that was with her. I slightly remembered her from the first night we met.

"This my girl Moni," she introduced her friend.
"Hey, what up." Moni waved, taking a seat down on the couch.

I looked at Shai, noticing that she was checking me out. She stared me up and down, from my Louie Vutton sneakers, to the Seven for All Mankind jeans I rocked, all the way up to the wife beater that masked my six pack. She could tell my body was toned, and from the way she was staring, thankfully, I had hit the gym up earlier that week to work off some of the frustration I was dealing with.

"Who plays the XBOX?" Moni asked, scooting over on the couch to grab the controller. Shai looked at me, I shook my head.

"I don't play games," I grinned. "Rell does," I said, pointing at him to Moni.

"Oh, you don't play either? Good cuz you and Shai made for each other," Moni laughed. "So Rell, you gon play me in a game?"

"Yo ass can't play no mafuckin XBOX." He smirked, getting up to turn on the game.

"What, you wanna bet?" Moni gave him a threatening look.

While they were discussing the bet, Shai pulled me into the bedroom. I leaned against the dresser, and she came in and closed the door behind her. She walked up to me and started to kiss my neck. I grabbed that ass so fast, I caught her off guard. I slowly slid my hand down in her Juicy Couture sweats she had on, and spread her cheeks apart. She engulfed herself in our passionate kiss. While doing so, I slid her thong to the side and let two fingers enter and explore her soft, wet insides. She gasped for air.

"Wait," she tried to push my hands away. "Let's wait til later on." she moaned.

I had forgotten about my flight that night.

"Damn, I ain't gon be able to chill with you tonight. I gotta flight to catch."

"Yeah right, you just trying to hit this ass right now. This pussy feels that good to you, you over there dying to dip that dick in it."

"Nall, I do gotta flight for real, I gotta take care of something."

"So what about our date?" she asked.

"It's still on, you and ya girl go get ready. We can go grab a bite in the Central West End."

I open the door to the bedroom and walked out behind her. She paused as she came into the living room. Shai looked back at me and started laughing. Then she looked at Moni.

"Moni, What the hell you doing?" she asked.

I tried to peek around to see what was going on. I thought they were fucking are something the way Shai blocked the entrance to the living room. I pushed her to the side and walked in to see Rell, butt-naked, and holding the controller. He was pushing the buttons hard as hell, too. Moni was still fully dressed.

"Damn," Rell shouted, "Ma-tha—fucka!" he had just lost again.

Moni looked at us, "Uh, yall might wanna go back in there, cuz I want my money." Then she looked at Rell. "Take that shit off nigga!"

"Girl fuck dat, let's go." Shai giggled, then tapped my elbow.

"We will meet y'all downstairs in 30 minutes."

I walked with them to open the door. When I came back in, Rell was putting on his clothes. I looked at him.

"Damn, nigga you let her beat you like that?" Rell was mad that she beat him.

"I got her ass, Imma use the code on her ass, watch."

Rell and I walked out of the building. We were waiting on Shai and Moni to come down. I noticed Heather getting out of her car and walking up to the building. When she noticed me, she began to plead her case.

"Papi, Papi, I'm so sorry, I didn't know-" I cut her off by grabbing her throat.

"Bitch, you set me up, I should-" I paused because Rell grabbed my hand. He looked around to let me know that I was tripping, acting

out downtown, so I let her go and tried to continue walking to the truck. She grabbed my shoulder, spinning me around to face her.

"No, no, he tricked me. I had nothing to do with it, Elan, Elan made the deal!" she yelled. "Elan—" she stopped in midsentence. She looked towards the door of the building. I turned around and saw Shai and Moni walking out of the door. Heather got quiet. I notice Shai pause and look at Heather like they knew each other. Heather looked and whispered to herself, "Diablo," then she looked at me, lowered her head, and walked away.

I looked at her as she got in her car and left. *That bitch is crazy,* I thought shaking my head. *Man, who the fuck is the devil.* I looked at Shai, she had a frown on her face.

"Who was that?" she asked. "That ain't somebody I'mma have to deal with in the future, is it?"

"That ain't shit for you to worry about," I said, getting in the truck. We were in Rell's Rover. I could smell the scent of marijuana as soon as I got in his ride.

"Damn nigga, why you ain't spray this shit?" I asked.

I really didn't have a problem with him smoking in cars like that, but sometimes it was too loud and caused us to deal with a routine search most of the time. That's why we had stash boxes in every car.

"Fire that shit up!" Moni said, getting into the truck. Shai just looked at me and shook her head.

"I got the same problem." she added.

We were walking up Euclid, a street in the Central West End of St. Louis. We walked pass the various nightclubs and bars on that street that were adjoined along the strip. When we got back into the ride, my phone started blowing up. I peeked at it, and realized it was Sheryl. I decided not to answer due to the previous run in with Heather. I didn't want to run Shai off to quick. Sheryl started to text me back to back. I grabbed the phone and read one of the text.

The text read, "Oh, you at the Central West End with some bitch, nigga you bet not have her in my shit, and you better come and get yours before I wreck it."

I didn't take her to be that stupid, but you couldn't underestimate nobody. So I texted her back.

My text read, "Bitch, don't touch my shit, where you at, I'm coming to get it.

Shai leaned over, "That's ole girl from earlier?" she asked. I didn't bother to hide it, Sheryl meant nothing to me for real.

"N'all, this other bitch I fucked with from time to time." I had to be brutally honest with Shai. Hopefully she would understand and recognize that I'm trying to keep it real with her.

"Damn, another bitch. That's two bitches in one night." she looked concerned. "Shit, I might have to kill me a bitch fo' fucking around with you."

Another text came in from Sheryl. She said she was downtown parked next to her car. I had forgotten she had low—jack put on her ride when it got stolen once before. She could locate her shit from anywhere. When we pulled up, Sheryl was already in her car. The door to my car was open with the keys still in the ignition. When I got out, she started yelling at me.

"I was about to leave yo shit nigga!" she approached me. "Oh, and Tyrek, I want my keys.. So you better give me my shit now!" she looked over at Shai, who was looking on. "And you bet not had that trifling ass bitch in my shit!"

I tossed the keys at her and gave her the house keys also.

"Bitch get the fuck out of here." I was getting tired of her nagging ass.

"N'all, that's the bitch," she said, pointing to Shai. She was trying to get a reaction out of me, and when she noticed I wasn't reacting the way she wanted, she started to threaten me. "I'll call the cops on yo punk ass nigga!"

After that comment, Shai got out of the truck. Rell and Moni rolled their windows down and had been laughing, until she said that. I didn't notice Shai come around the side of the car, but she placed a small barrel to Sheryl grill.

"Bitch, you ain't gon call shit!" Shai said, pressing the gun to her head. I noticed Shai wasn't even shaking or anything, she was too calm. I grabbed her arm, easing the gun down, because we were downtown, and I was pretty sure people were already watching Sheryl act a fool.

"What the fuck you doing, get yo ass in the whip!" I said, pushing Shai towards the car.

Sheryl didn't say anything. She was shaking scared. I thought she would surely call the police after that. I reached over in her car and hit the compartment. Sheryl didn't say anything. She just looked in amazement as I grabbed the money, gun, and work out of the stash. I closed it and then dismissed her.

"Get out of here, I'll hit you later." She looked up at me, and I could tell she was pissed.

"Nigga don't ever call me again." she closed the door and drove off. I turned to look at Shai, then at Rell. He was pointing to Shai.

"That's the one right there," he smiled.

Something was still bothering me about her though. She was too calm holding that gun to Sheryl like that. It was like she did it before. I got in the car to question her.

"What the fuck was that crazy ass shit?" I asked.

"That bitch wasn't gon keep disrespecting me, and then threaten you. She talking 'bout some she was calling the fed on somebody. Nigga you should've done something," she snapped. "Where's my gun?" she added, holding out her hand.

I gave her the gun back, but she was still annoyed by the incident and didn't say anything. I liked that she was down, but she might also have some issues.

"What y'all bout to do? You and Gansta Boo, over there?" Rell joked. Moni gave him an elbow to his side for the comment. "Aah, girl."

"Shit," I said, looking at Shai.

She was staring at me with a blank expression. I couldn't tell what she was thinking at the moment. Moni tapped on the passenger window where Shai was seated.

"I'm bout to go kick his ass some mo in the game," Moni leaned in. "You alright?" she asked.

"Yeah, we're going up to your spot," Shái said with a quick glance over in my direction.

I had about three hours before the flight. When we got up to Moni's apartment, her shit was laid out. I was reminding myself to ask what the fuck they did to make a living. She had flat screens in every room, even the kitchen. She had Italian sofas, the decor looked futuristic, and very luxurious.

Shai tugged at my shirt, pulling me closer to her. We started kissing, and then allowed our hands to explore each other's body uncontrollably. She unbuttoned my jeans and reached in to grab my dick. She ran her hand along the length of it.

"Mmm, shit when is it gon end?" she moaned, pulling it out to stroke it.

I was fully aroused, and wanted her like never before. I pulled down her jeans, right below her ass, and then turned her around to spread her cheeks apart. She had me so turned on at that moment; I dropped down to my knees, and stuck my face between her cheeks. As I sucked her juices dry from the back, I could feel her weakening. Her loud screams and moans for more caused me to grab her hands and place them on the wall. She was in a position and looked almost as if, I was about to frisk her. I leaned into her slowly and kissed her on the back of her neck, then shoved all of my dick inside of her.

"Ooh, shit!" she gasped, "Ooh, oh ahh shit!" she kept screaming at a high pitch. She tried to reach back and push my waist back some to stop the deep thrusting, but I smacked her hands away and kept pumping hard as I could. She was screaming like she was a virgin. I knew my shit was above average, but damn, she had me feeling like I was a porn star.

"Oh, ah shit, ah shit, I'm cummin, I'm cummin!" She let out a sigh, then a high pitched scream. Her legs buckled and she fell into my arms. As she turned around to look at me, I lifted her to her feet. She glanced down at my dick, grabbed it in her hands, then she leaned down and took it all in her mouth. She didn't even choke or gag as her deep throat covered every inch. As I disappeared into her mouth, she licked her tongue out while I was still resting inside of her mouth. She finally gagged twice, and then came up for air.

"Like that?" she smiled, and then she started right back. She put her hand on my dick and started sucking and stroking it at the same time. I couldn't hold back. I knew she could feel me hardening inside her mouth. She was reaching with the other hand to pull her titties out.

She kept on sucking, until I was about to cum, and then she pulled my dick out and aimed it at her breast. She stroked my shit all over her titties, and then she rubbed it on her thigh, and then her hand.

As we relaxed together in the jacuzzi for over an hour, we talked about everything. Shai told me about her dad, and how he was a big time hustler. She said one day she was in his room and stumbled upon all of his guns. At the time, she was eleven years old. She went on to say, she use to sneak them out to the backyard and aim at shit whenever her parents were gone. She said weekly, they were always on trips, so she was left with either one of her mother friends or Moni's parents. For the longest, she really didn't think her parents cared too much about what she was doing. Then while talking, she recalled a memory of a story about the last time she saw her mother.

"One day somebody came into our home and tried to rob my Father," she said, playing with my fingers. "All I could hear was gunshots, then my Mom screamed. I ran to get one of the guns from the bedroom. When I came downstairs, my Mom was lying there on the floor with her eyes wide open. She was looking at me, but she wasn't moving. She was dead. I saw a puddle of blood underneath her head, and then I noticed that there was a dude lying right next to her. I thought it was my father, but it wasn't. It was one of the robbers. My father had shot and killed one of them, before the other one shot him. I tip-toed around, only to walk right in on one of them standing over my father. He was yelling at him. That's when I aimed at his head and fired. He fell on top of my father, so I started shooting him again, then yelled for him to get off my Daddy!"

Her story was making me sad, but much to my surprise, she started laughing. I turned sideways to look at her, and she looked back at me.

"N'all, it's funny because I realize I could've shot my father. You should've seen the way he was squirming, trying to dodge the bullets and yelling for me to stop. Every since then, my father has taught me everything he knew or thought I needed to know about the streets."

I was speechless for a moment. In one way, I felt her, and in another way I didn't know if I could trust her or not. She might really have some serious psychological issues from that experience.

"So what about Moni, what's up with her?"I asked.

"Ain't nothing up with her, what you mean?" she asked.

"My homie ain't over there with a psycho is he?" I teased. Shai turned around.

"No, he straight, and I ain't no psycho either. Nigga, I went to therapy for my shit. Not for the killing, but for seeing my Mother like that. I couldn't deal with it for a while. I can deal with the killing though," she smiled at me. Something told me she wasn't playing.

She told me how Moni's family took her in after the murder and that her father was back and forth in her life. I felt compelled to share my life with her also. I informed her about my childhood, although it was nothing like hers. I also informed her about the depth behind my relationship with Rell, and how he once saved my life during a deal gone bad. We shared emotions for hours, and then I noticed it was time for me to catch my flight. I felt attached to her at the moment, so I didn't want to leave her.

"Fuck it, you wanna come with me for a day or two?" I asked her, getting out of the Jacuzzi. I knew I was pushing it by allowing her to come with me down to Phoenix, but for some reason I felt like I could trust her.

"I don't care! Where we going?" she asked, standing up. I watched the suds slide down her body.

"Phoenix." I said, smacking her ass.

We got dressed and went up to my apartment. I walked in to grab a few things and to let Rell and Moni know we were leaving. They were in the bedroom together, so
we decided to leave a note.
Afterwards, we switched cars and left for the Airport.

Chapter 6

When we landed in Phoenix, I sent an Instant Message to my connect. I was trying to figure out the name Heather yelled out, but at the time, it wasn't coming to me. We copped a room at the Double Tree, in downtown Scottsdale, and once inside, I called Rell.

"What's up," he answered, sounding like he was still asleep.

"Damn, Nigga she wore you out or something?" I asked, referring to the game.

"Man, she cheated like a mafucka. I had her down to her t-shirt," then he started to whisper into the phone. "You know I hit the code on her. She knew I was about to beat her, so she got down on the floor and started to play. bent over with her ass in the air, she ain't have on no panties my nigga, took my mind cold off the game." I could hear Moni in the background, "Shut up!" she yelled.

"A, did you remember the dude name ya girl Heather was yelling that had something to do with this shit?" I asked, hoping he could remember.

"Ella, or Elan, Elan! That's the name." Rell recalled.

"I—ight cool, Imma hit you up and let you know what's up. One!"

I hung up.

Shai was sitting in a chair, looking at me and tapping her feet against the leg. I sensed she had something on her mind.

"What's wrong with you?" I asked.

"Nothing, I'm good," she said, she got up, lying across the bed. I didn't think anything of it, so I got up and relaxed across the bed next to her while waiting to get a call.

The phone rang, and I got directions from someone on the other end of the line. I hung up and tore off the piece of paper I wrote the address on. Shai was all in my conversation, so I looked at her.

"I'll be right back in a couple of hours." I said. She leaned over and gave me a peck on the cheek.

"Imma shoot to the Mall if that's cool with you." she grabbed her purse and fumbled through her wallet.

"Yeah, that's cool, I'll be back," I expressed, walking out the door.

***

Shai waited until I was out the door, then picked up the phone to wait on someone to pick up.

"Hello, Meno?" she asked.

"Shai, donde estas?" Where are you, Meno asked.

"Estoy agui en Phoenix." I'm here in Phoenix, Shai said.

"Porque no vienes a vermo?" Why don't you come see me, Meno asked demandingly.

"Dame 30 minutos y ahi esta're." Give me 30 minutes, I'll be there, Shai said, and then she hung up.

***

I pulled up to the address. The same Big Mexican was at the door. He walked me into a room where my connect was sitting with someone.

"Hey senor Ty, want a drink?" he asked.

"N'all I'm good. What's up with this bullshit about going thru T—Mac?" I asked, walking over to the bar where he was sitting. Three other guys stood up and the Big Mexican was on my heels. The connect waved his hands for them to be seated, and they did. I watched as the Big Mexican walked back over to the door.

"Calm down, you do not understand the workings of the Mafia Mexicana, no. You are just born, Senor. Even you have to climb ranks, and T—Mac as you call him, has be with us for a while, longer than you. You have no say so."

"Then I'm out, I'm straight." I said.

The others started to laugh at what I'd just said, like it was a joke.

"Out, you are never out," he added. "The boss decides when you are out. He obviously hasn't decided yet, because you are still breathing," he laughed.

"Well tell Elan, if that's your bosses name that I'm out," I said, staring him in the eyes.

When I mentioned that name, the three stood up again. However, this time they had their hands on their guns. *Damn.*

"Where did you hear that name?" he asked, rising out of his chair slowly.

"Do it matter, I'm—"

"It matters if you value your life!" he hissed. I looked around at the others.

"I don't like threats," I warned. It was plenty of them and I was surely outnumbered, but I wasn't going to bitch up.

"That's a promise, not a threat."

The phone rang, and one of the men answered it. Seconds later, he handed it to the connect. He kept saying yes to whoever it was in Spanish. *That must be the Boss,* I thought.

When he hung up the phone, his fingers drug the length of the phone, then he looked at me and spoke.

"It seems like you have a little more power than I expected, huh?" he said curiously.. "You want your own line, you got it. But fuck dis up Senor, and Shai will answer to the Boss, not you."

When he said Shai's name, I squinted my eyes. I was wondering what she had to do with this deal. Maybe they had an eye on me the whole time and thought that Shai was my wife or something. Maybe they would threaten my family first. Whatever it was, I would find out if she knew something or not.

***

When I got back to the Hotel, she wasn't there. I must've paced for a couple of hours, trying to figure this thing out. I thought about Heather and when she saw Shai, the look they had, and then I thought about what Heather said before leaving. I thought about the puzzling looks Shai gave me whenever I mentioned Phoenix. After so much thinking, I knew the only one who could probably help me out with this was Heather. I decided to call her.

***

Shai stood over Heather, as Meno watched. Meno called Heather over after hearing that she blurted out Elan's name to Tyrek.

Meno gave Shai the honor to express how much of a devil she was. Shai raised the barrel to Heather head, and without hesitation…

-BONG-

As Shai and Méno walked to sit out on the patio, the guards picked up Heather's lifeless remains.

"Gracias Meno for giving Ty a chance, he is very dear to me." Shai said.

"You didn't know this before?" Meno asked, refering to his connection with the organization.

"No, I really had no clue, just was told to watch him for a while, but the thing with Heather surprised me."

"Well tell your friend to prepare for war, and you be careful. I don't care who wins, the product will keep flowing." Meno said, standing. It was time to go, so he signaled to his men. Shai stood and kissed him on the cheek. He looked at her, and then to the others, "Shai be careful," he paused. "Have you seen how your father is doing?" he questioned.

"He better be doing fine." she said, smiling at him.

"He is, don't worry, he is," Meno said, looking around to be sure no one heard him.

***

Shai came through the door of the hotel room. I grabbed her by the neck as she walked up to me.

"Bitch, you need to tell me what's going on?" I wasn't going to hurt her at all, just was trying to scare her into telling me everything. "I tried to call Heather and her phone is off. I got a new line and they say it's because of you, what's up?" I added, squeezing harder.

"You need to let me go, Tyrek," she fussed. "Now!"

I let her go, and she took a deep breath and sat the bags down on the bed.

"Remember when I told you about my father?" she said, sitting down on the couch.

"Yeah," I replied. I was still standing, my adrenaline was pumping, and I was pacing.

"My father is in Mexico. He has life in prison. Meno, the guy who the call Elan and my father started out together. When my father got caught up, he didn't rat, so Meno rose in the Cartels, and vowed to my father that he would look out for me. Meno wanted me to stay here in Phoenix, but I wanted to stay in St. Louis," she looked at me. "I met T-Mac some years back and introduced him to Meno and he gave him to Elan. At first, Meno didn't approve of me getting involved with the business, but I insisted I could deal with whatever came with it. So he gave T—Mac to Elan and gave me a percentage of the shipment. My job was to make sure T—Mac didn't fuck shit up," she added.

Shai stood up and walked to me, "Elan is the guy Heather hooked you up with." I sat down and took it all in, then she sat down beside me.

"Tyrek, my loyalty is to you. If it wasn't, I wouldn't have put my ass on the line to keep your line open," she added.

"Bitch I'm just another side deal for you! You really ain't got no loyalty to no one."

"No! You lie, I am loyal to you and I'm not getting anything off of your ass nigga." I got up and walked to the bedroom. She tried to follow, but I slammed the door in her face. "Ty, I swear I'm not getting anything!" she screamed through the door.

I had to think this out. *How loyal was Shai. She did get the deal back. The numbers was the same, but was her loyalty stronger for T—Mac.* My mind was racing. I didn't know who to trust right now.

About two hours later, I woke up to find Shai laying on my chess. When she noticed I was awake, she looked into my eyes. I just couldn't believe she would stick her neck out for me, for nothing.

"How much you getting out of this?" I asked.

"What!" she said, raising her head off my chess with a look of disbelief.

"You heard me! How much?"

"Nothing! Man Ty, I can't believe you! I ain't making shit off you. It's my ass on the line for your shit!"

"Just like T-Mac shit too?"

"I don't got shit to do with his ass no more, I only do what I have to do and that's it."

"And what the fuck is that?" I asked.

"If T—Mac fucked up he dies, but my investment is dead also," she said, "I didn't put my life on the line for T-Mac, like I did for you."

"So why the fuck you do it for me then?"

"Because I'm feeling you. The only problem I caused is beef between you and T-Mac. The Cärtel doesn't care about who dies; all they care about is the product. So if one goes, the other will be forced to move more product."

I studied her face for any sign of lies. Either she's telling the truth or she's a good liar. What could I possibly lose by fucking with her. If she has any hidden motives, then it'll be that much easier to kill her. As far as, T-Mac goes, she's right, I have to kill him, and I don't mind the challenge either.

"So how down are you for me?" I asked. "You down enough to help me take out T—Mac?"

"Yes, I'm down," she responded, looking me in the eyes,

***

We landed back at Lambert Airport in St. Louis, we got in the truck and drove back downtown to the Loft apartment. I informed Rell of the new deal that Shai set up for us. He assured me that I should trust her. As we talked, I came to an understanding that he and Moni had gotten closer while we were gone. I let him know we had to drop T-Mac. Also, once we did, due to the Cartels monthly supply to this area, we would be forced to move more work. But, we couldn't cause a drug war on the streets though, because that would get us both killed. We couldn't bring heat to the Cartel either.

Realizing that we decided we would plot to make the Cartels do the dirty work for us, by forcing T—Mac into an all out drug war without the Cartel's consent. Then they would send the hit on him and not us.

Shai called us down to Moni's apartment. She introduced us to her younger cousins, which were two wild niggas by the name of Chad and Boo. They were good for 20 bricks a month. I stretched my hands down to Memphis, TN., and Rell reached down to Southern Illinois. We had Mount Vernon, Centralia, and Cape Giradeau, Mo. on lock. Before we knew it, in a month's time, we were up to moving 200 kilos. Shai did everything in her power to prove to me that she was down with me and not against me. She was down for me for real, and with my every move. She showed me various spots where T-Mac had niggas pushing for him chilled. She helped me weave out the weak links that could be potential snitches in the long run.

***

I drove up St. Louis Ave, and Natural Bridge. Me and Chad were riding through to meet with this guy he knew who could put my plan with T-Mac into motion. Chad was very confident that Rico, the hit man, would immediately jump on anything he could. I told Chad to inform him of a few spots where T—Mac stashed and sold some of his work. And when he moved on them make sure he burned the spot down to ashes. I didn't want him to keep anything moving. I knew as long as he had to keep paying the Cartels out of his pocket, things would be more favorable for me in their eyes.

I parked up the street from Rico's house. I didn't want to be seen by him at all. I didn't want to know my intentions either. Chad got out and ran up the street to his spot. They talked for a while before entering the house. Chad told me that him and Rico hada' solid relationship.

He would normally put him up on shit whenever he needed some extra cash, and in turn Rico would break him off something. Chad emerged from the house shortly after he went in. He ran back to the car and got inside.

"So what's up?" I said, once he got in.

"Oh, it's all good. He's with that all day long," he smiled. "He said he gon' burn that shit down to ashes, and then turn a fan on a nigga," he laughed.

"Yeah, that's what's up." I said, pulling off.

Chapter 7

Shai and I meet Rell and Moni out at Frontenac Mall, which was a mall that had several upscale boutiques. Rell and Moni walked off to Nieman Marcus, while Shai and I walked through the mall area. Shai went into the Louis Vutton boutique, so I followed her inside to check out some billfolds and belts. She ended up spending a good ten grand on handbags, a belt and watch that I was eyeing.

"I been meaning to ask you, where the fuck you and Moni come up with all this money," I asked, watching her pass the cashier a stack of hundred dollar bills. "You spend this shit like it's nothing."

"I told you my father looks out for me," she said.

"I thought you said your father was locked up?" I looked puzzled at her.

"Well you know what I'm talking about, my father looks out by way of what he did, and in turn I get a fixed allowance."

"Shit, well that allowance must be fixed real well, considering the way you throw money around," I added.

"Here." She handed me the bags with the newly purchased items in them. "You should be glad I ain't spending your money and that I got my own."

"Yeah, how do I know you ain't spending my money."

I still believed she cut a side deal with Meno. I didn't just believe that she was getting taken care of like that by someone who wasn't benefiting off of her at all. It got to be some form of exchange going on to keep money like that flowing.

"I thought we were past that mess Tyrek?" she stopped, turning me around to face her. "You still think I got something out of your deal don't you?"

"It's all good, I ain't tripping." I said, trying to hug her. She stepped back from me.

"Nall, it ain't all good, you need to tell me what makes you believe that you just can't trust no one."

"I don't trust nobody but Rell, and that's how it is."

"Well that's too bad, because you can trust me. Haven't I proved to you that you can? If not, what more do you need me to do?" she added.

"Nothing, you've proved enough, just let this grow on me." I paused. "Give me some time with this," I gave her a peck on the lips.

We started back towards, Niemans to meet back up with Rell and Moni. As we approached them, I received a text, and it was from Jessica.

"Need to talk to you ASAP," it read, sending chills through me. *Damn, she must have gotten caught, and maybe trying to set me up. I* immediately thought, waiting a while before I replied.

After we ate, I decided to text her back, requesting that she meet me in a hour, off 270 and Halls Ferry, at the AppleBee's. Shai could recognize a look of concern on my face.

"You alright?" she asked.

"Yeah, I just gotta go meet somebody real quick. I'll be back later," I said, making eye contact with Rell.

We split up from the girls, and drove in Shai's Benz truck. While pulling out the parking space, Moni honked.

"You niggas could have at least helped us put these fucking bags in the car."

They didn't know we had our mind on something far more serious than that. It was no telling if we were going to see them for a while.

***

We arrived thirty minutes early to see if the cops were trying to set up a sting operation. I told Rell to park over at the White Castles that was across the street from our meeting spot, so we could scope out the area.

"She sounded like something was wrong?" Rell asked.

"Man, I don't know, but we ain't finna find out by being where they want us to be," I said, looking across the street towards the restaurant.

I saw her car pull into the parking lot, so I called her before she parked.

"Where you at?" she asked.

"Come to that liquor store over by the Sex store on West Florrisant."

"Nigga, I just past that up," she fussed, pulling back out to turn around.

I didn't see anyone following her, so I tailed her down to the store. I pulled up alongside of her and got out of the truck. Jessica was looking cute, with her dark complexion. She also had a nice body. Every time I saw her, it looked like her ass was getting bigger. We never fucked because I found out that she preferred pussy more than dick. So as a result of that, we always kept it business.

"What up, you hitting me up like that, had me noid as fuck,." I said as she walked around the truck.

"Nigga, you got me noid. My boss questioned me about my luggage last week. It's only so much I can do at a time." she pleaded.

"What he say? I thought you had him on lock?" I asked, leaning up against the truck.

I didn't think this was going to be a problem, but She expressed that with her bringing more luggage than usual on each trip, it was starting to raise some suspicion. Plus, I noticed she had some nice little Davin rims on her shit now, and them thangs wasn't cheap. They could raise some suspicion also.

"He just asked why I needed all the luggage, and I do got him on lock, but he got a job to do, and he takes customs very seriously," she stated, throwing her hands in the air, "He ain't gon let everything fly."

"Look calm down, we'll just have to think of something." I replied, because I saw that she was getting worked up. "You got some friends you work with right."

"Yeah,"

"Well make them an offer they can't refuse and bring them in, and we'll figure something out for your boss. I mean, he still wants to fuck you, don't he?"

"That's all he talks about."

"Well give him what he wants, Im'ma send you a chick over tomorrow. Take her with you and let him have a good time." I smiled.

She drew a slight expression of regret on her face.

"Alright, but it's gon' cost you big," she smirked.

"We good then, right?"

Umm hum."

"So I'll call you tomorrow," I informed her, getting back in the truck.

For some reason, I couldn't help but watch as she got into her car and pulled off. I waited for Rell to come out of the store. And sure enough, he emerged with a bottle of Platinum Patron, and two Monster energy drinks. It's like he read my mind, cause I needed a drink badly. Rell handed me a cup, and I mixed the two drinks together and took a nice long sip.

Afterwards, we shot down highway 270 to Bellefontaine, drove through the Sierra Vista Apartments, and then headed over the bridge to the Illside. While driving I was thinking about Chad and that situation with Rico. I wondered had he taken care of that already. I hadn't heard anything about it, so I called him.

"Yo, what up nigga?" I said when I heard him pick up.

"Shit, I been meaning to hit you up, ya boy good," he said, referring to Rico.

"Oh yeah, already?"

"Yeah, come thru or meet me somewhere."

"I—ight, give me a minute and we will meet downtown."

"I—ight then cool, I'll be there in an hour or two."

We hung up. Rell pulled up to Zeek's crib. He stayed in Madison, aka Mad town, so we chilled out with him for a while. Zeek had a crew of niggas that got money and got down with them guns. Whenever we had trouble, he was one of the guys we could depend on to handle that quickly. We chopped it up with him for a few, before hitting East Saint.

Coming up Collinsville Road, which is the strip where most of the clubs in the downtown area are located; we ended up turning on State Street, the main street. Quickly scanning the area, we popped the pistols out of the compartment, because it was a must on the Eastside. Niggas on that side are the grimiest on Earth. And since we were riding Missouri plates, we were an immediate target for a jacking. As we passed down 16th Street, we saw flashing lights from a distance in the rearview mirror. I didn't think they were on to us, but if it wasn't the niggas, it was the cops. The cop car swerved behind us, signaling for us to pull over. I could've floored it, but I pulled over.

A fat black muthafucka got out of his patrol car with his hands on his gun. We put the guns back into the glove compartment and locked it. When he approached, he didn't even ask for license or registration. He looked at both of us, with his hand on his gun, like he just wanted us to make a move.

"Get y'all hands on the muthafuckin dashboard!" he yelled. I looked at him like he was crazy as I followed his orders. "What the fuck y'all doing over here, y'all tryna sell something, or buy something?" He asked without allowing us to reply. "Looks like y'all might be doing the selling." He quickly leaned back to observe the truck and rims. "Yeah, I think I might got me something today. Driver, get out, and your passenger can keep his monkey ass right where he's at," he yelled.

I got out of the truck and he walked me to the front of the ride. I placed my hands on the hood, while he gave me a pat down. He pulled my billfold out of my pocket, and set it on the hood. Then he thumbed thru my stack of money and put it in his pocket.

"What nigga." he said. "Yeah, I got me a lick today," he taunted me as he patted down my legs. "Shit, y'all need to call me next time y'all floating across the bridge; I just might look out for y'all for the right fee." He said, now going thru my billfold to take the last few dollars I had. "Now, go'on get back in the ride," he pointed at me. "Okay, come on it's yo turn," he waved to Rell. After he searched him, he came to the truck and looked inside. He tried to open the glove box, but it was locked.

"Open it up, and let me see inside," he demanded.

We knew he was dirty, so he just wanted to find a few more reasons to get more money from us. He was probably hoping there was dope in it, so he could drop it off to one of his boys.

"Either open it or I will, and y'all don't want me fucking up ya ride and shit, so open the muthafucka," he added.

I knew we weren't going to jail, because if he booked us, he wouldn't be able to keep the money he'd just taken from me. So I opened it, and the guns dropped to the floor.

"Oh shit, some guns, don't nobody move, or this gon cost ya," he insisted, placing his hand on his pistol. "This shit just got serious."

I was getting fed up with his crooked ass, "Man, you already got all our money, what the fuck you want us to do!"

"Shut the fuck up before I book ya ass. I was just fucking with you nigga," he holstered his gun, then reached in his pocket and gave us his card. I couldn't believe this nigga had the nerve to give us his card after this shit.

"Y'all keep the guns, I got one already," he laughed, walking back towards his patrol vehicle to squeeze his fat ass back inside. And after a slight struggle and a few wiggles, he was back in and peeling off. As he left the scene, he hit his sirens at us twice.

"Pussy ass muthafucka," Rell said, "EastSaint off da chain."

Though his comment was true, the dirty cop was actually a benefit to us, because we were both looking at prison time had it been someone or anywhere else. We swung through 25th, and St. Clair Ave, to the liquor store to chill with Mike and Mamun. Pulling up in the lot, Mike was smoking a blunt on the side of the building. Rell went over there while I went inside with Mamun.

"What up fool?" Mamun said as I entered the door.

It was a normal neighborhood liquor store. Except they didn't have bullet proof glass, and they weren't worried about having any either, because they stayed strapped.

"Shit, what up wit it?" I said, grabbing a bag of chips from the rack. "Nigga you know we just got jacked by East Saint," I informed him, referring to the cops.

"Straight up?"

"Fuck yeah, that muthafucka took all the doe, too. Some fat black muthafucka."

"That's that same fat bastard that took our shit, then gon come up in here like he cool and shit, asking for shit." Mamun grimaced.

"I told that muthafucka he had to pay like everyone else, fat fucker," he fussed, "Shit but I see you still shining. I told you to stop fucking around with these lame ass niggas and get ya own shit," Mamun expressed, leaning across the counter.

About five females came into the store. They looked like they were all dressed up to go to the club, but I didn't pay them any mind. Instead, I went behind the counter to fuck with the laptop. One of them approached the counter to ask a question.

"Do you work here?"

As she stood there leaning over the counter, I glanced over at her, noticing enough cleavage to distract me. She was in a tight black dress, with some micro braids and heavy gloss on her lips.

"N'all you gotta check out down there." I said, pointing towards Mamun.

She looked at me, studying me for a moment.

"You know who got some weed around here? I ain't from over here," she added.

"Where you from?" I asked, noticing her friend all in our conversation.

"Girl you act like you from out of town or something," she said, leaning over the counter.

"Bitch! I don't be over here like that!" she fussed, looking over at me with a smirk on her face.

I walked around to the front side of the counter. The first thing I noticed was that her ass was way too big for the short dress she had on, which is why her ass cheeks could be seen right at the baseline near the split. She was standing with her legs crossed, leaning against the freezer. She had a flirtatious grin on her face, so I knew she was use to niggas trying to do everything in their will for her attention. But I was about to completely disappoint her.

"N'all, I ain't got none, but I'll check for you though."

As I walked by her, she let out a sigh of relief. I guess she hoped that I would emerge with her nightly fix to help her prepare for the club. She stared as I stepped by.

"Girl Monz gon kill you," one of the chicks said.

Monz, I know who Monz is. He fucks with T—Mac, I thought. That was one of the dudes Tre would holla at whenever I dried up. Curious, I turned back towards her as soon as I heard Monz's name.

"Where y'all going tonight?" I asked.

"The Bino, way in the back." one of the females sung while doing a two step.

I figured I might be able to catch Monz there, or try to get her to drop my number off to him on the low. She looked like she was going there to chase after the niggas, so she might be of some assistance to me. I walked in the back, through the cooler right into the storage room. There, Rell and Mike stood blazing. Both of their eyes were glossy and low.

"What up nigga?" Mike said, dangling a bag of weed. "Man, this shit's that killa boy."

He held the bag in one hand and his Beretta in the other. I snatched the bag of weed out of his hands, examined it, and noticed it had crystals all over it, almost resembling some form of white dust. The weed was light green with hints of orange and lime.

"Nigga let me get some of this shit," I said. Rell looked at me like I was tripping.

"Nigga you don't even smoke," he teased, leaving out the back.

"Hell naw! And you damn sho ain't bout to give my shit to them dusty ass bitches out there," Mike added.

Mike was the oldest of the two, and Arabic. He had long wavy hair, and Mamun had short hair. Both of them had bad attitudes and it was plenty of times I had to stop them from fighting, shooting, or pistol whipping someone.

"Nigga give me some of this shit," I insisted, opening the bag to take out a few choice buds. The shit was strong as fuck, too.

"Damn! Man, you owe me a hundred dollars for that shit nigga; straight up," Mike joked as he snatched the bag back to stuff it into his pocket. "Trick ass nigga, I know you bout to give it to them hoes," he concluded, exiting to walk back to the front of the store as well.

As we came around the building, Trell was placing numbers in his phone. The driver smiled when she saw me, almost as if she was checking me out.

"Nigga, she's been asking for you," Rell said, reaching in the car to open the passenger legs. She immediately smacked his hands, and he jerked them back out the car. I held up the bag, and smiled.

"N'all, she been looking for this, not me." I teased, dangling it in front of her. She grabbed it, and then passed it to one of her girls in the backseat.

"No, I've been looking for you," she flirtatiously grinned at me again. One of the females in the backseat interrupted her.

"Damn, you got some more of this, we'll buy it?" she showed it to her friend. "Girl look at this shit?"

"That's that AK." Trell said.

"Nall that's all I got for right now, we can do something later though. Here's my number, hit me up later," I gave it to the driver. "Oh, but this ain't for you Mami. Give this to ya nigga and tell him I got something for him, and it's a real good deal, too."

"Who is you?" she said, getting defensive. I laughed at her, because she was cute.

"Ah Ma' it ain't like that, this'll benefit both of you. Tell him Ty want to holla at him."

***

Chad waited outside the apartment building downtown. We pulled up minutes later, and I stepped out of the truck while Rell was on the phone.

"What up," I greeted him.

"Shit. Dude got down on that spot on the north side. That shit's in the Whirl newspaper, then he went over to the other spots and caught a few niggas down bad," he said. "He threw up that 3100 Mag. I know them niggas gone think it was behind that Tre and Bella beef. So they ain't really gon have a clue."

"Yeah, yeah that's sweet, so now we gotta hit this nigga hard. How much did he get hit fo?" I asked.

I wanted to hurt his pockets. I knew that would be hard to do though, cause T-Mac was paid. He'd been in the game for a while and would have enough doe to back his deals with the Cartels for a while. I just needed to make him feel the lost.

"Shit, he said it was the best lick he ever came across. I think that nigga said he got 2 or 3 birds, and some doe."

"Yeah, that ain't shit, but that's cool. We gotta find out where that nigga really got that shit at. Get at me tomorrow and we'll think of something." I shook his hand then walked back to the truck. "A Nigga, I'm bout to take it in," I said to Rell. "Holla at me tomorrow, early."

"I-ight Nigga. I'm bout to get up with them hoes from tonight. Imma see if ya girl gon be able to get at Monz for us," he said.

"Cool, be careful fucking with those hoes," I replied, locking up Shai truck.

Chapter 8

Shai had some shrimp from Playboy's on the counter in the kitchen. Playboy's was a local tavern in Baden. They had some of the best prawns in St. Louis. I opened the bedroom door to find her asleep. She had the covers pulled slightly over her ass, and when I got in bed, she just rolled over and placed her head on my chess. She didn't even bother to ask where I'd been? Who I'd been with, or even let me smell your dick? She wasn't all insecure like most chicks, and I was feeling her for that.

"What's up?" she said, barely lifting her head.

"Nothing, just thinking."

"Thinking bout what?" she asked, raising her head a little.

"Thinking about how you make a nigga wanna rape yo ass when you sleep with it all poked up in the air like that," I laughed.

"Shut up! You must be scared or something?"

"Shit, why you say that?"

"Cause you ain't try to rape me. And had you, I might've stuck it up there a little higher for you to do something with. I want you to wake me up with that thang all up in here," she said, gripping her ass to open it up for me.

I licked my lips at the sight of her seduction. It was very tempting, but I wanted to talk about something more serious, so I passed and changed the subject.

"On a more serious note, I need a sweeter deal to go up against T-Mac." She raised up on her elbows to pay more attention. "I need a deal that will get his workers a sweeter price, I figure if they jump ship, then he'll crash."

"I can take you to see Meno."

"Elan might not like that."

"Who! Elan?" she asked.

"Yeah, he ain't gon like getting cut out. Besides he told me to only deal with him."

"Elan, he is no good, a snake. He's probably allowing that deal to go through with T-Mac to charge you extra." She said, raising up on the headboard.

"T-Mac did try to extort me for a hundred geez behind that deal."

"Yeah, and he was probably getting sixty of that, he is greedy and not to be trusted." She looked at the time on the nightstand. It was 2 a.m., but she still picked up the phone to call Meno.

"Meno? Mi fidelidad esta contigo, usted es como un padre para mi. Si algona vez necesitaria algo usted me lo dana." Shai paused.

"Adelante Shai." Meno said.

"Quiero a Tyrek y estoy con el 100% es por eso que no deseamos hacer negocios con Elan. Te necesitamos en order para-" Meno cut Shai off.

"Lo que me pides no es simple. Necesitare habiar con alguien, dame una hora." Meno said, and then hung up the phone.

(Translation)

"Meno, my loyalty lays with you, you are like my father. If I ever wanted something. you would give it to me."

"Go ahead Shai."

"I love Tyrek, and I'm with him 100%, so we do not wish to do business with Elan. We need you in order to.."

"What you are asking is not that simple, I will have to speak with someone, give me an hour."

Shai let me hear the whole conversation on speaker phone. Although she thought I couldn't understand Spanish, I guess she wanted to assure me of her loyalty by not hiding the phone call. I looked at her in disbelief.

"You love me huh? You with me 100%." I smiled.

She looked in amazement.

"You know Spanish?"

"What you thought I was gon fuck with some muthafuckas and not know what they be saying about me." I pulled her on top of me.

She looked me in my eyes and softly spoke.

"I love you and I don't care if you don't love me now, you will later. I'm with you, or I'll die without you."

I took those deep words to heart. I thought about them and repeated it over in my mind. I looked at her and repeated them back to her.

"Estoy contigo o mi muero sin ti."

Just as I was lying there wondering how things would play out with Elan, so she answered.

"Meno?" she said.

"Si, the deal is 10," he said, and then hung up before she could say anything.

She stared at the receiver for a while, shocked at the quick ending of the call. She knew deep inside that he was not pleased to know her feelings for Ty, and it wasn't because of his race. It was because of his involvement with the Cartels. Shai knew that from now on, she was Ty's family, and the one that the Cartels would target if anything went wrong.

"What's wrong with you; you alright? Who was that?" I asked.

She looked at me.

"Is 10 sweet enough?" she smiled.

"Hell yeah! That's cool! Now I can cut into T-Mac's shit."

"And I might be able to get some niggas to jump sides," she said, straddling me. She leaned down to give me a kiss.

"Hold on," I said, holding my hands up to her face. "You might want to go brush yo teeth first? You know you just woke up."

"Shut up!" She grinned, wrestling to plant a kiss on my lips.

***

Elan sat tapping his foot furiously against the floor. He just received a call from his boss, El Chapo. He was informed that he would no longer take care of the St. Louis region. It had been handed over to Meno. He couldn't argue with El Chapo's decision, though he knew it was Meno's doing. Elan never trusted Meno, and vowed someday that he would take care of that little secret that Meno was hiding. He thought hard about his next phone call, and decided that it was time to carry out his plan.

***

T-Mac walked in his kitchen. He lived in Lake St. Louis, which was a rich community that housed some of the wealthiest and most successful people in the St. Louis area. Breakfast was prepared for him on the patio. He kept a few good looking women around his home that knew how to cook. He looked up to see Easy already outside sitting at the table. Easy helped himself to an early meal.

"What up nigga?" T—Mac said, taking a seat.

"Shit, you got some nosey ass neighbors. They are always looking at a nigga when he pull up and shit." Easy said, placing his glass of orange juice on the table.

"Nigga I told you don't drive no rides out here with rims on'em. You know if they don't like Nelly's ass staying out here, they definitely ain't gon like my ass." T-Mac chuckled. "I see ya boy cut out on tha deal." he added, informing him of the deal with Ty.

"Oh, yeah what you wanna do about that?" Easy sat back in his chair, giving T-Mac his full attention.

"Imma holla at Elan to see what's going on, then I'll let you know."

T-Mac took a bite of his sandwich, and then a woman came out to the patio in a gown.

"Telephone," she said, sitting the phone down and placing a bluetooth on his ear.

"Yeah," T—Mac answered.

"I promised you a long time ago that once I reigned over Meno, that you would be very well taken care of, right?" Elan said.

T—Mac sat up in the chair and glanced over at Easy. He knew a phone call from Elan that early wasn't good.

"Yeah, what's up?" T-Mac replied.

"Where is the bitch, Shai?" Elan asked. "That bitch put her neck on the line for that puto, Ty, then had Meno cut me out of the deal!" Elan yelled. "Listen, you take care of that bitch and I will forever be in debt to you," he demanded, and then hung up.

T—Mac wasn't shocked to get the information on Shai. He knew she was fucking with Ty, he just didn't know she switched sides. He took the bluetooth off of his ear. He knew by Ty having Shai behind him, he would be hard to stop. He could rise quickly with her, too. So T-Mac looked over at Easy.

"Shai, she gotta go."

Easy was surprised, because he liked Shai. But an order was an order, and he knew he had to follow them.

"I-ight."

***

I was up early, I had plans for Shai today. I had already been out to the Galleria, and made a stop off by the Channel &Co store. I bought a 10 karat yellow diamond bracelet, and a 3 karat yellow diamond ring. Once she set eyes on my gift, I knew she was going to melt. When I got back, she was still asleep. I left a note on the pillow along with the bracelet, which entailed a romantic scavenger hunt for her.

I arranged a reservation at the *Clayton on the Park* hotel. I booked the Presidential suite for two nights. After that I went to Bristol's and got a private booth, paid the waiter to hold the 3 karat ring for me while I waited for Shai to meet me at the Restaurant.

***

"Where the fuck is this muthafucker!" Easy yelled, hitting the dash. I was getting paranoid waiting in front of the Airport. He stayed armed and had been smoking. He was waiting on someone from Phoenix that Elan had sent to make sure what he ordered was taken care of properly. Easy was getting restless and was contemplating leaving until he saw a glimpse of a big balled Mexican.

***

Shai awoke to a cream rose and a note on the pillow next to her. She opened it and a diamond tennis bracelet fell on the bed. She picked it up and dangled it around her hand. It was gorgeous, she looked at all the diamonds. Each was at least a karat. She tried it on, and loved it.

"Perfect," she mumbled to herself. She picked up the note and read it:

Today you should have something for your wrist, something for your fist, and something for you to kiss. Meet me at Bristol's and you can have all of this, I'm waiting.

Shai rushed out of the bed and into the shower. She picked up her phone to text me, to make sure I knew that she was on her way.

I had been waiting for about 30 minutes already when the text came thru. The waiter was showing her co-workers the ring, and telling them I was planning on proposing to someone today. I told her to hold it and wait 'til I give her the signal to bring it to the table.

***

Pull over here, the Mexican told Easy. Easy had just gotten off the phone with T-Mac, and listened as he joked about how he felt like he was in the scene of a Tony Montana movie in New York. T-Mac insisted that he take care of the business quickly and get that muthafucka back to the Airport. He didn't want him parading around the city with a Mexican like that.

Easy sat watching as the Mexican screwed a silencer onto the .40 caliber handgun. He then cocked the gun, loading it with one in the chamber.

"Now we wait." the Mexican said more to himself. They sat back and waited. It wasn't long before their target emerged from the building. He rose up in the seat at the sight of Shai walking to her car.

"Mu evete!" he said, tapping Easy. Easy tossed the phone in his lap.

"Speak English muthafucka, What?" he said, rising up in the seat to get a look at Shai. "Yeah, you ready." Easy looked at the Mexican. He was adjusting the beam on the gun.

"Si." he replied.

***

I was getting impatient. I had been waiting for more than an hour now. Shai should have been here by now. I picked up the phone to call her again. No answer still, so I called repeatedly and it kept going straight to voicemail. So I tried Rell.

"What up," he answered.

"You seen or heard from Shai? If not ask Moni has she heard from her?"

"Moni said she was on ner way to meet you."

After giving me that information, Moni snatched the phone from Rell.

"She ain't there yet?" she asked. "Stop Boy!" she yelled at Rell.

"N'all, let me try her again." I said, hanging up.

***

Shai drove up Olive Blvd. She did not notice the SUV following behind her. Had she just looked into the rearview mirror once, she would have noticed that she was being followed. Her curious excitement from today's events had her off guard. As she prepared to turn on Jefferson to get on the highway, when she turned on the intersection, she heard cars screeching to stop. She turned around quickly anticipating impact from a careless driver, when she saw the flash of a muzzle from a gun pointed in her direction. Before she could maneuver the car to try and dodge the oncoming bullets, she felt a burn.

The half turn from her maneuver gave the car a straight path into a light pole. Shai layed stiff with her head pressed against the steering wheel. There were medics all around the scene, trying to pry her from the vehicle. The impact had crushed the vehicle, causing her to be stuck between the steering wheel and the seat. Witnesses say they saw a blue SUV swerve towards her vehicle, causing her to crash at the corner. None of them reported hearing any gunshots.

Detective Scott, who had been on the force for many years, and had seen his fair share of accidents pulled up and briefly looked around the area. He noticed cops over at the corner pawnshop talking to witnesses. He wondered if anyone had a description of the vehicle that actually caused the hit and run. As he watched them remove the young lady from the vehicle, an hour had almost passed. Once they got her onto a stretcher, the medics yelled for him to come over quickly.

"We got three gunshot wounds," one of the medics expressed, concerned.

The cops placed perimeter tape around the area. It was now ruled an attempt homicide. Detective Scott hurried over and took a look at her. *Damn, very pretty young lady*, he thought, looking at the medics as he waited for him to finish working on her.

"Is she alive, will she make it?"

The medics wiped the beads of sweat from his head.

"I don't know, she's unconscious right now."

Detective Scott swung around, facing the wrecked vehicle. He heard the tune of a phone in the car. At first he thought it was just the radio, until it repeated itself over and over again. He looked in and saw the phone on the floor. He put his latex gloves on, then reached in to try and grab it. He squeezed his arm between a bent in door and contorted seat to try and reach it, but his 6'2, 240lbs frame couldn't get it. He looked around to see if he could find someone to squeeze in between the small space, then he yelled to one of the medics nearby.

"Hey, reach yo skinny ass in there and get that phone." he said to the medic.

The medic looked up at him and cursed under his breath. Scott, was getting restless, but the medic grabbed the phone and handed it to him. He quickly scanned through the call history log, trying to see who the last caller was. Suddenly, the phone rang again.

"Hello! He quickly answered.

***

I was worried now that Shai didn't show up. I didn't want to think anything was wrong. She wasn't answering her phone at all. I decided to try one more time before leaving, and when I heard another man's voice on the other end, I froze for a moment. As my mind took in the male's voice, I finally responded.

"Who the fuck is this? Where Shai at?"

"Calm down, calm down, this is Detective Scott, Shai has been in a very bad accident."

"What type of accident?" I asked, fearing the worst as I sat back in the chair.

"I'd rather not say over the phone. Is it possible for you to come down to the station so we can talk in person?"

"What type of accident!?" I yelled, realizing the other patrons in the restaurant whose attention was now on me. Trying to get control of my temper, I settled back down.

"What is your relation to the victim, Sir?" he asked.

"Victim? What happened? She's my wife! What happened?" I asked.

"She has been in a wreck. She struck a light pole," he paused. ".. and she's also been shot three times. Sir, they don't know if she will make it."

I was already on my way out the door when he said she had been a victim. I was worried about Shai so much that I forgot about the ring. I made it back to the Loft, ran up to Moni's apartment and banged on the door. Moni answered.

"Shai been shot!" I said, walking in.

Rell came out the backroom, he could see the tears in my eyes. He stood there waiting on me to speak. I didn't know what to do, Moni was coming out the back fully dressed on her way to the hospital. She kissed Rell on the cheek.

"I'm going to be with her." She said as she walked out the door.
"What happen?" Rell asked.
"I don't know, I just had a conversation on her phone with a detective saying she was in an accident and got shot."

I could barely get the words out. It hurt more when I said it then when I heard it from the cop. I sat in silence for a moment, as Rell sat looking and waiting on my response. The phone in my pocket started to vibrate. It was Jessica. At first I wasn't going to answer, then I thought about the thing she had to do in order to keep the product flowing.

"Yeah," I answered as normal as possible.
"You wanted me to call, where the girl at?" Jessica asked.
"Here's the number, make sure you videotape it." I gave her the number and tried to hang up, then she yelled in the phone.
"Video! - Nigga, I aint videoing me!" she added.
"Just make sure you video him and her together, not you," then I hung up. I wasn't in no mood to go back and forth with her right then. I got up, and Rell rose with me.

"So what's up? What you wanna do?" he said, pacing.
Shai was like family to us now, it was no doubt that the city was going to pay for what happened to her.

"Get them thangs, fuck all this political shit."

Chapter 9

Rell rode over to the north side of St. Louis, on Mimicka. This was the set of Murdaville Ganstas. Rell had a few cousins who were M.V.G. He pulled up to a brick house got out and walked towards the porch. Scully, Rell's cousin, emerged from the inside of the house.

"What's up cuz?" Scully said excitingly, due to not seeing Rell in a month or two. Rell walked pass him, into the house.

"Shit, what's up."

Scully immediately sensed that something was wrong.

"What up nigga, you straight?" Scully asked. Rell walked up to the dining room table where a few M.V.G. members sat playing cards and drinking.

"Where Tarv at?" Rell asked.

Tarv was Scully's oldest brother. Sensing Rell was serious, and not in the mood for games, Scully called for Tarv.

"Tarv!"

Seconds later Tarv came out the back room.

"What up nigga? What the fuck you yelling foe!" he said, pulling up his jeans. Some of the others jumped up at the opportunity to see through the crack of the door, sneaking a peek at the female laying naked across the bed. Tarv reached back to close the door. "What up Cuzzo?" Tarv said, giving Rell a handshake.

Tarv was big, chubby and dark skinned with a low cut. Scully was skinny and dark skinned with a lot of tattoos. His name Scully came from him robbing people with different types of scullys on. Rell looked at them both, reaching under his shirt to pull out several stacks of money. Then he placed it on the table, right in front of the others. Rell placed his hand over the money to get their attention off of the amount on the table.

"Serious business," Rell said, looking at Tarv then at Scully. "I want ya boy Easy and his crew knocked. First one, get plenty more." then he tossed stacks across the room to the others.

***

I walked into the I.C.U. at Barnes Hospital. At first they wouldn't let me in since she was a victim of a shooting; but I created

64

such a scene, and demanded that as her husband they let me see her, so they did. Though I was only allowed a few minutes to visit. I couldn't take seeing her that way. My knees were weak, after seeing Shai helplessly lying there with several I.V.s stuck in her arms. I couldn't take my eyes off all the tubes they had running into her body. I removed Noni's bag from the chair and took a seat. I sat there thinking about losing her and while going over my feelings, I realized how much I really loved her.

I'd never felt like this before about any woman at all. I knew if I could, I would take her place in that bed. I sat there for a little while longer before walking out into the hallway. I saw a nurse and questioned her about Shai's health. She said it would be a day-by-day process and that she didn't know exactly when the doctor was coming in to provide me with any more details. In regards to living, it was up to God and Shai. As I sat down in the seat by her room, I placed my head in my hands. I didn't notice the man bending to sit next to me, but after a few seconds, I just heard him speak.

"I take it you are the one I was talking to on the phone?" Detective Scott asked. I looked up to see who it was, and noticed it was the detective. Unmoved, I placed my head back down. "Feeling guilty, huh? Was it meant for you?" he asked.

I knew he was trying to probe me for information, but I didn't want to snap, so I got up and tried to walk away. That's when he got up and followed.

"You know you're a lowdown pussy ass motherfucker when your wife is in there fighting for her life, and you know those bullets was meant for you. Now you don't want to help us find the motherfuckers that did this." he retorted.

I paused and turned around at the comment. I couldn't hold my emotions back. I hit him so hard, he slid across the floor. Two blue suits rushed me and wrestled me onto the floor. Afterwards, they placed cuffs on me. The detective got up laughing it off.

"Boy! Now you really got to come downtown."

***

Jessica was leery of her little sex-capade with her boss. Karra, the female I sent with her was told not to put Jessica in the video. Jessica was satisfied, and stood aside to watch the whole thing. Jessica

65

was glad Karra was there too, because Karra was far more freaky than her. She switched positions every minute and sucked her boss dry. Once they were done, they left him with a copy of the tape. Jessica glanced over at Karra several times. She was curious as to how old she was. She was sure that Karra wasn't of age and that was why Tyrek wanted her to tape the scene, and advised her not to be involved with it. She knew it was getting too deep for her to be involved, so she wanted to figure a way out. When she pulled up to Karra's apartment, Karra reached into her purse and grabbed the video memory chip to give to her.

"Here, Tyrek told me to give you this. He said you might need it later." then she got out.

Jessica wanted so desperately to ask her how old she was, but she decided to let it go. She watched as she walked into the building, then she pulled off.

***

"Sit yo motherfucking ass down!" the detective yelled at me. They had me in the interrogation room for hours. I couldn't move, my ribs and chess were hurting from the brief ass whooping they gave me on my way downtown. I could taste blood in my mouth, too.

"You know I haven't seen a hit like this in years," he leaned over towards me. "Now somebody wants you dead bad enough that they would hit yo pretty ass girlfriend." He sat down on the side of the table. "Now, you can let us know what's going on, or we can wait til we find yo ass floating in the Mississippi. And if we do, we can only hope to find some evidence. Most likely we won't though, because of the way these motherfuckers move about," he got up. "Yep, they would've been knocked ya girl and you, and got away with it."

I kept my head down, waiting on my lawyer to come. It seemed like they weren't going to let me go, until I said something. I must've gone through another hour of this shit before my counsel finally stormed through the door demanding that they release me. They all stepped out of the room, then the door swung open and a slim bald guy in a suit stepped in and signaled for the detective. The detective stepped out for a second then came back into the room and grabbed the folder. Then the other guy quickly entered the room.

"Yo you're free to go."

As I walked out of the building, the detective approached me. *What the fuck now*, I thought to myself. *Damn, he's going to arrest me for hitting him.* He starred me in my face.

"Imma get a good look at you so I can recognize you when the coroner finds you," he angrily stated, walking off.

***

I was awaken when the nurse tapped me on the arm. She was changing the I.V. bags, and I didn't even know what time it was. She gave me some bandages for the wounds the cops had given me on the way down to the station. I sat up and checked my text messages. There were several from Jessica, questioning why would she need the video. I ignored it, then thought about the fact that I still hadn't heard from Rell. Stressed from the day's events, I walked outside to get some air. An ambulance was pulling into the emergency entrance and paramedics were wheeling someone in on a stretcher. I distanced myself from the commotion and called Rell. Thankfully, he answered on the first ring.

"What's up?" he said.

"Why you ain't hit me up?" I asked.

"Shit, figured you was going through it, so I gave you some time to ya self. Since you up, meet me on the East. We got a situation."

"What's that?" I asked.

"Can't say. Couple of hours," he hung up.

I wasn't in the mood to deal with no bullshit. Especially with the way I felt at the time. Anything coming my way right now was getting deadened. After clearing my thoughts, I went back up to spend time with Shai, til it was time to go meet Rell. I held her hand, hoping that she would show me a sign that she-was still fighting for her-life, but she didn't. I laid her limp hand down beside her, gave her a peck on the cheek, then headed for one of the spots off Churchlane, in Edgemont.

"Nigga shut the fuck up!" Rell yelled. Los was lying on the floor. I came through the door to find Rell pacing over him. "I knew yo mafuckin ass wasn't built for this shit, Nigga." Rell smacked him. "You don't know how to follow rules."

"What's up," I said, looking at Los on the floor, bleeding.

"Ty! Man help me tell—," Los was cut off by a swift blow to the jaw by one of the homies who was standing near.

"Shut the fuck up nigga!" Rell said, turning towards me. "The nigga got in the whip, talking all reckless to me while somebody was on his phone. When I picked up the phone to see who it was, they hung up."

"Man, it wasn't nobody! Straight up, I swear," Los screamed.

Rell nodded to one of the others standing around. The guy approached Los and kicked him in the mouth.

"Aww, mamufuk," Los mumbled.

"I'm tired of this nigga, he'll fuck around and get us knocked." Rell added.

"Do what you do. You know what it is with me; ain't no room for error," I cautioned. "But we need to find Easy. I want that nigga and T-Mac," I whispered to Rell.

I felt the phone vibrating in my pocket. I backed away from the commotion and took the phone out to see who it was. Calls were coming in back to back, and I didn't recognize the number. It had a weird area code, 011—52. *Who the fuck could this be.* I thought to myself, glancing over at Rell.

"Holla at me when you are done here," I stepped outside and walked to the side of the house. I could hear the faint muffling of gunshots in the background, then Rell emerged from the house shortly afterwards. As he walked up, I held the phone in the air to allow him to see the weird area code.

"That's Mexico." he said, looking just as puzzled as I was.

"Hello," I answered the phone.

"Senor Ty?" someone said.

"Yeah, who is this?" I asked. Then, it was a brief silence.

"Meno," the voice answered. I looked up at Rell. I could sense this phone call wasn't about business. He seemed angry. "What happened to Shai, better not been because of you. Revenge should have already taken place." then he hung up. I knew Meno wanted blood just as bad as I did, and if I didn't do anything, then my blood would be spilled.

The M.V.G. niggas been sniffing out Easy spots, but hadn't been able to catch him. They did stumble across a spot where some niggas hustled for Easy and T-Mac. Some of them were out smoking and talking shit. Two of the M.V.G niggas got out around the corner from the block they were on and started walking in their direction. The others rode up the alley, and got out a couple houses down from the spot. One of the cats noticed the two M.V.G niggas walking up and tapped the others.

"Derrty who the fuck is these niggas?" one of the guys asked, passing the blunt to another.

Everyone drew their attention on the two guys walking up the street. It was not common to have strangers walking up the block like this, so it raised flags. On que, one of the MVG's that crept up the alley broke a bottle in the gangway behind them. Everyone turned around to the sound of the broken bottle and that's when the two walking up came from under their shirts.

"Murdaville!" one of them yelled as the barrels started to erupt in gunfire. They tried taking cover in the gangway, but the other MVG's were waiting. They ducked, trying to dodge bullets and ran into two AR-15's.

The dudes walked up on the guys and shot them close range. Then a car sped up and they got in and left the scene. Speeding out of the alley and down the street, two guys hung out of the window. Others on the block were out, so they drove by shooting at them also. And while leaving they also yelled, "Murdaville Nigga!"

When I arrived back at the Hospital, Moni was in the hallway talking to Chad and Boo. Chad's eyes were bloodshot, so I knew he was mad. They had every right to be too. And being that they were Shai's cousins, I figured they would want in on what was going on.

"What's up wit it." I said to Chad and Boo. We walked down to the cafeteria. Chad didn't waste any time, and he quickly asked me what happened?

"Look Homie, I really don't know shit. I think she got hit over some shit we got going on. I think the boy T-Mac had something to do with it," I explained.

"I know that nigga, well I don't know him, but I heard of him," Boo said. "He be pumping over on the south side. Plus I heard this bitch mention his name, because I think she fuck with the nigga's nephew or something like that. But anyways, she's always talking bad about the nigga."

I came to the edge of the seat when I heard that information.

"Who is this Bitch? You think she'll get at him for you?"

"She stays off the Laide, the Bitch and that nigga be in Ofallon Park every weekend," Boo said. The Laide, was a street called Adelaide in St. Louis. Most of the niggas over there were 6—0's.

"You trying to get them fingers greasy?" I asked, trying to see if they wanted revenge just as bad as I did.

Both of them mentioned at the same time, "Hell yeah! Nigga what's up?"

"We gon kidnap this nigga." I said.

***

It had been over a week and I hadn't heard anything from Meno. I was assured that he'd cut us out for now, or at least until this beef blew over. Our next shipment was coming tonight through Jessica. It was confirmed that she had two suitcases or 50 bricks for us. For weeks she had been bitching about how her boss had been questioning her about the extra luggage and that if he caught her flirting with the other workers in customs, she would be fired. I informed her of the video and told her to keep it in her possession whenever she came to work. That way just in case he start tripping again, she'd have it. Though, I was hoping she wouldn't need it.

Once the plane landed, Jessica grabbed her luggage.

"Girl, you need some help?" one of the co-workers asked.

"N'all, I got it," Jessica grunted. "Shit," she mumbled at the weight of the luggage. She was tired and frustrated at the thought of being in too deep. She wanted to stop and wondered whatever happen to Heather. She recalled that she never saw her taking the occasional trips like she had been. She also knew that the loads were getting bigger and bigger, and it would only be a matter of time before something went completely wrong. She knew she had to make a decision, would this be her last trip or what.

Jessica had built a nice nest egg, and was ready to quit. At ten grand a trip, she was straight. Jessica walked through the terminal and noticed her boss approaching her. She knew he was up to something.

"Ms. Wallace," he called out. *Damn he called me by my last name,* she thought to herself, realizing that wasn't good. "Ms. Wallace, can I see you in my office?" he asked with a demanding tone. "Bring the luggage with you." he added.

She walked through the door to the office. Pleased to see it was just the two of them, she relaxed. Johnson walked up to her, then he looked her in the eyes.

"Ms. Wallace are you transporting something on my flights?" he asked.

"What!" Jessica replied with a straight face.

"You heard me clear as day," he reached for the luggage and slung one of the suitcases on the table. As he started to open the luggage Jessica blurted out.

"Wait, before you look at that. You need to look at this first," she took out her IPOD, opened up the videos and then pulled up the one of him. He looked at it for a few good minutes, then sat on the table in front of her with a smirk on his face. It was as if he was proud to see her possessing the video, then he started laughing.

"I know you don't think this is blackmail." he said, handing her the IPOD. "Listen Jessica, sex with a little slut isn't a crime. It ain't gon do shit to me."

"It ain't just a little slut you fucking pedophile," Jessica said, putting the IPOD back in her purse.

"Pedophile?" he stood up. "Bitch! What you say!"

"You heard me clear as day. That girl was only 16, and Bitch if you touch me or arrest me, I guess we can try to get correspondence to write each other in prison," Jessica closed the luggage and pulled it off the table.

"You set me up, you filthy whore!" he yelled in a low—tone.

"N'all, you the filthy whore." she grabbed the luggage and walked out of the office. She knew this was the last trip she'd be taking because it was becoming too much to handle.

"16 fucking years old Tyrek, where the fuck did you get that girl." Jessica was shaking and yelling as she paced in her apartment.

"Chill the fuck out, she ain't really 16, she older than that. You straight ain't you. The only reason we had to do it is so you wouldn't get caught. I was trying to look out for you."

"N'all you was trying to look out for that shit you selling," she said. "I can't do this no more, it's over - I'm done."

Rell looked up when she said that, he knew she knew too much and the way she was acting, he didn't trust her to hold water. As she took a seat on her couch, she talked to Tyrek.

"This is the last one Tyrek. I'm done. My boss will not tolerate me-working there after what just happened. Shit, I'm probably already fired."

"I doubt that -he don't want to take no chances with those charges. Besides, what the fuck you gon do, huh? You see the money is good, do just one more."

"Ty, you ain't see the look on his face, I can't," she explained, getting up from the couch. "Let yourself out," she said, walking into her bedroom.

When she closed the door, I felt she was closing the door on our entire operation. She was cutting my supply off completely, and not taking into consideration how her decision would affect me. I didn't even have to look at Rell. He was already thinking the same thing I was thinking. He walked into the kitchen, grabbed the icepick from the counter, and headed back in her direction. I didn't hear any sounds of struggle, just a body drop. He came back into the room, wiping the icepick off.

"What we gon do now?" he questioned, getting frustrated also. Everything was falling apart. Shai was the only one who could put things back in order. And at the moment, she was busy fighting for her life.

"I don't know for right now. We gotta find a way to get it in or we gon lose the streets." I said, taking my phone out of the console of my car. We rode down to the River Front, and sat there talking for a while. Rell saw SL drive by.

"There go ya boy," Rell said, pointing in the direction of a burgundy Mercedes SL 500, which was speeding down the street. It was headed towards the Casino.

"Come on Nigga, remember that nigga fuck with Easy!" Rell sprouted out in excitement.

We pulled up to the Lumier's Casino, which was one of the most elegant Casino's in St. Louis. We followed SL into the Four

Seasons Hotel, though he didn't look like he was staying there. He walked to the front desk, then came back out.

"What you wanna do?" I asked. Rell looked at the area, and didn't think Downtown, or the River Front was a good place to do anything.

"Let's follow this nigga," he said, leaning back in the seat. SL hopped on highway 70, heading west. He got off on Jennings Station Road, and turned into the neighborhood. He rode the block until he got on Fletcher. He parked in the driveway of a brick house, got out and snatched a bag out the trunk.

"I know he wasn't riding dirty in that." Rell said.

"N'all, this nigga's picking up some money. I bet it ain't nothing in that bag," I said. "Hit the box and grab them burnas."

Rell hit the power to the radio three times and the console lifted up, revealing two semi-automatic Smith & Wesson's. We grabbed the guns and Rell pulled the icepick from his pocket.

"What the fuck you got that for?" I asked, curious as to why he still held on to it.

"I like this little muthafucka."

SL waited on Kaymi to bring the money out of the backroom. Kaymi, was Geo's girl, who was also a nigga that coped from SL. He loved coming over while Geo was gone, so he could secretly indulge in their love affair. Geo considered SL to be a very close friend and trusted him around his girl, and SL played on that weakness.

He sat on the couch as Kaymi came from the back. She sat the money on the table and tightly pulled the string.

"Where Geo say he had to go?" SL asked.

"I don't know. He left with Rock," Kaymi replied, handing him the bag of money. She took a seat next to him on the couch, and immediately, he admired her.

Kaymi wasn't a bad looking female. She was of caramel complexion, with a nice body. As she sashayed through the house, she wore BCBG sweats that were so tight on her ass, SL was distracted. She had on a shirt that matched, and also showed all of her cleavage. SL counted the money, and then slid it in the Prada bag.

"So what's up?" he said, opening up her legs and rubbing his hands down her thigh to her pussy.

"I don't know how long he gon be gone," she said, moving his hands away. SL stood up and unzipped his pants.

"Well then I guess I can't get no pussy, huh?" he pulled out his dick as Kaymi looked at him.

"You ain't shit," she grinned, kneeling to suck his dick. SL moaned in pleasure.

"You ain't shit either... Damn!"

***

I stood on the side of the house, peeking through the   window. SL had his pants down as I tapped Rell to tell him that we should creep around back. We would have called some of the guys to handle this for us, but we needed this chance and had no problem with handling business like this. We were never too far from fucking something up, no matter how much money was made. Once we made it around to the back, much to our luck, the door was unlocked. I slowly opened the door and snuck inside.

We crept through the kitchen and came up behind SL. They were too busy getting off to see me coming. SL had his head tilted back with his eyes closed, while Kaymi was sucking him dry. I waved for Rell to come around with the guns drawn.

"Don't move!" I said, as the barrel touched the back of his neck. His eyes opened wide at the feeling of the cold steel.

"Oh shit!" Kaymi screamed, wiping her mouth and hopping back on the couch.

"Geo, Man what's up," SL said, thinking I must have been Geo catching them in the act.

"This ain't no muthafucking Geo Nigga!" I gritted. Rell eased around to the front of him with the icepick in his hand. When Kaymi saw the icepick, she balled up on the couch.

"The money's right there Dog; right there in the bag. You can have that shit," SL pleaded.

"Nigga that lil money ain't shit! I wanna know where Easy at!" I said. SL glanced around to the side and recognized Rell.

"Damn, Homie! What's up? What's going on Ty man? What's this all about?" he asked nervously.

"You know what it is, Easy where he at?" Rell gripped the icepick.

"Come on Dog, I thought we was—aww shit!" SL yelled, as Rell poked him with the icepick. Kaymi started moving side to side from the sight of him getting punctured.

"Just tell'em please!" she shouted.

"Shut up Bitch, fucking with you-aww shit!" Rell hit him again. "Come on Man, please, man please quit poking me with that muthafucka."

"Then tell us where he at!" I said, pressing the barrel to the back of his head.

SL quietly stood for a moment. Then he saw Rell looking like he was going to poke him again.

"I-ight Man, look, he ain't got no spot. We just meet in different places. Please Man, come on and just take the doe and let me go," he begged.

Rell looked at me with the look I was familiar with. Once the talking was over, he hit SL twice with the icepick in his upper chest, instantly puncturing his heart. Like dead weight, SL dropped to the floor. He began coughing and wheezing for air as Kaymi pled for her life.

"No please- no! I didn't see shit. I swear, I didn't see shit!"

Rell looked at her for a second, as if he was taking in consideration if she'd say anything or not. Without warning, he raised the icepick on her and struck her twice also.

"Aww!" was her final screams.

We grabbed the money bag, and ran back to the car. Rell reached around and threw the sack on the backseat.

"What the fuck is up with you and that icepick, Nigga?" I asked.

He looked up at me then at the pointed object.

"I don't know. Shit, Nigga I might be practicing for prison," he laughed.

"Nigga you stupid." I giggled at his comment.

Chapter 10

I couldn't sleep, so I tossed and turned all night long. This shit was getting to me and I couldn't focus. My connect froze up on me and I was trying to find another source. I knew I created a complicated situation with the connect by cutting out one and going through Meno. *Fuck it, what else could I do; especially when I got a deal that sweet. I had to make something happen*, I thought, so I decided to call Elan. I picked up the phone and sent him an I.M. to let him know that I wasn't in Phoenix, but I needed to talk to him A.S.A.P.

I waited over a couple of hours before he finally hit me back. When he first called, I was hesitant to pick up. I knew he was going to give me the third degree and I wasn't in the mood for that shit.

"Hello," I picked up after a few rings.

"What is more important, loyalty or life, Senor Ty?" Elan asked. I was caught off guard by the sudden question, which I didn't fully understand him.

"What?" I questioned, wondering what was his intentions were for asking me about loyalty. I thought the connect was all in the family, that it didn't matter who I coped from as long as I coped.

"Answer the question?" he demanded. I thought about what he asked, figuring it was a trick question. If I said loyalty, then he would say I didn't remain loyal to him. If I said life, then he would say I should've remained loyal. So I gave what I thought was the best answer.

"Both."

"Good answer, though you know I'm not pleased with the recent events." he paused. "You disappointed me Senor Ty." I couldn't say anything, I figured I'd just let him speak and hopefully I'd have a pipeline by tonight. "What can I do for you?" he asked.

"I need you to extend your hand to me, open me up a line," I asked, hoping it was possible. I heard him chuckle into the receiver.

"How would Meno feel about this?" he asked.

"Look you know I'm dry," I said, getting annoyed at all the questioning. "I need your help, so what's up," I added after taking a deep breath. It was a brief silence on the phone.

"Be here tomorrow and we'll talk." he said, then he hung up the phone.

It was becoming tiresome with all the back and forth between the connects. But that's how it is when you're dealing with an organization. They all wanted a piece of the cake, and was willing to backdoor a motherfucker instantly to get it. Now Elan was my only shot. And after what Meno said to me, I was paranoid about going down to Phoenix to holla at him. It could be a set up, but I had to take that chance. Elan hung up the phone. He knew by getting Shai out of the way he would be able to corner the operation. Elan wanted Meno out of the way, so he could continue to plot his way to the top of the organization. He couldn't just kill Meno, because that would have been a suicide mission, so he had to play the game and take Meno's business down.

As long as Shai stayed out of the way, Meno would not do business, he would only concentrate his attention on her from a distance. He knew Meno's secret, and that was that Shai was his daughter, but he was just waiting on the right time to let everyone know. It was only a matter of time.

***

"So let me get this right, y'all let some niggas come through the hood and get down on y'all," Easy paced back and forth, then slammed his hand on the wall. "Doing drive bys, and done chased y'all niggas in the house and shit!" he paused, looking around. "Some MVG niggas at that, what the fuck they doing over here? Them niggas from the north!" he looked around again. "Y'all got some beef I don't know about are something. One of y'all fucking one of they bitches or something!" Easy joked, but nobody laughed. They knew better than to take Easy for a joke. "I guess it's the same niggas sticking mafuckas with ice picks and shit." Easy glanced at his crew, he wanted them to see how serious he was. "Next time read the Whirl, it better be a massacre on Mimicka!" he said then walked out of the house. He hopped into the Ext. Escalade, and drove off.

He read in the Whirl, a local newspaper in St. Louis. There was an article about a police officer who got a call on a female named Jessica Wallace. She had been hit with an icepick. He was trying to figure out what that had to do with SL. He knew things could get wild

77

in the city during summertime, but niggas just didn't use icepicks like that. He thought about the act of poking someone with an icepick. *That's serious*, he said to himself.

***

I was on my way to the Hospital, trying to decide if I was going to get a bite to eat first. I haven't had a good meal since this shit kicked off. I was about to swing by Applebee's in the Central West End, when Rell called.

"Where you at?" he asked.

"I'm bout to get something to eat; I'm hungry as a muthafucka. Then, Imma swing by the Hospital. What's up?"

"Skip that, we need to rap real quick."

"I-ight, where you at?" I said, pulling over waiting for him to direct me to a meeting location.

"Meet me at the Church's Chicken on Delmar and Skinker, in the Loop," Rell said.

"Bet, I'll be there in about 10 minutes," I replied.

"I'll be waiting on you."

"Good, grab me a box of Chicken while you wait."

***

When I got there Rell was inside the restaurant ordering the food. I peeped in his truck and seen Chad and Boo with some chick sitting in the back seat with Boo. I instantly assumed that was the chick he told me about in the cafeteria that day.

"What up fool?" Chad said, hanging out the window.

"Shit, what up?" I replied, walking over to hop in the driver's seat. "Who dis?" I asked.

I stared at her as she looked out the window. She was a pretty high yellow chick, with a piercing on her bottom lip.

"This Jeremy gal," Boo smiled. The girl smirked at Boo when he mentioned Jeremy.

"Who the fuck is Jeremy?" I asked, looking at Chad.

"T-Mac's nephew." Chad said. I looked at her when he said that. She saw the look on my face when I heard T-Mac's name and it gave me a nervous expression.

78

"Let me holla at you." Chad said, getting out the truck.

I got out the truck and stood between the two cars. Delmar and Skinker was a very busy intersection. I didn't want someone riding pass and noticing us standing there.

"She's willing to set up Jeremy for some change. I told her I would hit her with 10 geez and she hopped on it." he said.

"Give her some more and make sure she's all the way with it," I said, reaching into my pocket to hand him some more money. "Here, give this to her and tell her we can hit her with some more if she plugs us with him now." I added.

"Yeah, got you." Chad got back into the truck, and Rell came out with the box of Chicken.

"My Nigga what's good," he said, handing me the box of food. "What you thinking?" he asked, noticing something was on my mind.

"You know I'm rolling out that way tonight," Rell smirked at the start about Phoenix. He didn't like it and knew it could go anyway.

"What, Nigga you trippin," he said. "I'm coming with you. You don't know what the fuck they might be on."

"N'all, I gotta plan to get us back in with Elan." I opened the box of chicken, grabbing a piece.

"I-ight Nigga, if you don't make it back in a couple of days, I'm coming," he said, smiling. "And Imma have'em screaming some Mexican shit when I put that icepick on they ass."

***

I stayed at a different Hotel in Scottsdale, this time. I had to switch up the routine, so I had to be careful. When I sent Elan a message, I told him I was at the usual place to see what happened. He just played it normal and told me to come to the house. I was hesitant at first, but I had no choice but to go.

I pulled up to the house and the same big dude escorted me back to where Elan was sitting. To my surprise it was just him and another guy. I hadn't seen this dude before, but he was in a suit just sitting like he was observing us talk.

"Senor Ty, want a drink?" Elan asked, then poured a shot of Tequila. "Please let's toast to a new beginning of business."

"New business, that's what I'm here to discuss—" I was cut off by Elan.

"Yes, yes we must have loyalty amongst us even in this cruel business," Elan said. "When a rule is broken, sanctions are permitted," he added. I looked around when he made that comment. I thought I was about to see dudes swarm the room and come in to get my ass.. But nobody came.

"Sanctions are my way of punishment and you deserve a sanction. So, I go up on the price, 10 percent," he said, smiling. He stood up and walked around the seat.

"Ten percent, that's twelve five a ki," I said.

"Plus, the 2 grand for shipment," he added, holding up one finger.

"What fourteen five, come on Elan," I said. Elan froze in his movement and turned around to look at me. I forgot that he never told me his name, it was Shai that told me.

"I see Shai has informed you of my name," he said. "Estoy contento que me discise de esa puta," he added, laughing along with the other guy. (Translation- I'm glad I got rid of the bitch.)

When he said that, I almost fumbled my glass on the table. Both of them stared at me.

"You al'right Senor Ty, is the price too much?" he questioned, firing up a cigar. I was holding everything in, so I swallowed my drink.

"Nall, that's cool. I-ight," I pinched my nose to try to block out the thoughts of taking the Tequila bottle across his head. If I did, I knew I wouldn't make it out of the house alive.

"I need you to get it to my doorstep," I said, standing up to sit my glass on the table.

"No problem, just ten grand a trip," Elan smiled. He was putting a tax on everything; so I played his game. I didn't have much of a choice and had to ride with him for now, or at least until I find a way to kill him.

***

When I got back to the Hotel, I was heated at Elan's role in the situation with Shai. To know and not be able to do anything about it was killing me inside. I knew now that he had that done for cutting his

80

ass out of the deal. I couldn't believe why I didn't put that together at first. He used T-Mac to get Shai.

Being that it happened right after the deal. Now I know I needed to figure out a way to talk with Meno. Without Shai, there was no way to get in contact with him. I laid on the bed and waited til it was time to get back to the Airport.

Stop the flow, and then I'm a dead man. That's exactly what they tried to do, Stop my flow.

Chapter 11

After I arrived home, I immediately stopped at the Hospital. I was excited and hurt. I had figured out valuable information for Shai and was not able to tell her anything. Moni said the doctors informed her that Shai would be fine, they were just waiting on her to come around. It was time for me to get on my grind again. Although, T-Mac had the ups right now, I couldn't let that stop me. I made a call to Memphis, which is where my cousins stayed. I told them to come up for the weekend, because we needed to talk. My plan was to send everything out of state, because I was in no position to compete. I called up everyone I knew that stayed close by in small towns down in Southern Illinois.

I hustled hard, had to stack my doe, and at the same time stack T-Mac's shit also.

"Man, I wanted to kill that muthafucka!" I gritted as I told Rell about the details of the meeting with Elan.

Rell knew a little Spanish also. Like me, he'd learned those key words we needed to know in order to understand what was being said. And that helped out a lot and taking the time to learn another language was beginning to pay off. Once I informed him of the new ticket, Rell stood up.

"What, that's some bullshit! Nigga we can't rock like this for too long," he said, pissed about the prices, but I knew if he came along with me, we probably would have never made it back to St. Louis.

"We gon get wit- his girl," I asked. "Peep, we gon rape every spot T-Mac got and substitute for the loss we taking."

***

"B, what it do cuz?" I greeted my cousin from Memphis with some dap and a hug.

We met downtown at Calico's, it was a nice restaurant in the downtown St. Louis area. It was also a good spot to eat and chill at. I guess I liked it cause it had more of a social gathering type feel than dining. B loved the seafood pizza there too, so every time he came to town, he had to get one.

"What up Main- why you don't come to the town?" B asked, stepping inside the restaurant. We scoped out a spot next to the fish tanks and took a seat.

"Nigga, I been grinding," I said, opening up the menu to glance at the list of entrees. Rell glanced over in the direction of the bar, then got up to holla at some female who was waving him over. "I got something coming through in a minute; you still got the East on lock?" I added.

"Hell n'all, it's tough Nigga," B waved for the waitress. "Ain't shit poppin like that."

"Hello, are you guys ready to order?" A slim waitress approached the table. B took a look at the menu.

"I don't even know what I'm looking at this for. Let me get the uh, seafood pizza," he smiled. "Oh, and a side of hot wings also."

She looked over at me.

"And you, you ready to order? Didn't you come in with a party of three?" she asked as she quickly surveyed the restaurant, lying her eyes on Rell over at the bar.

"Yeah, let me get the wings also, no pizza," I said.

"Ok, and just tell him to wave whenever he's ready to order," she said, walking off to place the orders.

As the waitress was talking it felt like someone was staring at me. I looked around and B noticed Monz coming our way. He had another nigga with him.

"Who dis, ya man?" B questioned. I stood up.

"N'all, but don't sweat it, I got this."

I saw Rell step behind me. Monz walked up and pulled a seat out from the table.

"What's going on Homie," he nodded, sitting. He looked at me with a puzzled look. "A, what up with you shooting your number to my gal, relaying the message that you wanted to rap with me? What we got to rap about?" Monz asked.

"Business," I said, sipping my water. "It wasn't nothing personal."

"Yeah, that's cool, but I don't fuck around on that tip no more. The numbers them people throwing at a nigga is vicious. One of my niggas just got thirty. Catch me on that green, ya know," he said, looking at me then at B. It was if he was sternly stating his point.

"Ok, I got you, hit me up though. I may be able to do something with you." I wanted to leave the air peacefully, even though he wasn't a factor anymore, I figured I still may be able to use him for something later on. After Monz got up, Rell sat down. The food came, and we ate and chopped it up about how we would get it to Memphis. B had a white bitch that would drive around town for him, so he said he could get her to move it on the highway for him. I told him that would be up to him, but I didn't trust no white bitch at all, not like that. When shit hit the fan you can almost be sure that they will tell everything.

Leaving out of Calico's, Rell and B spotted a pair of chicks walking in. They instantly broke for them. Usually I'd be in high pursuit also, but I was going through it. My mind was on Shai and getting revenge. After putting their Mack down, they got back with me a little later.

"Dike ass bitches," Rell said, returning.

"Damn Main! Shit! Y'all need to let a nigga watch or something," B yelled, walking in our direction.

We got in the car and stop by a clothing store called Fresh Image. We spent a few dollars before we headed out to the house in St. Charles. It's been a while since I'd been out there; at least a month or so, so I grabbed a pile of mail from out of the mailbox, and walked in the house. I threw the mail on the table, and sat for a moment to admire the house. It was a nice home with 3 bedrooms, 2 and a half bath, and a basement that I'd decked out with furniture and fish tanks. Rell sat down in the living room.

"Damn, what the fuck is that smell?" he asked. I walked through the house to make sure everything was as I'd left it.

"That's the spinach dip yo muthafuckin ass had last time we were here Nigga. You left it on the counter," I fussed, picking up the molded tray to throw it in the trash. I wrapped the bag up inside another one and sat it out in the garbage.

"Nigga, we ain't gon be able to do shit with this load," he yelled into the kitchen at me. I was coming back in, when he expressed his frustration with the prices.

"I know! We gotta move it though, then try to get something better or we gon have to fallback," I flopped down on the sofa.

"I think we should fuck with that weed, I know some niggas that's coping like a 100 at a time. Shit, we can get some of that money," Rell hinted.

"So you making money outside the brothers now, huh?" I joked, doing my impersonation of Nino Brown.

"Nigga fuck you," Rell laughed. "N'all, straight up though, that weed is the lick."

Getting into the weed game wasn't a bad idea. But it was just too damn bulky for me. To get that shit back, we needed a van or a truck.

B butted in, instantly looking at the aquarium.

"I know some white boys who grow that shit; and it's some fire to Main." I glanced over at B. I never thought about growing, I was getting desperate.

I heard the beep to the alarm go off. That meant a door or window had opened. I got up to see what it could be. I walked into the kitchen to find Terrence, my next door neighbor, coming in. He was only 12, so he'd come over while I was gone to feed the fish and maintain the aquariums. Usually, I'd give him a hundred a month to help out. He didn't want his parents to know he was doing this cause he feared they would have a fit. So he kept the extra key that I gave him under the pot in the backyard. Everyone in the neighborhood thought I was a Music Promoter, and that I was constantly on the road.

"Oh, hey Ty," Terrence said. He was a real cool kid, who was quiet and attentive. What I liked the most about him is he always came in to feed the fish and then left. He never nosed around or anything like that. He made sure he got his money every month too. A good loyal, trustworthy hustler he was.

"What up Lil T? How you doing?" I asked, patting him on the head. I reached into my pocket to give him some money. It was more than likely that him stopping by wasn't a mistake. I know he came to collect. As I peeled off four fifty dollar bills and gave it to him, I had to talk noise.

"Make sure you don't spend it all at one time, i-ight," I said as he grabbed the money.

"Al'right," he said. "Thanks." then he left back out the door. I looked out only to see him hiding the key back under the wood flower pot, and then he crept back over into his backyard. I walked into the living room, tapping B on his leg.

"Yeah, let's get to know how them white boys get it poppin on that weed." Then I looked at Rell. "And we gon find a plug on that commercial green also. We gon lock some shit up around here," I stated, and then heard a knock on the front door. It was immediately followed by another knock, but it was even louder than the first one. I quickly hopped off the couch.

"Who the fuck-" I hurried over to the door, wondering who it could be. No one knew of me staying here, so Rell and B, followed me to the door. "Chill! I'll get it," I said, cautioning them to stay back. I didn't want them causing no trouble out here in the St. Charles area or the police was going to be over here on our ass quick. I looked out the window, and it was a woman standing there in her gown with an overcoat on. She looked pretty decent, as for as looks, so I opened the door.

"May I help you?" I asked.

"Hi, I'm Mrs. Sutton. I stay next door," she said. I immediately figured this was Terrence's mother. "Yes, how are you doing?"

"I'm ok, thank you. I was just wondering why would you give Terrence this much money just for watching your house and feeding your fish?" she said, pulling out a wad of cash from her coat. Terrence must have been saving every dollar, because it looked like he had saved up at least two thousand dollars.

"Yes, I gave it to him, but I think he must have saved it up all the while, because I've never given him that much at one time. I'm sorry for not asking you first. Maybe I thought you wouldn't mind." I stepped out on the porch.

"No, no it's ok, it's just that it's a lot of money for a young boy to have and I didn't know what he was doing."

"No, there's nothing going on, I gave it to him and like I said, he must've stacked it up."

"Stacked?" she questioned, as if she was judging my choice of words. "Look, I don't know what's going on, but I would like it if you never gave my son anymore money," she added.

"Airight." I said as proper as I could, trying to be sarcastic. She smirked at my sarcasm and tried to hand me the money, but I didn't take it. It was Terrence's money, he earned it honestly, and I wasn't going to take it back. Once done, I turned around and went back inside the house.

***

Everything was coming together with B in Memphis. Now I just needed to stretch down to Mt. Vernon. I had a homie down there that was getting it in for me. After sending B back to M—town, we shot down to Mt. Vernon. We met up with Jus, on 12th Street and Murda Ave. It was just a field on one side with a house in the open. Across the street were houses, but they hustled out of the house in the open. These niggas was going hard, like on some eighties shit.

At anytime it was at least 20 niggas standing around with smokers all up the block. Jus, took us over to 17th Street, to a spot they called The Trap. It was a little studio home, but it rocked over there as well. I could tell that is why they called it The Trap. Jus loved this spot because on any day he could get a nine off in dubbs. To think about it, getting a quarter Ki off in dubs in one day, *Damn that's big; especially in a little town like this.*

"I ain't gon be over here in this hot ass spot all day Nigga," I stood by the door watching the traffic. I didn't want to get caught up, and all the traffic made me nervous.

"I'm ready," Jus said, walking from the back room. "I'll be back in a minute," he stated shooting a quick look over to the female sitting on the couch. She wasn't all that fine, but she was thick.

We went around to his house and got the paper. He had forty stacks, so we tossed him two bricks for that.

"Holla at me when it's over and we gon do something big." I stuffed the doe in the bag, then realized I had the same Prada nap-sack as SL did. Rell grab the doe and went to the ride and stashed it in the compartment. I shook up with Jus, and told him to get at me later.

***

AFFILIATED MAFIA MEXICANA

"Man, fuck Nelly, he got all that doe and ain't signing all these rappers coming out in the city. Fuck'em I don't care what he do for the city, he ain't putting none of the artist on. Chingy, J-Qwon, or whateva his name is, the new lil nigga, got dreads like everybody else, riding lil Wayne dick and shit," Cooly, my barber fussed. He was talking shit again, just as I was coming through the door of the shop to get a haircut. Cooly looked up at me and nodded.

"You next."

That was the big homie. He'd been my barber for a long time. He also used to grind, but had made enough change to where he was comfortable and stopped. He got him a custom Barber/Beauty Salon and been talking shit and cutting hair ever since.

"Come on nigga! What up Derrty, you been M.I.A?" Cooly said, throwing the cover over me.

"N'all, I been trying to get shit together. Been rough on ya boy."

"Yeah, I gotta holla at ya before ya leave."

"What up?" I curiously asked.

"We'll talk in the back," he cautioned. After Cooly finished cutting, he walked me to the back office.

"Come on Cooly, I gotta be somewhere at two," some guy yelled who had been waiting for a while.

"Shut up you fat muthafucka, I told you I do appointments, now you gotta wait. I'll be right back," Cooly said as he walked off. Cooly was a lot older than me, he was 37 and I was 26. So I looked up to him and his opinion mattered.

"What's going on Young Blood?" he asked as he sat down at his desk. I took a seat, too.

"Shit everything's cool."

"Not what's going on in the streets, I hear you beefing."

The word can get around quick, especially if you about something, then everybody be in your business. One person says something, then they start to put two and two together, then bam, ya business is out in the streets.

"You know how it is out there Cool." I didn't want to talk about the situation. Cooly picked up on the hesitation, and chimed in.

"Look, get ya shit together. I told you this shit ain't for everybody, and it don't last forever. You can't make doe dead or in jail."

Cooly was right, he always kept me grounded and focused.

"It ain't like dat. See, a nigga got mad cuz I stepped on the turf. But it don't matter anyway at the moment cuz I'm fucked up right now. I gotta find another plug. Tryna fuck with that weed, you know somebody?"

Cooly kept his ear to the streets, and always had ties from when he was in the game.

"You fucked up," Cooly laughed. "You ain't fucked up, you greedy, ain't no telling how much doe you got," Cooly thumbed through some papers. I knew when he did that he was thinking hard. I knew he didn't like getting involved with the streets either, but he always looked out for me. "I gotta cousin out in Texas. He stay in the Valley, outside of Roma, and I know he gotta plug. He been trying to convince me to come down, but I ain't on nuthin. I'll get at him to see what I can do for ya."

"My nigga," I reached over the desk to touch fist with him. "That's what's up."

"But you need to think about getting out of the game. This shit ain't gon last long, and you can't spend all that doe in the joint," he paused. "You know how much they spend in there every month, just two hundred and ninety dollars Nigga. You better think about what you're doing and the potential consequences."

Chapter 12

"What you mean, it's over E?" I argued with the Mexican who was responsible for the shipments. He said Elan sent him a message, saying our line was cut. We moved all the shit now Elan was cutting us dry.

"I don't know, I don't know just give me the money and you talk to him," he said.

I gave him the money, but Rell wanted to take the money and send him back to Elan in a bag. If we did that, me and him both would probably be dead men. I had a feeling T-Mac had more influence than I expected. With Shai down, it was no way I could get it back running. The weed game was the only shot I had until Shai came back around. I stood there empty handed, watching the truck pull away. I had to go hard with the weed for now, and make T-Mac pay for this setback.

***

Chad nodded at Jeremy, "There's that nigga over there." Jeremy was stunting in O'Fallon Park. It was time to get some revenge. His chick told Boo that Easy came over and stashed some work at Jeremy's house the other day for T-Mac. She said it was money and drugs there because Jeremy would pull it out to show it off to her like it was his.

The only way to get it was to snatch his ass up. He stayed off 270 and Old Halls Ferry Road.

Chad looked over at Rell, "How you wanna do this?" he asked.

I was sitting back in the cut chilling. We were in a Tahoe with tinted windows, watching some chicks parked on the side of us who were scoping us out. Rell looked over at them, I knew he was contemplating something.

"Wait a minute," Rell said as he got out the truck.

O'Fallon Park was packed, it was where people would ride through to show off their whips. It was mainly a Crip set though, and most of the niggas was from 44 Bud, the Laide, and The Fair. I leaned out the window to holla at'em.

"What you doing Nigga?" He held up a finger and walked over to the chicks that were parked next to us. They were chilling and smoking weed. They were the average hoodrats, who looked like they might be banging too. He leaned in the window of their car to talk to them, then reached in his pocket and pulled out some cash. After that, all the chicks got out of the car and followed Rell back over to us. They looked like they might have had at least 5 kids a piece. But when Rell approached with them, he was still smiling.

"Give me two geez," he said.

"Man, what the fuck you on," I replied, pulling out the money to pass it to him. Once he had it, he turned around and gave it to one of the females. She was giving me too much eye contact as they split the money up. As soon as they were done, they started off in Jeremy's direction. Rell looked at me.

"Watch this, I told them to just go over there and get to stripping for him," he started to laugh. "I told them to just start dancing on all of them and to keep it on the low that it's his B-day. The one in the blue gon pull him to the side, take him over to the car, and give him some head, that's when we gon bag that nigga."

The bitches walked over there and started doing what they were told to do. Them niggas started to laugh, pointing at their stretch marks and pouring beer on one of them. A different one turned around to bend over to dance in front of some niggas and got kicked in the ass. She was a real hood bitch though, because she turned around and served that nigga quick. His homies were trying to get her up off him, but she was viciously swinging and kicking his ass. I kept my eye focused on Jeremy. He was laughing at the confrontation as he stood alone by his truck. The girl in the blue approached him, grabbing on his pants as she tried to feel his dick.

She was on her job. She whispered something in his ear then pointed over to her car. Jeremy smacked her on the ass and started to follow her over to the ride. Both of them got in the car, and she leaned over and went to work. Jeremy had his head leaned back in the seat with his eyes closed. When he opened them, he saw two barrels in his face.

"What the fuck!" he yelled, looking surprised.

The chick raised up at the commotion, "What baby, oh shit!" she yelled in a low whisper. She looked at the barrels and drew back in the seat. Boo walked around to the other side of the car and opened the door.

"Get yo ass out Nigga!" he demanded, pulling Jeremy out onto the ground. Jeremy quickly took off the chain he had on and threw it at Boo.

"Man, what's up, you can have this shit!" he pleaded.

"Shut the fuck up, and get yo ass up and in this ride."

Chad pulled him by his collar and pushed him inside the truck. We smashed off, as I looked back at him, smiling. He looked around in shock and was caught totally off-guard. I could tell he wasn't aware of the situation. He looked at me as if he was trying to put a name to my face. I chuckled and looked over at Rell.

"Damn, that lil nigga look just like his uncle." Jeremy's eyes widened when we pulled up to his home.

"What we here for?" he asked. I reached over and hit him in the mouth.

"Nigga you know what we here for, you think we stupid. Get yo ass out of the truck and go get us that shit!"

Jeremy grabbed his mouth, pleading for us to let him go.

"Nigga, get yo ass out!" Rell hit him in the head with the butt of the gun, as I grabbed him and walked him up to the door.

"Who's inside?" I asked, quietly putting the barrel under his chin, while looking around to be sure there wasn't any neighbors watching.

"Nobody." he mumbled. He was crying like a bitch. Rell opened the door and walked in, as Chad and Boo followed behind. Ready to get moving, I pushed Jeremy inside.

"Nigga get that shit, where is it at?"

Jeremy tried to play dumb. "I don't know, I swear man straight up." He stopped talking when he seen Boo come out the room with a duffel bag full of kilos and money, then I slapped him with the gun.

"Nigga straight up, huh! Oh you straight up!" he was squirming on the floor, holding his hands up like that would stop the bullets. I didn't understand why niggas did that.

I didn't want to pop him because it would have made too much noise. So I bent over and started to pistol whip him. I smacked him over and over with the tool until he was lifeless. Rell was grinning, but Chad and Boo was looking in disgust at how gory it was. I felt a tap on my shoulders, and it was Rell. *I must have snapped out for a minute.* But I regained my composure, and then I stood up.

"Bitch ass nigga," I huffed, I was out of breath and had spots of blood all over me. The gun was dripping with blood, so I looked around. "Bust open some of them bricks and leave some on the floor," I said, throwing the gun in my pocket. "Wipe down whatever you touched and let's roll. Take the truck over to Murdaville and tell'em to torch it."

I tossed the gun in the river on the way across the bridge. We went to Chad and Boo house in O'Fallon, Illinois, which was about 20 miles outside of St. Louis. They had a decent layout, and you could tell they didn't design the house at all. They had paintings on the walls and little wooden sculptures to match the hardwood floors. We split the work up and counted the money. It was a little over 200 grand. I sat back thinking of the upcoming beef that was about to occur. That 200 grand didn't even put a dent in his pockets, but the loss of his nephew was going to make him feel like I felt about what he had done to Shai. I got up to go to the bathroom.

While walking through the house, I noticed it was big in size and in a good neighborhood. I looked at some of the pictures on the wall. I stopped at one in particular. It was a picture of Shai at a young age. She had a strong Hispanic resemblance back then and was standing next to Chad and a Latino male. He had on a linen suit, like he played in Miami Vice. It was halfway buttoned down, and he had a chain on with a cigar in his hand. He looked familiar, like I'd seen him somewhere before. I studied the picture for a little while longer, then it came to me, that was the guy with Elan from the restaurant the day we first met.

"Meno," I whispered to myself, not knowing Chad was standing behind me.

"How do you know Meno? Shai mentioned him to you?" He asked as he stood next to me looking at the picture. "We was on this yacht he rented, now his ass owns one. I ain't seen him in years though. After Shai mom, my auntie, died he hardly came around. He keep her loaded though, but she don't even acknowledge him as her daddy."

"Her daddy?" I asked curiously.

"Yeah, her ole man." he said as he walked off.

For the rest of the time there I was wondering if what Chad had just told me was a lie or not. Her Dad, damn, why would she lie about something like that? Now I was thinking, *did this bitch lie about everything she told me.* I thought about all the times she landed big deals with Meno, just by a phone call. Was she playing me, just using me to get money and keep her family business going?

I couldn't figure it all out, so I called Moni to see if she was doing better. She said she'd come around, but was barely able to talk. She also said the Shai had written my name out on a chalk board asking about me. She asked was I ok, and said she wanted to see me badly. That made me feel a little better about our relationship. I looked over at Rell, as Moni asked for him, I threw him the phone, wondering to myself, *was Moni playing this game also.* All this deceit had me questioning what or who I should trust.

***

Cooly had left messages for me to hit him back ASAP. He wanted to inform me that he had talked to his cousin and that I should swing by to see him as soon as I could. I pulled up to the Barbershop in a Van, about 4 deep. I saw how Cooly came to the door as I was getting out of the vehicle. He knew that I hardly rolled deep like that unless it was trouble in the streets.

"What up boy?" Cooly said, opening the door to the shop for me to enter. He nodded for me to head towards the back room. "I'll be back in a minute," he said.

I walked into his office and took a seat. I stared at the pictures on the walls for a while. Admiring his change from a street dealer to coaching his son's Youth Baseball Team. I thought about how peaceful his life must be at this time, considering that he got money, a business, family, and he was doing something that would not threaten to put him in the grave. I envied him for a moment, because I wanted that same life for myself, but I felt I was in too deep to have what he had. He came into the office and took a seat behind the desk.

"Damn, I see you still causing trouble," he said. I knew he was talking about the Jeremy situation. We didn't even have to speak on it. "My people said fly down and pick out a flavor. They gon give you a real smooth ticket too, so don't worry about it."

"Cool, Imma get down there by this weekend." I said, sitting on the edge of the seat.

"He wants you to hit him up when you land, and he'll either come get you or direct you to a meeting spot." Cooly passed the number over to me. "I-ight Nigga be cool out there, cause if something happens to you, you gon force me to come out of retirement," he laughed.

***

Shai had been laying up in the Hospital bed for weeks. To ensure her safety, Moni put an alias name on her after that shit with Jeremy went down. She had been wondering what was going on with Me, and why I wasn't coming to see her that much. She didn't know that I had stayed the majority of the time she was unconscious. And Moni was filling her in on the things Rell wanted her to know. Shai was doing better and getting restless.

Although she suffered minor injuries from the crash, she still was prepared to get out and get revenge. The three gunshot wounds had grazed her and one went straight threw her shoulder. The most serious injury was done to her brain during impact. She damaged her cerebral cortex, causing her to fall in a comatose state for a short period of time. They ran several cat scan and found no further damage to the brain.

Shai was up and moving about. She became infuriated by what her memories of that day brought to mind. It took her a minute to piece it together, but moments before the shooting, she recognized the driver, it was Easy, along with a big bald Mexican. In the elevator on the way up to the room to see Shai, I felt a bit of nervousness and excitement. I didn't know how she would react to the news about Elan and his role in her accident. I also didn't know if she would be pleased with me going at T-Mac's nephew like I did. She was always with the political side of the game, and war wasn't her first priority.

When I walked in the room, she was peering out of the window. Her arm was in a sling and she looked a little pale. I was glad to see her alert though.

"How are you?" I asked, approaching her at the window. She didn't turn to face me, she just spoke.

"Why you ain't been here to see me?" she asked. "You should have been the first person I saw besides Moni!" she hissed. I knew this wasn't the same woman. I walked closer to her, placing my hands on her shoulder softly. I was trying not to hurt her wounds.

"I was coming up here, but so much shit has been going on—" she cut me off.

"I wanted you here," she said, pulling away from my hold. I felt her cold attitude, and questioned her motives.

"Why you ain't tell me Meno was your Daddy, why you lie to me?" I asked. I wanted her to know that I was dealing with issues also pertaining to her. She turned around to face me.

"Who told you that?"

"Ya cousin Chad."

"You two must have gotten real close for him to tell you that," she walked over slowly to the bed and sat down. "I told you that to protect you, if my father finds out that you know I'm his daughter, he'll have you killed. He fears that others will use me to get at him. So anyone who is not family that knows will die; even the one that told you."

I sat down beside her and leaned in to give her a kiss. I realized how much I missed her.

"So I'll act like I don't know."

"Exactly," she said.

"Look we need to talk about what happen to you-" I said, taking a deep breath.

"I know what happen to me, and once my father finds out, T-Mac and Elan are dead men." She got up and slowly walked off to gather her clothes.

Chapter 13

T-Mac watched as his nephew's body rested in the casket. His sister, Jeremy's mother had been blaming him for her son's death. His cheeks were red from her smacking him twice already. He sat at the wake as others came through to pay their respect. He watched each person individually, looking for a sign of forgiveness. He knew Jeremy was set up, he just didn't know who did it. Whoever it was, they were close. Jeremy didn't have anyone over to his house, just his girl. That's when it hit him. La'Chelle, was nowhere in sight. After the wake, he had to pay her a visit.

La'Chelle was at her mother's house. She wouldn't leave since she took that money and Jeremy had gotten killed behind the information she had given. She was scared for her life. She felt real bad, because Boo promised her that nothing would happen to Jeremy. Her mother just thought she was going through it from losing a loved one.

"I'm bout to go to the store Baby, do you want something," her mom yelled up the stairs.
"No, I'm ok," she responded.
"Alright, I'll be right back in an hour or two."

La'Chelle wanted to go to the wake and the funeral, but she was feeling so guilty, she couldn't bare to face his mother. Her mom stayed in University City, off Dorset Rd., which was a suburb in the north county of St. Louis. It was a good neighborhood, one she felt safe enough to hide out in. La'Chelle went down to the kitchen after she heard a knock on the door. Her mom hadn't been gone for more than 10 minutes, so she was shocked to have guest.

"Who is it?" She yelled, and without looking, she opened the door. "Oh my God!" she screamed, trying to close the door. T-Mac, blocked it and grabbed her by the arm, slinging her to the floor.
"Please, please, I didn't know!" she yelled.
"Didn't know what, didn't know what!" T-Mac gritted.

He looked around realizing she may not be home alone. He didn't want to get caught up in the moment. The area was a watchful neighborhood, so he calmed down.

"Chill, I didn't come here to hurt you, just wanted to know what happed," he said, holding his hands up in the air. La'Chelle got up on her knees and crawled to the couch. She sat down in front of the couch, knees balled up to her chest, then T-Mac sat down on the couch across from her.

"What happened?" he asked, getting a little frustrated.

"It-it was Boo," she stuttered.

"Who, who the fuck is Boo?"

"Boo, this dude I was messing with before Jeremy. I didn't know he was going to hurt him. Boo promised that they wouldn't hurt him," she started to cry. T-Mac hid his anger the best he could. "Where he be at, you know?"

"Most of the time he stays on the Eastside. I didn't know they were going to do it. He had me meet some dude. He was dark skinned with low hair. I think his name started with a T."

T-Mac thought of Tyrek instantly. He gritted his teeth and got up to walk out. She jumped at his movement, watching him as he walked out the door. He hurried to his car, and before getting inside, he nodded at the truck parked across the street. Seconds later he left.

Easy got out the truck with another guy and walked in the house. La'Chelle was still balled up in fear. She raised her head up at the intruders.

"No, no! I swear I told him the truth! Nooo—," her screams were silenced by a gunshot.

***

Phi, Scoop, and Terrel were rolling in the truck they were supposed to torch a week ago. They didn't know why they were suppose to torch it, it was just the orders. They decided to cruise the Tahoe for a while, because it was far too nice of a truck for them to just torch it, so they rode it at night, but today they got comfortable and pulled it out in the day.

Phi knew not to be in the hood with the ride. He knew Scully would probably fuck them up for not torching the truck already.

"Let's go pick up Nika freaky ass, she keeps hoes with her," Scoop suggested, rolling a blunt.

"Hell yeah, go get that bitch," Phi tapped Terrel.

T-Mac had every resource he had on the streets involved in finding out who and where Boo was. He had several police on the payroll, so they informed him of the vehicle that the witness said they seen leaving Jeremy house that day.

Terrel stared out the rearview; he noticed a SUV swerving in and out of traffic towards them. They were coming up to a stop sign. Terrel wanted to floor it, but decided not to, fearing that he would be downed by the others for being paranoid. He watched as the SUV rolled up. The windows were tinted, so he couldn't see who was inside. He glanced over at them for a moment then realized that he may have been paranoid.

He watched and waited as traffic passed through the intersection, then he looked over at the SUV again. The driver had rolled the window down. It was a female, waving at him. Phi saw her and rolled the window down to talk to her. She wore a halter top and her breast could hardly fit inside the fabric. She had on lip gloss and pixie braids in her hair. Since their attention was fixed on her, the masked gunmen who crept out of the other side of the SUV to come up from behind the Tahoe was not seen. Terrel heard a car honk from behind, and when he looked in the rearview mirror he saw the gunmen setting up to fire upon the truck.

Before he could floor it, they opened fire. The people in the cars behind the Tahoe ran out of their cars for cover. Once the gunmen was finished shooting, one of them walked up to the truck and checked inside. Then he got back into the SUV and sped off. The bystanders quickly ran back over to the truck to check on the passengers. They were all slumped over in the Tahoe, and clearly dead.

***

"Hey baby," Shai cooed, sitting down on the couch. She had just been released from the hospital and we decided to stay at the Loft until we found something else far away from the bullshit.

"How are you feeling?" I asked, watching her move around better than the last time we talked. Seemed like every day she felt better and was getting more restless. At times she would punch the bed and grit her teeth. I never saw her display so much anger before, but I guess I would too if I had gotten shot up.

"I'm good, I'll be better when I get me some," she put on a fake smile.

"Shit, I've been ready to do that. If you ain't come out of that coma sooner I was gon climb on top of you and fuck you out of it. Shit, the nurse was gon come in and catch me banging that ass." We laughed, and I was glad I put a smile on her face, a real one.

"Shut up, where's my cousins at?" she asked, wondering where Chad and Boo were. I pulled out my phone. "Hold on, I'll hit them up," I said.

Chad was pulling up to the spot Boo and him, had been slanging out of. He parked the car in the back and got out. He was off 29th and Renshaw, on the Eastside. It was a dead-end street. A typical dope spot, filled with all the latest electronics. They had shorties hanging out to watch for the police. Chad hadn't seen any when he was pulling up.

"Hello?" he answered, as his phone rang.

"What's up boy, where you at?" I asked. Shai was putting a finger up to her mouth, trying to tell me not to say she was home.

"I'm across the waters, at the spot," Chad said.

"I need to holla at you ASAP, come through, I'm downtown."

"I-ight give me a minute thou," Chad said. He was pissed that niggas wasn't nowhere to be found. No look outs, nobody grinding, and he felt like something was wrong.

He went to the kitchen and threw the empty baggies and chicken boxes away. He pulled the baking soda out of the cabinet and turned the entertainment system on, listening to Jeezy. *It's that d-boy bullshit yeah I'm still on it, gotta half of brick left, do anybody want it'*, he quoted the song to himself. He rolled up some weed while the water boiled, then went to work. After he cooked up everything, he put it up in the stash and called Boo to see what the fuck was taking him so long to get to the spot. He dialed once and it went straight to voicemail. He figured Shawn was with Boo, so he tried Shawn's phone, and again, no answer.

***

"Man, where the fuck you going?" Boo asked Shawn. Shawn was riding through Brooklyn, IL. A very small area between East Saint, and Madison.

"I know where I'm at Nigga, just gotta make this stop real quick," Shawn said. Boo watched his movements. He didn't completely trust Shawn at all, so he felt like he was always up to something.

"Have you seen my phone?" Boo asked, patting his pockets.

"Damn, I know I ain't lost that muthafucka, shit." he looked down in the seat and on the side of the passenger seat.

Shawn knew where his phone was. He'd taken it off the seat and put it in his pocket while Boo was in the store earlier. He pulled over to a house on a back road in Brooklyn. It was a small house, looked almost condemned.

"Who the fuck stay here Nigga?" Boo asked.

"Come on, check this shit out," Shawn said, getting out of the car.

"What shit, Man you better get yo ass back in this mafuckin ride and let's get back to the spot." While Boo was talking, he reached for the gun he had stashed under the seat and slid it in his pocket. He really started to get suspicious of Shawn actions now, and was near shooting him. He decided to get out and follow Shawn up to the door.

"Who you say lives here?" Boo asked with his hands in his pocket on the gun.

"This bitch, she said she'll let us use it for a new spot Nigga, it be rolling over here."

Boo stared at the house as he walked closer to the door. He looked up the side of the walkway and at the windows to see if he saw any movement inside. The house was in bad shape, it wasn't even fit for a spot. He watched as Shawn pushed on the front door and went inside. He looked over his shoulders across the street at the neighbors having a barbeque out front. He felt something didn't seem right and was skeptical about following him inside. He took a step towards the front and paused at the sight of a shadow coming from behind it.

He did not hesitate at all, Boo reached for his gun and aimed it at the door.

"Nigga!" he yelled as he pulled the trigger and backed away quickly towards the car. He pointed into the windows, shooting recklessly while opening the car door to get inside. He checked for the keys, but Shawn had them. He ducked at the sound of tapping into the steel of the vehicle. They were shooting back at him. He didn't know how many niggas were inside, and when he looked back across the street at the neighbor's barbeque, he saw someone ducking inside of their car from the gunshots. Boo open the car door, taking aim at the house again to make a break for the neighbor's car. He opened the door, startling an elderly man.

"Get over, move!" he yelled to the man bent down low in the driver's seat.

"Ok, ok, please just don't shoot me!" he pleaded. Boo threw the car in drive and sped off. He could see two dudes in his rearview running out toward a car to chase after him.

"Shit!" he looked around at the vehicle he jacked. It was a piece of shit.

He knew he couldn't make it that far in the car. He looked back, they were gaining on him. He hit a corner and shot over some railroad tracks, onto a dirt and gravel paved road. He sped up as much as he could, and was able to see the main road ahead that lead to the Racetrack and Truck Stop.

He looked back again and saw the car chasing him had slowed down. Boo sped onto the main road and headed to 25th street, to the liquor store. He didn't want to take the old man to the spot, so he got out and left him on the lot with his car. He went inside and used the phone to call Chad.

"Nigga where you at?" he asked soon as Chad picked up. He was breathing heavily and his adrenaline was still pumping.

"I'm at the spot, where the fuck you at?" Chad asked. "What's up? Why you breathing hard as fuck Nigga, you i-ight!"

Boo peeked out to see if the old man was gone, he saw that he was on the payphone, probably talking to the police. He hung up quickly and ran out the store. He paced across the field and over the highway, heading down the street on Renshaw. Chad was on the porch looking up the street at Boo running. He went inside and grabbed the AK-47 from under the bed and ran back out to the porch.

"What up nigga, you alright?" Chad asked again.

"Man, that bitch as nigga Shawn just tried to set me up," he took a deep breath. "The nigga took me to some spot in Brooklyn and tried to trick me into the house, if I didn't peep the set up out, I could've gotten knocked. Shit I had to jack some old nigga for his whip to get here!" he paused. "Nigga, I had to pop my way up outta that muthafucka, them niggas gave chase and everything. They wanted me cuz, I think it's behind that thing with Jeremy."

Shawn rode back to the abandoned house. He was pissed that Boo had gotten away. He didn't just set Boo up for the money, him and Jeremy used to kick it when they were little kids. Shawn was raised up on the Mac. So originally, he was down with they set. His family had moved over to Madison when he was young and since then everyone thought he was from there. That's where Chad and Boo thought he was from also.

Easy knew Brooklyn would be a perfect spot for the set up. He knew people out there that he could trust. All the cops were crooked out there, so he wasn't worried about them reporting shots fired. He was disappointed in Shawn for not making sure that Boo was carrying. After Boo got away he told them to chase them down. When he saw Shawn pull back up, he knew Boo had gotten away.

"He on his way to the spot." Shawn said, coming through the door. Easy was quiet for a moment. He looked at Shawn, as he weighed the benefits of keeping him alive.

"One of us got killed today because of you," Easy said. "You ain't check to see if he had a gun on him," he added.

"He didn't at first, he must've had that stashed in the car," Shawn said, looking around to see who was hurt, or for any signs of blood. He looked back to Easy. "Who got knocked?" Shawn asked.

"You," Easy let the gunshot follow immediately after his words.

Chapter 14

Shai and I waited on Chad and Boo to come over to the apartment. She wanted to surprise them, because they did not know she was release from the hospital. She was telling me that she would call Meno soon. She knew she had to approach the situation differently now that Elan had something to do with the hit on her. The Mafia Mexicana had certain ways they dealt with their kind, and if she just up and accused Elan of staging a hit on her, it could cause friction between the bosses and both Meno and Elan could get killed.

I heard a knock on the door, so I got up and checked to see who it was. I peeked out and saw Chad and Boo standing there waiting on me to open the door. I signaled to Shai that it was them. She got up and ran to stand behind the door to surprise them. When I opened the door, she jumped from behind it as they came inside.

"What's up cuz?" she said, smiling, but the smile quickly dissolved into a serious expression once she noticed the look on their faces. Something was seriously wrong. "What's going on with y'all?" she asked.

"Cuz, some niggas tried to knock me, and that nigga Shawn set me up," Boo said as he walked pass her into the apartment.

"Where were you at?" I asked. He sat down and explained to us how it went down. I knew it had something to do with T-Mac. It was no doubt blood would be spilled behind Jeremy's death, and by any means necessary. One thing for sure is that he would target anyone close to me. I glanced at Shai and noticed how mad she was at hearing this, I didn't want Chad or Boo getting hurt behind some beef with me and T-Mac, and I knew Shai would never forgive me for that. And I definitely didn't want her to get hurt, but now there was no way to talk her out of it.

Shai got out her keys and said she was going to Moni's apartment. She left in a hurry, and I could tell it was a lot on her mind. So out of respect, I let her go alone. Shai walked quickly to the elevator. She needed to talk to Moni to see if she could stop the war before it got out of hand between Elan and Meno. She felt it was all her fault, and knew that if anything happened to her cousins, she wouldn't know how to take it. Shai thoughts had her spaced out as she fumbled through her purse to get her keys. She wasn't aware of the loud moans going on as she walked in the door.

"Moni we—", Shai stopped in midsentence after seeing Moni spread eagle on her back with her legs in the air, and Rell pounding her.

"That's why you wasn't answering your phone!" she yelled to get their attention as she turned away from the sight.

"Damn Shai! What's up girl," Moni smiled embarrassed. Immediately, she covered her and Rell up.

"Somebody tried to kill Boo." Shai said, holding her hands over her eyes. Rell hopped up and put his clothes on. He quickly kissed Moni on the cheek then looked at Shai.

"Where they at?" he asked.

"They all up at the apartment right now," Shai said. Rell bolted for the door.

Shai went to sit on the couch. She rubbed her hands over her head. "Girl Ty knows about Meno," she said as she took a deep breath. Moni looked up.

"Does Meno know that he knows you are his daughter?" Moni asked.

"N'all, and he ain't gon find out either. I think Meno is in trouble with the family," Shai said, taking another deep breath. This situation was quickly wearing her down and she was finding it hard to breath. She needed to calm down, so she sat back on the couch. She took another deep breath to calm her nerves. "By me cutting Elan out of the deal, I might have started a war between both Elan and Meno, and Elan is the one who sent the hit on me."

"What!" Moni stood up in shock. Moni knew that it was very few who survived a hit from the Mafia Mexicana. When they came, they did not stop until you were dead.

"Yeah, the best thing to do now is to cut Elan a deal and to ask for a peace between Ty and T-Mac. That way the product can continue. That way if T-Mac breaks the peace then the Mafia will deal with him and not Ty," Shai added. "And T-Mac will break it cause he wouldn't be able to sleep right letting the man live who killed his nephew."

Moni looked off from Shai.

"Did you ever tell Ty about you and T-Mac?"

Shai looked towards the floor, although she tried to tell Ty several times, she didn't know how to. She couldn't just tell Ty that her love for him was a mistake. She couldn't tell him that she was really sent to keep an eye on him for T-Mac, but ended up falling in love with him.

"No," Shai said, looking up at Moni with a serious look on her face. "And he will never find out either."

***

"Nigga I'm on sight with T-Mac, Easy, and I don't give a fuck!" Boo yelled as he paced the room. I was trying to calm him down, but his adrenaline was pumped and he wanted revenge. They were too wild and didn't understand the the position we were in, we couldn't afford to be careless.

"Look Nigga when we was just spot hustling, I didn't give a fuck either. It was anyone can get it at any time. Now everybody know a nigga, we got money so the shit we do gotta be smart and elusive. Nigga, we fucking with that paper, so we can't be like that right now," I looked at Boo and Chad seriously hoping they got the point. They were still young, and the youngsters never understood the consequences behind their actions. "We gone handle that situation, we just need to chill for right now. It's more complicated than y'all think," I added, getting up to speak privately with Rell.

We walked to the backroom and out to the bedroom patio. Rell stepped out and closed the door.

"So you really ain't trying to bring it to these niggas. You know how we do. Nigga, I ain't never got too much money to the point where I can't blow a nigga's shit back," Rell added.

"Man did you know Elan had something to do with Shai's hit?" I leaned against the rail. Deep down I felt the same way they did - fuck these niggas, but the Mafia was a different thing. "Yeah, so this changes a lot of shit. Now that Shai is doing better, she gone deal with the situation. Meanwhile, we gotta go to Romo, TX. to see what's up with that green. We can leave Chad and Boo with the last of the work, and let them push it while we're gone."

"I—ight, but nigga if I see one of them niggas, I ain't gone hesitate or wait for them to pull they shit. I'm dumping," Rell said, leaning over to dap me. I looked at him with a slight smirk.

"Shit, me too nigga."

I rested in my room for a while. I needed to get some peace and quiet to think for a minute. My mind was racing with conflicting thoughts. It had been doing it for weeks now, well, ever since Shai's incident. This organized shit was a lot different from fucking with a regular connect. All the politics that went along with this shit was bullshit. I looked up as Shai walked into the room. She was looking at me with a wondering stare. She laid down by my side and took out the tennis bracelet that I'd bought for her the day of the hit. I instantly thought about the ring. *Damn.*

"I never got a chance to thank you for your gift, did I?" She said, unbuttoning her jeans. She wiggled them off to the floor and kicked them over to the corner. She leaned up and pulled her shirt over her head.

"Ouch shit!" she moaned as she grabbed her shoulder. She was still in pain from the wounds. She straddled over me. I pulled her down and rubbed her body, letting my fingers study her scars.

"You should've seen the ring I had to go along with the bracelet." I said, rubbing my hands along her curves.

"Where is it?" She asked.

"Probably at some Pawn Shop, or somebody's wearing it on they shit right now—"

"What?" She leaned up to look into my eyes.

"I was going to surprise you, so I gave it to the waitress at the Bristol's. When you arrived, I was going to wave her over to bring it to the table."

"Were you going to propose?" She asked.

"Well like I said when I found out about the accident, I left. I was like fuck that ring. I forgot all about it," I tried not to smile, but Shai looked at me then threw a punch to my side.

"Nigga, don't try to avoid my question. Were you going to propose to me?"

"Yeah, I was going to propose! Why?"

Shai looked at me. I could see the tears forming in her eyes. She wiped them away before they fell.

"You trying to make me cry," she smiled. She grabbed my hand to stop me from rubbing her wounds. "Will you still love me with these wounds?" She asked.

"Who said I love you, I mean I was gon marry you because you got some fire not—" I said jokingly, before she interrupted me.

"Nigga you better love me!" She said, elbowing me in the side. "How did you know Elan had something to do with me getting shot?"

"I had called him to get a line, because Meno cut me off after he found out about what happen to you."

"You what! Why did you do that?" She sat up.

"I didn't have no other line, what the fuck was I supposed to do. Elan was the only route. Shit it didn't last long that muthafucka cut me off after a few trips."

"Elan didn't cut you off, Meno did. That is going to make the bosses look into the situation. Meno had to cut you off, you can't switch like that, it makes the other look incompetent. A Cartel drug trade is like the stocks, if a broker has the clientele over the others, he rises in the company. You made Meno look bad in the eyes of the bosses," Shai got up and grabbed her phone. "I gotta call Meno."

Shai got up from the bed and started to pace the room. As she called Meno, she nibbled on her bottom lip. I could tell she was thinking.

"Hola Meno." she spoke as soon as Meno answered.

"Shai? Como esta usted?" Meno asked how are you?

"I'm fine, I'm fine, Ty is taking care of me," she said, hoping that would convince Meno to trust me. Shai knew that Meno still trusted no man when it came to her. She wanted to convince him that Ty was different.

"Senor Ty, si que paso?" Meno asked Shai, he wondered what happened.

"It's best we talk in private, it wasn't from this end, it was from your end." Shai explained.

"What!" Meno spoke in a low angry whisper. "You are right it is best we talk in private, I think it is eyes there now."

Shai look to Ty. She knew if what Meno was saying was true that it could mean Ty could very well be in trouble and the Cartels might be preparing a hit on either one of them, Ty or T-Mac. She feared it would be Ty, simply because T-Mac had too much history with them.

"Calm down please, I need you to bring this to an end, Ty only acted in revenge. I know you can understand that. He didn't mean to bring a problem to the business."

"That may have been because of me," Meno said. "I didn't know what happened so I talked to him myself. I will send a jet for you soon so we can talk more about this. I will do what I can, and I will open something up for him so the bosses will understand that Ty has their business in his best interest." Meno paused, Shai knew what he wanted to say. She missed him also. And now that eyes may be watching, they had to be careful on what was said over the phone.

"You be careful and advise senor Ty not to cause any additional problems. There will be eyes on him now," Meno sat the phone down.

He thought about the situation and how it was too close to exposing the secret of Shai being his daughter. He tried so hard to hide her identity for so long, now Senor Ty was putting it all in jeopardy. He would do any and everything to prevent anyone from finding it out and he also wanted revenge for what happened to her.

Shai informed me of what Meno told her. I didn't believe shit about eyes watching us. This is St. Louis, Mexicans will stick out here, it's no way they can stay incognito, especially on the North, West, and East side. I definitely didn't trust no peace treaty shit. I wasn't about to let my guard down for no man.

"This nigga gon want blood, just like I want blood, fuck a peace treaty." I warned while getting up and slipping into my vest.

"You don't understand, if either one of you do anything, you will die. You have gotten yourself involved with an organization that does not tolerate arrogance or disrespect. So this is not just your life, it's yours, mine, Rell's, Moni's, and everyone who you consider family." Shai paused, trying to get me to understand what she'd just said. I can tell she was getting frustrated with me.

"If T-Mac doesn't honor it then you will witness their wrath." Her expression said it all, get T-Mac to break the treaty.

***

"Fuck peace! How the fuck Meno gon issue a peace treaty sitting way in fucking Mexico? Who the fuck he think he is!?" T-Mac snapped, speaking with Elan over the phone.

"Look Meno is getting weak and it's time for him to move on. I will promise you entire reign over the Midwest once I succeed him, especially if you stick with me," Elan said. His plan was coming along well and T-Mac could be easily used. He was beginning to be a very valuable pawn in plotting Meno's demise. "Keep the peace for now, and I will let you pull the trigger later." Elan added.

T-Mac slammed the phone down. Easy watched on as T-Mac fumed in anger.

"Fuck peace! That nigga gotta go." T-Mac gritted. They were sitting in the theatre inside of T-Mac's home. T-Mac sat back in the seat as his favorite movie played on the 100'inch screen; King of New York.

"Fuck it then, I'll go at these niggas," Easy said, leaning up in the seat. He loved beef, that was always his MO..

"N'all, let me think, it's gotta be a way I can have this nigga dropped without it looking like we did it." T-Mac stood up and watched the screen, showing the scene of Frank getting revenge for the murder of one of his crew members. That scene brought him to the thought of revenge for Jeremy. He got so angry he reached for his phone and threw it into the screen.

"So you gon let this nigga make you fuck up ya house, or is we gon kill this nigga," Easy stated sarcastically.

"Not right now nigga," T-Mac warned. "Elan got a plan, but I don't trust his snake ass. Even though the benefits are lovely, for right now let everyone know it's hands off until I say so," T-Mac ordered. "I'll give Elan a month, then it won't be no talking."

***

I had gotten a call from Cooly letting me know that his cousin was ready. While preparing to take the trip, I had to get someone to take the money down for us. I didn't want to take that chance anymore. I knew plenty of niggas who got relaxed and started to make the trips with shit on them on their own, now every now and then I find myself shooting their family some doe because they in the Feds. Rell insisted that I get Karra to ride the Greyhound Bus or Train. Karra, the 16 year old that Jessica used for leverage on her boss. She was already groomed in the streets. She had been a prostitute since 13, and I knew her since she was 14, when I interrupted her pimp from beating her ass one night on the lot of a strip club. She had matured early and was abused by family and men at a young age. Although my lifestyle wasn't right, I took her in and put her up in an apartment to get her off the streets. For a while she did ok, went to school and worked, but she always fell back into that street life. I guess that's how it is when both parents are addicts and you got no other relatives. That's how it was for me except we are both on different side of the spectrum, which is why I could relate to her. Besides that, she could take care of herself and was very crafty at what she did.

I knew I could trust her with this. She was always loyal to me besides the fact that she loved to scheme for a living. I didn't tell her what was in the bag. I figured if she knew it was a hundred stacks in the bag she might get thirsty. I had it sewn into the luggage and packed her clothes inside. The train would take about a day, so we would be there to meet her and send her back on a plane.

"Imma turn y'all on to this shit, but ain't no room for error, and don't ever rock this shit up. It's too much time, the type of time that make niggas snitch," I schooled Chad and Boo, while getting the five kilos we had left over out of the ceiling at the stash house.

I never knew them to hustle at this level, so I wanted to let them know what to prepare for. Shai got a line open with Meno, so once I got back I planned on having both sides of the game sowed up. I'm bout to turn it up a notch.

"Don't trust a mafucka, not even that On Star shit in the rides. Don't talk in them cars like that. If a nigga talking to you all wreckless and shit don't fuck with him. We should be back by the next ship, so stack ya doe," I added.

We were heading out the door. I grabbed the Louie duffel and took it down to the ride. Shai and Moni was waiting on us to drop us off at the airport. I was worried about Shai and what she would be up to while I was gone. I didn't want her to get hurt again, that would send me on a spree. I decided to leave that thought alone and let her handle things the way she wanted.

***

Landing in Texas, it looked like a big ass desert down in the valley. I couldn't tell if I was in Mexico or the U.S. It was Mexicans everywhere. We hit Cooly cousin, he directed us to a nearby Hotel. He would meet us there then take us to see the plug. We got to the Hotel and got a suite. Karra wouldn't be arriving for another eight hours or so. We checked to see where the Train Station was and drove pass it a few times so we would know how to get there.

Cooly cousin, Randy, was sitting in the lobby waiting on us to come down. Randy looked kind of like Cedric the Entertainer, a little bit chubbier, darker, with a low haircut. He had a Mexican guy with him. He was short and a bit slimmer than Randy was. Randy took us to a restaurant that his friend's family owned. We sat down and ordered some burritos, which were the biggest I had ever seen. Mexican music played faintly in the background while couples, families, and others sat alone eating.

We sat in a back corner far out of ears reach, while we talked about the kind of mota we were interested in getting. The Mexican we meet was named Rueben. He showed us two different kinds of weed. One was dark green and had a little bit of seeds in it, the other was light green with a hint of orange with hardly any seeds. He wanted 400 for the dark and 600 for the light.

"How much of this can we get?" Rell asked, holding up the light bud. We wanted to see how much was available and if it was plentiful. I knew that weed goes on a drout for weeks sometimes months.

"This is plentiful, no problem. It comes from the Familia, this doesn't move well here in Texas thou. They do not like this kind. They love the dark green and brown shit. So I would have to order this from across the border," Rueben advised.

"What are you talking about, Familia?" I asked, wondering if I was getting involved with another fake ass Pablo wannabe that wanted to control me with politics and shit.

"See there is so many Cartels, and each one runs a territory. Basically, they fight over land and distribution of who controls the East or West. The good shit is mainly shipped out to the west coast, while the bullshit is mainly east coast or down south. We keep the cheap shit, you can make a pretty penny off of it." Rueben explained.

"So by us getting this here, it won't be a problem with the Cartels," I asked.

"No, me selling you this won't be a problem. The problem would be if the Familia was to force everyone to sell it, then it will be war, which politics will not allow that to happen," Rueben smiled.

"Good, let us get 200 of them," Rell said, playing with the buds. "And keep it around for us. This is all we want, unless you got something like this or better," Rell added.

"How would you get it back, your rental truck outside? I have a cousin that can put it in the doors and dash of the truck for you." Rueben suggested.

"Yeah, we need that," I said, looking at Randy. Cooly told us he would look out for us, and he did just that.

***

We watched as passengers got off the Train. We looked for Karra. "Damn, this bitch got us," I said, speaking out loud. Just as that thought cleared my mind, I noticed her getting off along with the bag in hand. "Oh, there she go."

She spotted us and began to head in our direction. She began to pick up a light jog as she got closer to the car. I looked past her to see if anyone was giving chase, but saw no one. She quickly got inside.

"Damn, what you running for?" I asked, feeling the adrenaline starting to pump through my veins.

"Nothing, I got to piss Nigga," she said, sliding into the backseat and closing the door. "I've been holding it for a while now. I didn't want to leave the bag at all," she added.

She handed the bag over to me. It was still intact and had the small lock still in place.

"You ain't have no problems on the way here, did you?" I asked. I looked at her and noticed that she was looking a lot older than she was the last time I saw her. She looked like she was in her late twenties.

"Nall, it was straight. The private cart was cool."

"I—ight Imma take you to the telly, you got yo license right, I might need you to do something else," I asked.

I knew it would be risky for her to drive back with the shit, but at the time I didn't have a choice. I needed her to handle this for me.

"Yeah, I got it," she said, fumbling through her purse to make sure.

She had a fake I.D. that I'd gotten for her when I got her the apartment. She needed that in order to get it because at the time she was too young, and she was always ducking Juvenile and Children Family Services.

Once we got back to the room, I informed her of the change in our initial plans. She was confident that she could handle it. I never used her in any situation like this before and was curious as to how she would handle it if she was to get pulled over by a cop while driving with package.

"You think you can drive for about 12 hours or more?" I asked.

"Yeah, I can do that." she said, looking me into my eyes. She was very attentive and that was one of the reasons why I believed that she may be able to pull this off.

"You can't be swerving and shit. If you get tired just pull over to a gas station and get some coffee or stretch. Anything to keep you awake, but don't rest for long."

I decided not to tell her what was in the ride. I'm sure she already knew and she didn't ask either.

"I got you," she said, lying across the bed to give me a wondering stare.

"You good?" I asked.

"Yeah, I'm straight," she said, moving to her side and placing a hand on her head.

"Cool, I'll be back in a minute."

Karra watched as I left the room. She long to tell him how bad she loved him and how she would do anything for him, or how she wanted to be his one and only. She laid her head back on the pillow and drifted off into a day dream. The same one that makes her fall asleep peacefully every night. She slid her hand into her jeans and slowly began to play in the juices that flowed from her body at the thought of her and me making love.

***

We pulled up to the restaurant. Before we could get out the truck, Rueben came out and told us to follow him. He took us around the corner, a couple of blocks away from the restaurant to a little house.

We got out and went inside. It was nobody but Rueben and another Mexican. I laid the bag on the table in front of them. They unzipped it and took a look inside, smiling at the money.

"Mi pedro," Rueben said as he shook our hands. He then opened a door to a room which was filled with the bales of the weed we asked for. It was all wrapped in plastic. He gave Rell a razor to cut the top and check to make sure we were satisfied. Rell went through all of them individually to make sure it was the same or better. All together it was 8 bales, and all of them were good. Rueben reached down and grabbed a bud from one of the bales.

"We call this popcorn," he said, holding up the bud that resembled a popcorn kernel.

I grabbed some of the money out of the bag.

"We call this stacks," I said as we all laughed. Rueben wasn't new to this. He ran the money threw the money machine in minutes.

"It's all good." he said, extending his hand out to us. We shook, then I asked about the cousin he said he knew that would hide the weed in the truck.

"Yeah, let's get that taken care of now." Rueben pulled out his phone and placed the call to his cousin. Shortly after that we met with him in his garage. In no more than 30 minutes the entire truck was taken apart. The inside of the doors, the rear bumper panels, the dashboard, the console, the entire vehicle.

We didn't know we had to break down all the weed from the bales into two pound bundles and re—package them all into little plastic wraps that resemble footballs. I was tired as fuck, after breaking all of it down and making sure it was football size. When we finished, his cousin put the truck back together. The only difference was that you couldn't roll down none of the windows except on the driver's side.

When we got back to the hotel, we stopped and cleaned the truck out and sprayed it down inside and out so that it would look and smell new. Besides the fact that we smelled like weed from all the work we'd just put in, you couldn't smell it at all inside the vehicle. That is what mattered the most. I was exhausted and was trying to remember how he took the ride apart. It didn't matter at the moment; I would have to just get someone to do it for me, once I got back home.

I entered the room and tossed Karra the keys and waited on Rell to bring the other rental around. I didn't tell her we were going to follow her, I didn't want her to get nervous at knowing we were watching her drive. I decided to tail her simply because I didn't want to take any chances with her twice. We planned to leave at night because Texas Troopers stay on the highway trying to profile mafuckas. At night it would be hard for them to see who was driving. As long as we made it out of Texas, we were straight for the rest of the way.

Rell called to let me know he was waiting downstairs. I went back in the room where Karra was to tell her to get ready. When I opened the door she wasn't there. I checked the bathroom, and she was standing in the mirror observing her body. As she pulled her pants up, I noticed that her pussy was shaved and her clit was bulging.

"What's up?" she said, pausing before pulling them up to her waist. I knew she wasn't saying hello. She had been trying to throw that pussy at me since I met her, but I refuse to fuck her. She was fine and very attractive, but she was also young and it didn't feel right to me.

"Let's go." I said then closed the door. She came out the bathroom stumping her feet and mumbling something under her breath. So I grabbed her arm and swung her towards me.

"A, you straight! Cuz if you ain't you can catch a mafucking plane!" I yelled, looking directly into her eyes. She needed to know I was serious and didn't mind sending her on her way.

"I'm good, it's all good. I'm ready." she said. "I'm just tired of you acting like my daddy or somebody. Nigga I ain't attractive to you?" she asked, looking up at me with a seductive stare. She was attractive, her ass was firm and large like Serena Williams. I wanted to, but I couldn't because that would cause a lot of problems. I smacked her on the ass and she smiled.

"Come on let's go," I said, hoping that little smack was enough to satisfy her. Anything to get this work back.

Chapter 15

While Rell and I were in Texas dealing with Karra crazy ass. Chad and Boo were holding up their end. Chad had a nigga he fucked with that moved work off 22nd Street, on the Eastside. The niggas name was Steph. Everything had been going smooth, so they had been getting most of the work off to him lately. Boo worked Edgemont and 59th Street. Over there he had a solid connection with the Bloods in that area on 59th. Although they had a good piece of the city, Steph was the main one moving shit. He moved 8th's in a day at his spot.

Chad and Boo didn't think about selling everything all at once, they wanted it all, so they crumbed niggas.

On this day, Steph woke up with a slight headache. He was partying at the Onyx the night before with Chad and Boo. They left him with a quarter ki, and told him that they would be back, but never made it there after hooking up with a few chicks. When he came in last night, he was so high that he forgot to put it up. After he got back from the club, the spot started to jump. He didn't have much time, so he began to break down and rock the drugs so he could make a few dollars. What he also forgot was that the money he had in his pocket was marked, he had broken one of his main rules, never serve anyone he didn't recognize.

He had served an undercover three times last night. He got up and stumbled to the kitchen to get a bottle water. He noticed that the refrigerator light did not come on when he open the door. He quickly checked the water faucet in the sink, nothing.

"Shit!" he mumbled.

Steph moved the curtains and peeked out into the backyard, and he saw the task moving in quickly to the back door, so he ran towards the front. As he reached the living room, the front door burst open.

"Police, get down on the ground!" A cop yelled as they entered the house.

Steph ran out of the living room, down the hallway. One of the cops tackled him into the wall. They cuffed him and led him out with no shirt on and put him in the police cruiser. Steph watched as task force agents came out of the house shaking each other's hands. Unfortunately for him, they laid numerous amounts of drugs, money, and guns on the hood of one of the cruisers. He knew it was over with for him. With priors already, he would not see streets for a while.

Boo was on his way to the spot to pick up his gun he'd left over there last night. He didn't want to ride dirty like that up in Belleville. He was in a hurry to get it after that situation that happen a while back, and he was still paranoid. As he turned the corner, he stopped up the street when he saw all the police at the spot. He looked on as they led Steph out of the house, then quickly backed up and turned off the street. He dialed up Chad.

"What up?" Chad answered. "Nigga what you doing up this early?"

"Man, ya boy just got raided." Boo said, peeping back in his rearview to check and see if anyone was following him.

"Straight up, where you at?" Chad asked.

"I'm just leaving from over that way, it's all unmarks over there."

"I'm getting up right now, I'll meet you in a minute," Chad said, then hung up the phone.

***

Shai sat in Wing Stop on Grand, in south St. Louis. It was one of her favorite spots to eat. She waited patiently on the person she was meeting. She noticed the black Navigator sitting across the street. She knew he would not come alone like she advised. She only hoped to get some answers as to why someone she thought was her friend wanted to hurt her. She took all the risk by meeting him, but she felt like she needed to know. She sat inside the restaurant for 30 minutes, waiting on his arrival. He came in alone, looked around and noticed no one but Shai sitting inside, then he smiled.

"Where ya boyfriend at?" Easy said, sitting down across from Shai. "I know you ain't come here alone, you ain't that stupid."

"I know you ain't come here alone either, where ya crew?" She asked, being sarcastic.

"They on my hip," Easy said, patting his side.

"Then that's where my boyfriends at, in my holster," she sassed. "I can't believe you nigga!" she gritted, beginning to grow angry at the thoughts of seeing his face in the truck that day.

"What the fuck you talking about," Easy smirked.

"You know what the fuck I 'm talking about, Nigga! I saw you," Shai was growing more angry at his cold attitude.

"Hold on, you think because we got a little history, that I'm suppose to flip sides whenever you flip—"

She cut him off, "I ain't flip, I was never on any side but my own!" her tone grew a bit loud and the lady at the register looked up in their direction. She noticed the stare from Shai and quickly got back to minding her business.

"I gotta do what I gotta do. Just cuz we fucked don't mean shit. It was a bigger picture involved. You need to be taking this conversation up with ya nigga."

Shai thought about what he said. She felt like Ty didn't have the resources to truly stand a war with T-Mac. She didn't want to underestimate Ty, it's just that she knew T-Mac had an influence with the Cartels and with the streets that was a lot stronger than Ty's. The only way to keep Ty safe for now was to make peace.

"Is T-Mac going through with the peace," she asked.

"Bitch you got some nerve! You expect me to tell you what my nigga gon do- What you think; you dealt with these mafuckas long enough." Easy rose from the table. "This the last conversation we gon have."

She watched as he walked out the door.

"You right! This is the last conversation we gon have," she mumbled to herself. She only wanted to spare a friend. Easy and her didn't just have sex, she had gotten pregnant by him, but decided not say anything. She ended up getting an abortion and kept it quiet. So she had feelings for him, she cared for him, but not anymore. The conversation was something she needed. She needed to believe that he was better off dead.

***

Steph sat in the interrogation room handcuffed to the table. The officer opened the door and took a seat besides Steph. Steph sat nervously in the room, shaking his leg. He wasn't built for prison, he was too much of a trick and he was soft.

"Steph? Is that what they call you?" The officer asked. "I am Agent Boone, with the U.S. Marshal's Office."

"Marshals? What the Marshals want with me?" Steph asked curiously.

"You just graduated, to the Feds, your case is going federal." The Agent said. "You had over 200 grams of crack, 3 sells, guns, and we took the marked money out of your pockets. Looks like you will be taking some time off for a while. Unless you got something to tell us that may help you out a bit," he added.

"Man, what I'm looking at?" Steph asked.

"What you looking at? You're looking at possibly spending the rest of your life inside; especially with your priors," the Marshal leaned back in his chair and studied Steph for a second, he'd seen so many crack before and knew that Steph would be easy. He just hoped Steph had something good for him; something that might even aide in him getting a promotion. "Come on give me something and help yourself. How many kids do you have?"

"Man, don't play me with that shit, I've been in this situation before, I ain't trying to do a day in prison!" Steph took a deep breath.

"Oh, you got to do some time, now how much is the question, who's is it?" The Marshal asked, leaning up in his chair. "Give me somebody and we can go from there. Now you don't want to do a day, you can work for us, get us some sells, something major."

"Fuck dat! You trying to get my killed!"

"Alright fuck it then, you the one said you ain't trying to do a day."

Steph sat nervously thinking about the deal he was just offered. He knew working the streets was risky and could get him killed. He also didn't want to do 30 years in prison.

"Fuck," he mumbled quietly. He looked up at the Marshal. "My connects are some niggas named, Chad and Boo."

"Good, now all we need to do is a buy from them, how much do you usually get from Chad and Boo."

Steph began to inform him of all the transactions and things that took place when dealing with Chad and Boo. They planned to let Steph back out onto the streets so he could get a buy from them both. They held him until the wiretap was approved and advised him to set up a phone call to Chad.

Chad and Boo sat waiting on Steph to call so they could post his bail. Snitching never crossed their minds about him. They were naive, but smart. They both had a different impression about Steph. Chad glanced at his phone vibrating in the console.

"This him right here." He said, picking up the phone. He noticed Steph cell on the screen, and was hesitant to answer.

"What's up Nigga, why you ain't picking up?" Boo asked.

Man, this that nigga cell, he should be calling from a jail phone. What's up with thats shit, Chad wondered. Chad decided to pick up. "Hello," he answered.

"What up Nigga," Steph said hesitantly, as he watched the detectives marking the money and listening in on the call.

"Shit, how you get out?" Chad asked, glancing over at Boo. He could hear a difference in Steph's tone. He didn't sound the same, but he brushed it off due to the arrest.

"Out, how you know I got locked up?" Steph asked nervously.

"Boo saw the crib getting raided this morning. You alright or what?" Chad asked. There was a pause on the other end. For a moment Chad thought he heard Steph whispering to someone, he looked at Boo feeling suspicious about the conversation that was taking place.

"Man, they ain't have no warrant when they ran in there so they had to let me go." Steph said, reading off a pad one of the cops slid over to him. "Man, I need to holla at you though, they took everything," Steph said anxiously.

"Imma hit you back." Chad said then hung up. He looked at Boo, "I think that nigga just tried to set us up. Let's get rid of these phones."

They drove across the bridge and tossed them in the river. They stopped at a corner store and got a few pre-paid phones and decided to call Shai instead of Ty and Rell. They didn't want to bring any heat to them while they were on the road.

He dialed Shai.

"Where you at? I need to holla at you, it's important." Chad said, driving through downtown St. Louis.

"I'm at Landry's with Moni, come down here and don't be looking all crazy either," Shai didn't want them embarrassing her in the posh setting they were dining in.

***

121

Steph hung up the phone. He knew that Chad wasn't dumb enough to fall for a set up like that. He snapped at the cops for pushing that bullshit script about a warrant across the table. He knew this wouldn't work unless he was on the streets.

"I need to get out there that's the only way I can get you the buys." Steph begged.

"I don't now if we can trust you like that. I will have to talk with my boss." The Marshal left the room and came back within 30 minutes. He sat down and slid some release papers across the table. "If you think about running, you can forget about the deal later. You got a week to get a buy, every call better be used from this phone. It's wired, so we can hear the conversation whether it's on or off. Get us those buys, and you got one week to do so," The Marshal said, getting up from the table.

Steph grabbed the phone and was walked out by another officer to discharge. They unshackled him and let him go. The first thing that crossed his mind was getting some money together and getting far away from there as possible, but in the end he knew he would end up facing prison time for the rest of his life. He had to do something, and quick.

***

"You think this nigga telling?" Shai asked. She knew what it sounded like. She was just seeing how sure Chad was in assuming the situation. Chad explained again what happened.

"I know this nigga snitching!" He said, taking a quick look around the restaurant. He was paranoid and wondered if someone may have heard him. "This nigga talking about how they ain't have a warrant when they ran up in the crib and shit, then talking about he trying to get straight fresh out of some bullshit like that."

The more Chad spoke of the situation, the more he began to feel the adrenaline pumping in anger. He wanted to do something about it, he wanted blood.

"So just don't fuck with him. He don't know about us do he?" Moni asked.

"Hell n'all, it's just the principal. I gotta bang this nigga." Chad said, looking at Boo. Boo shook his head in approval. He knew this situation was on Chad to handle. And he never really like Steph, didn't trust him at all, and it was now proven just why he felt the way he did. Now they had to take care of the situation before Ty found out. The only line that played in Boo head right now was, *it's no room for error.*

Shai didn't want to hear her cousins talk like this. She was shocked to hear that he wanted to kill with ease. She knew they were off into many things and even encouraged some, but killing was something she would never encourage for her kin. She had to realize quick that this was a part of the game.

"You should wait til Ty gets back first," Shai advised. She felt with Ty being there things would go well.

"They grown girl, you might as well let them handle it," Moni said, she could sense Shai protective attitude towards the situation.

But she knew they were going to do it anyway, no matter what was said. Besides, Moni knew they had something to do with Jeremy's death, she knew they had no problem killing.

Shai listened to Moni as she stared off into the parking lot. She was fixed on a Black Navigator. One similar to the one she saw that day she met with Easy at Wing Stop. She thought back to what Meno warned. "It is eyes on you now." She quickly looked away from the parking lot at Moni, then to Chad and Boo.

"Y'all be careful." she whispered, glancing back towards the parking lot.

She noticed the Navigator was gone. She knew now they had to be careful when speaking to each other. The Cartels had a great deal of intel devices, one of them being Sonic Ears, a small satellite dish looking device that can hear anyone from a distance when pointed in their direction. She had to warn Ty and quick before he said something that could get him killed.

***

We made it out of Texas with ease. I didn't have to worry too much about Karra, she was driving like a professional. We decided by taking Interstate 10 to Louisiana, it would be a much quicker way for us to get out of Texas. It was also a riskier way, being that Interstate 10 is a popular and frequently traveled highway. We just had to make it to Highway 51, then to 55, and then take that all the way back to St. Louis.

While driving through Louisiana, a state trooper got behind Karra and followed her for a while. At first, I started to panic a bit until Karra called me on the phone. I leaned the seat back a bit and answered.

"It's a cop behind me, but he ain't pulled me over yet. He just following me for right now," she said. It's a good thing she didn't sound nervous. She seemed more relaxed than I did.

"Just do the speed limit and don't panic," I said. Soon as the last words left my mouth, the cop hit the lights. "Damn, he just hit the lights!" I said it aloud, forgetting that I was still on the phone with Karra and she wasn't supposed to know I was tailing her.

"How you know he hit the lights, you following me?" she asked.

"Yeah, but don't trip though just pull over," I advised. I looked at Rell. He knew what I wanted him to do. He slowed down then waited til the cop got out of the cruiser. As the cop approached Karra, Rell picked up speed. He turned the wheel quickly to change lanes, then turned it back once more in the other direction towards the officer. The car swerved within inches of the cop, almost knocking him into the air.

Just as we thought, the cop jumped on top of Karra's vehicle dodging the quick brush with death. He then got back onto his feet and ran back to his cruiser in pursuit. We didn't give chase at all. We pulled right off the highway onto a truck stop and got out of the ride. The officer pulled up and hopped out with his hands on his hip and ordered us back into the vehicle. I open the door to get back inside slowly, while looking towards the highway. I saw Karra cruising by as I sat back in the car. I called her quickly, to tell her to get as far away as possible, but to pull over in the next town, then call us once she got there so we could meet up.

The Officer wrote us a ticket. Rell told him that I was asleep when it happen and that he had been driving for hours, so both of us were tired. Rell apologized several times, putting on a good act, even going as far as to ask to pray. The cop fell for the script, but did not let us go until we consented to a search of the car. After the cop searched our vehicle, he let us go. We went in and got some coffee and came back out. Before we pulled off, he radioed a K-9 patrol, which was pulling into the lot. I wasn't surprised; I figured he wasn't going to let us off that easy, and after a near death experience like that. They ran the dog around the car twice and the dog didn't bark. So the officer apologized for the waste of time and let us go.

We met up with Karra, about 100 miles up the highway. We rode the rest of the way with no problems. Karra was laughing at how we played the situation with the cop. I told her, it was no room for error, and that we should stay off the phones until we get home.

We arrived back in the Lou, at dusk. I went to this shade-tree mechanic crib named Larry that I knew in St. Louis. We went there so I could take the weed out of the car. Once we got it out, I took it over to Rell's aunt's house in Jennings and put it in the garage. She had a deep freezer in there that we could keep on low, so that way the weed would stay fresh.

I was extremely tired but I wanted to stay awake to surprise Shai. When I got to the Loft it was no one there. So I went in the room and got me some sleep. Before leaving Rell, I'd told him to drop Karra off and hit her with some change. Then I laid down, trying not to think about anything. I needed to clear my thoughts, but my mind was still racing. I wasn't comfortable at all and paranoia crept back into my mind. I noticed when I was in Texas, I felt relieved, but now that I was back home, the killer instinct has kicked back in.

Chapter 16

Steph knew to watch his back. He figured Boo and Chad knew something was up. Chad had hung up the phone when he asked for some work. He knew he was stupid to even think that would work, he shouldn't have ever trusted the Feds, because they were only going to get him killed. He was now on pre-trial probation for his case. He was tired of going downtown to Free and Clean to piss in a cup every time his color came up. He was already feeling stressed out and paranoid for snitching on a few dudes he knew, just to get some time knocked off, so he was laying low at one of his chicks crib.

On his first real offense, he was looking at 180—252 months, and for doing his dirt, he was looking to get half of that knocked off for turning informant. He still didn't want to do that time, so he was out there still in the streets, hustling.

We was getting it in with the weed. The 200 pounds moved in less than a week. I didn't think the weed game was this sweet. Rueben had gotten us a mule after Karra went crazy on me and shit. She had gotten several attitudes when I refused to fuck her. She even followed me to the loft once, calling herself surprising me with a trench coat on and nothing else on underneath. She was getting out of hand, so I told her to take some time off. That sent her into a furry and I haven't heard from her since. I figured I didn't need her with this new mule. As long as the money made it, we got the product every week.

Shai also got the plug back from Meno. And Chad and Boo was taking care of that along with Rell managing them. I dealt mainly with the weed. The 200 pounds quickly went to 5, then to 800. Before I knew it, I was directing an 18—wheeler, unloading it off the truck. Six months had passed and we'd already made a mill. Shit was too sweet. That was just in weed profit alone, which was reaping more than the work.

Chad and Boo had been doing their thang. Them young niggas were shining. They bought two old schools and had them put on 26's. They sat so high off the ground, I thought them niggas would need a ladder to get inside of them whips.

I had moved out to South County, in a secluded private neighborhood that housed mini—mansions. I loved the new neighborhood because the neighbors weren't in your business. The houses were far apart from each other, too. It was the only peace of mind I had back home in a while. I felt safe out there, like I didn't have to watch over my back, I could sleep well at night, too.

***

Karra had moved out of the city after our fight. She couldn't stay there and watch the man she loved and cared for ride around the city with another bitch. She was only hoping that I missed her and was looking for her. She was staying in Carbondale, IL. with her cousin.

It was a college town, and she knew she could do her thang there. She had always been crafty at setting dudes up and getting money. She learned from one of the best chicks in St. Louis. Her having game started in her days as a prostitute. She would go into the pockets of her tricks and rob them for everything.

While down in Carbondale she had started fucking with a couple of niggas from Chicago. A couple of dudes named Kendrick and Moon had both approached her several times, trying to holla. They were flashing their little mall jewelry from the Chinamen. They were hoping that she would bite. She didn't mind them at first, but when the money started to run thin, she got to skeaming and was looking for a come up.

Karra had been taking sleeping pills and anxiety pills to calm her down. She figured it was time to put them to some real use. So she called up Moon, told him to come over and pick her up.

***

Shai's birthday was coming around, and I wanted to throw her a big party. Rell and Moni had plans to rent the Skybox, a club downtown, which was owned by Nelly and some other celebrities. After that, we were all going on a trip out of the country. I didn't pick where I wanted to go yet. Bora Bora, in Tahiti sounded real good though.

As I rested in the Jacuzzi, Shai entered the room. She was naked and had the look of seduction on her face.

"You still haven't given me none. What's up with that?" she asked, leaning over to kiss me. I never did talk to her about why I hadn't touched her. I care for her too much and I didn't want to touch her until I knew she was completely healed and ready.

"I was waiting on you to heal. You know I don't want to hurt you, cuz when I get in it Imma fuck the shit out of you," I smiled, pulling her closer to me. I was getting aroused just from the kiss and realizing how long it had been since me and her last made love.

"Nigga I was ready the first day I got out the hospital," she said, slowly kissing down my stomach and reaching for my dick.

She lifted it to her mouth and deep throated it all. I was already hot from the Jacuzzi flow, but she made it even hotter. We were both sweating, but still going at it. I had to stop her, both of us anticipated this moment and was ready. But I knew if I kept going I wouldn't be able to hold anything back, it would be over before it even started. I picked her up and carried her into the shower. It was big enough for six people, so it was ample enough room for me to do what I wanted to do with her. She reached over and turned on the cold water.

"Aw, shit!" I yelled when the water hit my back. She started to giggle while kissing my neck. Then she reached down to put my dick inside of her.

"Mmmm," she moaned. I began to lift her up and down on me like I was lifting weights. I leaned her back against the wall and went to pumping harder. She could only take so much before she pushed me away and put her legs down, then turned around and bent over. I know she wanted me to finish, but I couldn't help myself. I dropped down to my knees and dug my face in her ass like I was R. Kelly. I spread her cheeks open and got to eating like a homeless person. She yelled so loud it turned me on even more.

I came up for air after a while and began to hit it from the back. I couldn't take too much more of her. I was fired up enough to explode all inside of her. It felt so good that I laid my head on her back and kissed her continuously, moving my hands along her body, until I slipped out from inside of her. Shai turned and looked at me. She told me she loved me and at that moment, I knew I didn't want to be with anyone else but her.

***

"Damn, girl let me see something." Moon asked while he was driving back to their house. They were in Moon's outdated Escalade.

"Where ya boy at?" Karra asked, wondering about Kendrick.

She needed him to complete her plan. These niggas was green and real soft. They probably wasn't even from Chi-town for real. Karra decided to let Moon see what she was working with, she spread her legs open, revealing her shaved pussy.

"Damn, Kendrick's at the crib. We bout to be there in a minute though," He said, reaching over to try and feel that thang. When they pulled up to the house, Karra looked at the bullshit 2 story brick home. It had a lot of land around it, and resembled a farmer's ranch. She got inside and glanced around at the taste they had, which wasn't much at all. The house had no decor, just couches and televisions and the bedrooms had just a bed and dresser. It was hardly furnished at all. Kendrick walked up to her.

"You want something to drink?" he asked, taking a look at the mini skirt she was wearing. It barely covered her ass.

"Y'all got some X?" Karra asked. She was in need of something that would help her through this night.

"Hell yeah, is you rolling cuz bitch I might be, bitch I might be," Moon replied, quoting a song from Gucci Mane. He pulled out a bag of pills, took out a few and handed them to her.

"Where y'all bathroom at?" she asked.

Moon pointed in the direction and Karra slipped out of the living room into the hallway. She looked up in the bedroom up the hall, then back to the other bedroom in the opposite direction. She was trying to figure out where the money might be hidden, most likely in the back bedroom. She went in the bathroom and took out the sleeping pills. She crushed the X up along with the sleeping pills, then slid the powder in a pill bottle. She came back into the living room and walked up to Moon. She stood in front of him and bent down to unzip his pants. Kendrick looked on in amazement while Karra looked at him.

"Pull your dick out Nigga," she said, easing it into her mouth to suck Moon's dick.

She swallowed it whole, letting out a little giggle at how small he was. She slurped and slobbed, smacking her jaws with his dick then sucking it some more. Then she got up and went to work on Kendrick, doing the same thing she did to Moon. Just as she thought, that little treat got both of them in her little trance. She decided now was the time to make her move.

"Let me get some ice for y'all." She got up and went into the kitchen. "Imma fix a drink for us so I can really get going. Shit that X ain't working like I thought. I'm ready to fuck!" she spoke as she trotted around the kitchen looking for glasses and ice. She took out the crushed pills and poured them into two of the drinks and mixed it around. She grabbed her glass in one hand and held theirs in the other. She sat the drinks on the table in front of them so they would not see her crushing the X Moon gave her into all of the glasses. She wanted them to not get suspicious when they tasted the pills in the drinks. She poured the last bit of the crushed X in her cup and took a gulp. Moon grabbed his and Kendrick followed, they both took gulps of their drinks, trying to speed up the night, Karra knew all she had to do was play around with them for a little while longer because they would be out in no time.

They sipped away as Karra sucked them dry. She made a suggestion to move into the bedroom, figuring that whatever bedroom they take her in the money would be stashed in the other room. She knew they were green. She laid them down and started to ride Moon reverse cowgirl style, while Kendrick stood on the bed and got his dick sucked. Karra was getting annoyed and angry at Kendrick. He was getting disrespectful, by smacking her face with his dick and forcing it down her throat.

"Oh, you don't like that or something?" Kendrick asked in a menacing tone. Karra just looked at him.

He pulled her hair back and smacked her with his dick again. She didn't do anything but smile. She knew she would be the one getting the last laugh tonight. They went back and forth for the next five minutes or so, then they were out cold. They were lying naked in the bed next to each other not far from the position that Karra wanted them lying in. She got up and took some Vaseline and rubbed it down Moon's ass, then she rubbed Kendrick's dick with the rest of it.

She pushed them closer together on the bed, turning Moon over on his side so his ass would be facing Kendrick. They looked like they had just had sex. She got out her phone and took several pictures of them laying there together, looking like they were spooning. She then put the phone in her purse and slid on her clothes.

Immediately she began searching the house. It wasn't long before she stumbled upon the money and drugs. Like she thought, they were small time hustlers, faking like they had change for real. She found the money stashed in the dresser drawers and closets in shoe boxes. The most common place to hide drugs and money. She looked at the money then dumped it in her bag, it was no time to count it, she would have to do that once she got far away from the town as possible.

It couldn't have been any more than a hundred grand and the drugs, she didn't know, but she knew who she would sell them to though. She had many ties to the streets and knew plenty of hustlers that would love to buy it. Before she left out the door she sent a picture of the two lying in the bed to Moon's phone and left a note on the dresser. She grabbed her bag and threw it over her shoulder and hurried into the living room, grabbing the bag of weed on the table and headed out the door.

Kendrick woke up with a blurry vision and a headache. He didn't even notice Moon lying next to him naked. He stumbled out of the bed and into the bathroom. He lifted the toilet seat to take a piss. When he grabbed his dick, he felt the Vaseline. Then from the other room he heard Moon yell.

"What the fuck!" Kendrick came running back into the room to witness Moon wiping his hands across his ass.

"What up, Joe?" he asked with a weird expression on his face. Both of them were trying to figure out what was going on.

"Nigga, it's Vaseline in my ass, all in the crack and shit!" Moon said. He glanced around the room and noticed Karra was nowhere in sight. "Where that bitch at!" he quickly began to search the house. He couldn't remember anything from last night and all he was thinking about was if she violated him or not. "Imma kill that bitch!" He came back into the room and noticed a note by his phone. He reached for the phone, then the note.

Kendrick didn't bother saying anything about the Vaseline on his dick. He didn't want to raise the assumption that both of them had sex together. He could think of the many things he wanted to do to

Karra right now. Almost instantly, he decided to check the stash. He went into the other room and noticed it was flipped upside down. He saw the Nike shoe boxes overturned and the dresser drawers hanging out empty.

"Muthafuckin Bitch!" he yelled. He punched through the wall after realizing that she'd gotten away with a hundred and forty grand and a half of ki of coke. Kendrick immediately reached up into the attic for the 357, he had stashed. He walked back to get his clothes and get Moon. When he entered the room Moon was reading the note Karra left for them. "Nigga I'm bout to go get this bitch, let's go!" Kendrick ordered.

"Hold on, hold on," Moon paused, continuing to read the note.

Y'all had a helluva night, good looking on the come up. I never had it sweeter than you two gay ass niggas. If y'all try to look for me or do anything to anybody I know, Imma put y'all ass on blast on You Tube and all over the Internet. Fucking Vaseline Villains.

Check ya phone.

Moon quickly checked his cell and saw the picture mail. He clicked on it and up popped a picture of him lying in a bent position with his ass pointed and damn near touching Kendrick's dick. He hurried and deleted the picture; he couldn't stand to look at it. He also didn't want Kendrick to even see it at all. He was too embarrassed to show it.

"Imma kill that Bitch, Dog!" Kendrick yelled, pacing the room with the gun in his hand.

"Dog! Let it go, just let it go," Moon looked up from the phone, realizing that getting the money wasn't a problem.

He was the one on the picture looking like he was taking it from behind. He couldn't let that get out at all. He had the connect and he had the means to move it, Kendrick was just his right hand. Never could he let that shit get out there.

"What Nigga, you crazy! You just gon let that Bitch get you like that!" Kendrick yelled.

"She got ya manhood to Nigga. We can get that doe back, we can't get our manhood, fuck dat bitch. If I catch her somewhere yeah, it's like that, but for right now I'm not bout to fuck with her," Moon explained. "We'll get that bitch, don't sweat it."

Chapter 17

'Money ain't no muthafuckin object Nigga. Money ain't no muthafuckin object- tell'em money ain't no muthafuckin object. I got bricks in the dashboard pounds in the closet, Yo Gotti and Rocko.

The music from Yo Gotti, blared through the speakers in the '09 745Li BMW. Me and Rell were rolling through the Lou, chilling. I was feeling myself, the doe was piling fast and I was getting a sense of relief from the beef. But I stayed on my toes. That didn't stop me from getting my shine on every once in a while. We rode down Natural Bridge, when I thought for a moment I saw Karra roll by me in a new Challenger. I made a U-turn and punched the gas to catch up with the Challenger. I rolled down the window and blew the horn. It was Karra, she looked up from a blunt and smiled in shock to see me trying to flag her down. I signaled for her to pull over. She had a crew of females with her bouncing and listening to music. She pulled over to Lee's Chicken on the intersection of Natural Bridge and Kings Highway.

"What up Baby," she yelled, getting out of the car.

She stepped out in some booty shorts and a cut up top by Juicy Couture. I glanced down and saw she was wearing Gucci shoes also. I immediately went to wondering where she got the money from and whose ride she was driving. My guess was that some young balla was trying to lock her down. I got out the car and walked around to the other side.

"Where the fuck you been?" I asked. She began to look at me with a frown.

"Nigga I told you, you ain't my daddy. What you talking about where I been? Why you wanna know, you ain't fucking me," she said with a jazzy attitude. She was really feeling herself. Her friends looked on with occasional winks. "What's up Rell?" Karra spoke as if to ignore me. I had to admit I liked her style. She knew how to get a man's attention.

"I know I ain't yo daddy," I said, shaking my head. I was getting fedup with her and really didn't give a fuck where she had gotten the shit from now. I knew it was no saving her. I started to walk off and get back into the car.

"You can be my daddy!" One of the girls yelled from the car Karra was driving.

"Bitch, who can be yo daddy!" Karra yelled and opened the door to the car. She reached in and two pieced the girl, hitting her in the face. The girl didn't even fight back; she just leaned back in the seat and balled up holding her face. "Don't even talk to him, he's off limits, Bitch!" she added.

That was the first time I saw Karra act like that. It shocked me that she was protective of me. I walked back over to her and grabbed her.

"Chill the fuck out," I pulled out my phone. "What's ya number," I asked. I wanted to keep an eye on her. It was just something in me that wanted to protect her and make sure she was safe.

"Why, you finally gon hit this pussy Daddy?" Karra started laughing. "You too Rell, both of y'all."

"Shit, I ain't got no problem—" Rell smiled, but was cut off by me looking at him. He knew that I didn't look at Karra in that way. And didn't want him to either.

"Chill out Nigga," I said to him. Karra sucked her teeth and looked at me with that same frown again. "Karra you like a little sis to me, so you need to chill out with that bullshit and keep in touch with me. I need to know you a'ight from time to time."

"That's cool," she said, standing up from leaning on the door. She smiled at me, then looked at Rell, "Holla at me."

"Rell ain't gon holla at nobody," I said, getting into the car.

When I got inside, Rell looked at me.

"She just want me to holla at her, that's all," he said smiling.

I watched her as she got into the car. She rolled down her window.

"Don't sleep on me Tyrek, Imma get it," she said then she backed out. Karra rolled up the window and looked in the rearview mirror at the bitch she'd just hit. She was still nursing her wounds. Karra stared for a minute until she looked up at her to stare through the rearview. "Bitch, that's my man, don't ever disrespect me like that again, or I'll kill yo ass," Karra said.

Little did they know, but she was dead serious. Karra was infatuated with Tyrek. She thought jealousy would get him to hit, that's why she tried to fuck with Rell, but even, that didn't work. She knew by him feeling as if she was like a sister to him, it would be a lot harder than she thought to get him. She thought all she would need is one chance to fuck him and she would do everything in the world to get him to fall for her.

"Ya girl came up didn't she?" Rell inquired. I watched her ride off in the car. The Challenger had some 22' inch rims on it and everything. She came up somehow; I just hoped she wasn't in trouble.

"Yeah, she came up," I said, pulling out of the lot. I knew she had a crush on me, but I didn't think it was that serious. When I saw her beat the girl that was riding with her, I knew then that she had a problem. She also showed me real leadership qualities and I liked that, but it worried me at the same time.

***

We went out to the crib for a bite to eat. Moni and Shai was cooking, so Rell and I sat in the theater and looked at the game. Moni was in the kitchen with Shai cutting vegetables and talking with her. For a while, she was thinking how things may go sour with Rell if Ty found out that Shai use to do work for T-Mac, and especially if they found out about the relationship with Easy. She was beginning to care for Rell and didn't want anything to get in the way.

"You ain't never tell Ty about Easy did you?" Moni asked. It caught Shai off guard and she nearly dropped the glass of wine she was sipping.

"Oh, hell n'all! Shit, I know he would be pissed if he knew that." Shai said, "Besides, I will not have to worry about Ty finding out anything. I got a plan to get to Easy and T-Mac, once I let Meno know about Elan's bodyguard, Ramiero."

"Well I know you gon tell him you pregnant," Moni said.

Shai looked at Moni.

"Damn Girl! What are you, a fucking inspector or something, why you think I'm pregnant?" Shai asked.

"Girl, you been throwing up for the past week or so." Moni said, taking another sip of her wine. "You need to put that wine down." she added.

Shai was trying to keep the sickness a secret, but she knew Moni wasn't stupid. She was going to get another abortion, fearing that Ty wouldn't want a child. But she thought about asking him first just to see. She just couldn't bring herself to ask him though.

Moni knew how Shai felt for Ty also and figured Shai would be making a mistake by assuming Ty wouldn't find out about the relationship with her, T-Mac and Easy. And she knew Shai didn't tell Ty about the pregnancy also.

"Girl Imma tell'em, I'm just waiting on the right moment," Shai promised.

Shai knew she had to tell him soon, or Moni would. She would do anything to preserve the relationship with Rell and Ty. They both loved them and Shai understood Moni's concern. Moni was more like a mother to Shai rather than a sister, and even though they were the same age and childhood friends, she looked out for Shai's best interest. And she knew Ty was right for her. He loved her and she could tell.

"Well the right moment better come up soon, because no matter what I'm going to have a little nephew or niece and you two will stay together to raise it," Moni said.

"So when you gon let Rell pop one in that ass?" Shai teased, smiling. "I want a little nephew or niece too."

"Soon. He acts funny sometimes though. So I gotta make sure he's right for the taking." They laughed.

***

Chad and Boo had been looking for Steph for some time now. They found a spot that he had been laying at. They never bumped into him, so they decided to lay on the spot until he showed up. It was getting to be risky leaving his ass out there, knowing he could come back and testify against them if one of them got caught.

They were making too much money now to let this nigga bring them down. Months had passed and the word was that he was working. So they knew it was a perfect time to get rid of his ass now with everyone he set up, or attempted to, because it would be hard to find out who did it.

"So you gon swing through tomorrow?" Steph asked, getting out of Lisa's car. Lisa blushed. "Hell yeah, Imma call you," Steph said, getting out of the car. He grabbed the to-go bag from Applebee's out of the backseat.

"Alright Baby," Lisa said, giving him a kiss, right before she pulled off.

Steph looked around then walked up the side of the house. He noticed the motion detection light did not come on when he walked up. He looked up at the light and noticed it was broken. At that very moment he heard footsteps coming up from behind him.

Chad and Boo came from the other side of the car that was parked in the driveway. They had been there for a while, waiting on Steph to return. Chad hopped out and smacked Steph with the gun.

"Snitch ass nigga, open ya mouth!" Chad said, shoving the pistol in Steph's mouth, right before firing the gun. He stood over him looking at his work.

"Snitch ass nigga," Boo looked on smiling at Steph lying lifelessly on the ground, then he squeezed 5 shots into his body.

"You don't get no points for that, he's already dead Nigga." Chad said.

"The next one mine then," Boo said as they ran off into the night.

***

Shai's birthday was tomorrow. Moni had gotten the party all set up with the club. She'd invited the elite of St. Louis. Paying a lot of celebrities to show up and show out. She was going to have appearances by Nelly, Tha Lunatics, Chingy, Huey, and some of the Rams players. It was going to be a star studded event. I was a bit nervous because all the hype around the party, I didn't trust T-Mac. If he thought like me, he would definitely be out to get even that night. I got all my niggas from out the way to come for the party; my cousins from Memphis, Minnesota, and the rest of the click from around the city. We were mainly on security for tomorrow. I wanted to enjoy the party also, but I didn't want anything to happen to Shai. I trusted no one to take care of her but me. If T-Mac thought he was going to try and drop a mafucka tomorrow, then he was going to have to swing through with an army.

I had a whip custom designed specifically for this night as a gift for Shai. Shai and I would be pulling up in a bullet-proof Range Rover on 24's. Along with that, I bought her a Chanel bracelet, and a Cartier ring, both worth over 20 grand. I got her a new 6 series BMW drop. Her favorite color, white with off—white interior and white and chrome 22—inch rims. To top it off, two twin one of a pair, Patek Phillippe his and hers watches. No other couple in the world would have these watches on.

Rell was pissed when I let Moni take a peek at the gifts. He had to break her off some bread to go get her something. He knew he would have to show out for her birthday too, which wasn't too far away. Somehow Shai got wind of the gifts and I had to hide them at Rell's house. She searched the entire house for the gifts.

She was anticipating the presents and had been acting strange lately. I had a feeling she was pregnant, but I didn't want to ask her. I figured she would let me know once she felt the need to. She was a complex person and she needed time to do things her way. I was getting the hang of dealing with her. I think the only other person who understood her better than me was Moni. Sometimes she would get real bad attitudes, get mad and want to hurt somebody. She told me she would go to therapy because she was still having problems with the memories of her mother.

The club was packed. The line at the Skybox was out the door. The Skybox was on the Landing, an area in Downtown St. Louis that consisted of restaurants, bars, and clubs. It was owned by Nelly, Marshal Faulk a former Rams player, Darius Miles, and Larry Hughes, both NBA players. Nelly couldn't be there, so we paid to use his private V.I.P. section. Nelly's overlooked the entire club. Which was perfect for watching out and making sure the night went as planned.

I had niggas outside and around the corners on look out. Shai actually thought all the security was insane. She had been trying to convince me to chill and enjoy the night. I couldn't, as much as I tried, I had to assure myself that she would be alright. We were coming up Washington, on our way to the club. The Rover was like an armored tank. I could feel the extra weight in the ride. Even with the Brembo brakes and new suspension, the ride was still kind of heavy. When I pulled up, Rell came out followed by a short guy in a tuxedo. The guy rolled out black carpet and opened the door for Shai. She got out and we made our entrance.

I bought the bar out, so all the drinks for tonight were on the house tonight. The food was also catered from some of the most favorite eateries in St. Louis that Shai liked to eat at. I personally had 30 bottles of the Ace of Spades, 20 bottles of Richard Hennessy, and cases of vodka, Patron, and additional champagnes and liquor. I went all out for her.

I told her I would blow a Mil, easy. She didn't believe me. I almost did it though. Hell if it wasn't for her, I wouldn't be where I am today.Shai wasn't drinking at all. She was only drinking virgins all night. I knew she was pregnant. I took her to the couch and we sat down.

"Why you ain't having nothing to drink, I spent all this money on these drinks for your birthday..?" I asked, letting the words trail off into a wondering expression.

I wanted to see if she was ready to tell me the truth. Shai looked at me then to the ceiling of the club.

"What's wrong with you?" I asked.

"Nothing," she said, grabbing my hand. "Nothing," she paused again. "Ty, I'm pregnant." She waited to see my expression. When I didn't respond immediately, she exhaled. "If you don't want to keep it I understand. It's all good, I was thinking about getting an abortion anyway," she added.

"What, why would you do that? Why would you think I wouldn't want to keep the baby," I asked.

"I don't know. Just thought you might not want to bring a baby into this mess. What if our baby witness us getting killed or if we leave it alone out here, like my parents left me?" Shai exhaled again.

"What, that's what happened to you, but that's not going to happen to us. We're keeping the baby," I said. I felt hurt by the way she felt and wished I could change things but I couldn't. All I could do was console her for as long as she needed me to. The experience with her mother and father was very hard on her, actually something she will never get over.

When I said we were keeping it, her face lit up. She kissed my hand, and I could feel her tears as her lips touched my skin. I leaned down to her and whispered.

"I love you."

I looked up to catch Rell's attention, feeling this was the perfect moment to introduce the gifts. I signaled for him to bring them over. First, he brought over Moni and his gifts, which was really for all of us, four roundtrip tickets to anywhere on the globe, their treat. Then he brought over my gifts. She opened the two jewelry boxes. She damn near gave me an earache, the way she screamed when she open the Cartier box.

She put the ring on and held it out in front of her, then she took the bracelet out and dangled it in the air. I put it on her wrist. Then I reached down and gave her the twin boxes. She tried to reach for both of them.

"N'all, hold on now this one's mine, and this one's yours," I said, handing her the black and gold incrusted box with 'For Her' on the engraved lid. She opened the box and looked at her watch. It was all diamond encrusted. She looked at mine and noticed they were a matching pair. She begged me to put mine on, that way she could wear hers tonight. She took off the Franck Muller and put the Patek Phillippe on my wrist. Then I took out the keys to the 645 and gave them to her. I had the car pulled around front, so she could see a glance of the ride with the birthday ribbon on the hood. She looked and squeezed the shit out of me.

"You trying to get raped tonight," she whispered in my ear. I smiled.

"You choking the shit out of me," I said, trying to loosen her grip from the hug she had on me.

The night was going well, except for Chad and Boo hadn't showed up. I was getting worried about them. Shai had asked about their whereabouts throughout the night, and I didn't want her to start getting worried, so I had Rell text and call them both, but he got no answer.

"You heard from them yet?" I asked Rell. Shai had just asked about them again. I could tell she was beginning to wonder also.

"You know I haven't' heard from them since they said they dealt with that one nigga," Rell said. I thought for a moment and realized that I hadn't heard anything from them either. I figured they were laying low.

The club was packed, and everyone was having a good time. The floor was jumping and the DJ played St. Louis' local music, it got the crowd hype. He started with Young Ro, Kenny Knox, Mr. Lab, Nu Money, Pretty Thugs, and oops. A few celebrities raised their glasses to me in respect and gratitude for the affair. Plus they were probably shocked that I was shining like them without looking like I fucked off anything.

I watched the door heavily. Finally, I saw Chad and Boo creep in. A sense of relief came over me. They slid to the bar and asked the bartender where we were sitting. The bartender pointed in our direction. I raised my hands in the air, so they could see me. Then I waved at the security to let them pass.

"Man, what's up Nigga?" Boo said, he had a couple of gifts in his hands. He sat them down and dapped me up. Chad gave me a shake and hug.

"Where the fuck y'all been, we been blowing ya phones up?" I asked.

They were looking a lot like money now. I could see they had been stacking hard. Chad stood Louie down with a diamond 'World is Mine' emblem hanging over his belly, and a diamond Rolex on. Boo had Prada on with earrings the size of golf balls, along with a diamond Cartier on.

"We been laying low for a minute, ya know," Boo said. Chad went over to hug and kiss Shai. He gave her the gifts they brought. Boo followed to watch her open them. I still had my eyes fixed on the door. Something just didn't feel right tonight. There was no way that I would have a party like this without someone from T-Mac's crew trying their hand. I just kept thinking, if it was me, I would be lying outside waiting.

I could hear Shai screaming in the background from the excitement. I looked back and noticed Moni approaching me from behind.

"So y'all gon have the baby?" she asked.

"Yeah, hell yeah," I said. Moni took a sip of her drank.

"I appreciate you treating my sister like this. She ain't never had a party like this. She could've did it for herself, or I could have did it for her, but we were always private, ya know. Ain't nobody ever looked out for us like you and Rell." Moni added.

"It's all good, Sis. That's my wife," I said. Moni looked up at that comment. "But don't tell her yet," I added. "Damn!" I mumbled under my breath at seeing Karra come through the door with Easy.

"Damn, what?" Moni asked. She looked towards the door also. I quickly stood in front of her so she couldn't see them coming in.

"Can you go get Rell for me, I got another gift," I asked. Moni nodded and walked off.

Seconds later Rell walked up.

"What up, Nigga," he immediately noticed the look on my face.

He trailed my eyes to the stare I had fixed on Easy and Karra. Karra must have been making herself real popular around The Lou. She was becoming a St. Louis diva. She was in the Whirl a few times already as the Whirl Girl of the week. Now she was fucking with Easy.

I went down with a couple of guys. I knew if Easy was in here, then T-Mac wouldn't be too far behind. Easy stood by the bar with a couple of dudes, and I saw Karra slip away to the bathroom, so I followed her. Rell stayed with his eye on Easy. I moved through the crowd quickly to catch up with Karra before she entered the bathroom. I snatched her into a corner before she entered.

"What the fuck are you doing here with that nigga!" I asked, angry as hell. She looked at me like I was tripping.

"Who Easy, that ain't nobody. Just a nigga I fuck with. Why you tripping, we ain't fucking!" She said with an attitude.

"How long you been fucking with him?" I asked. She was standing there like she was the shit now. I could tell all the hype was going to her head. I gripped her arm a bit harder.

"Stop Ty, you hurting my arm," she said. "What you jealous?" she added.

"Bitch, jealous. Me and that nigga beefing!" I was ready to smack the shit out of her. When I mention we was beefing, she froze up. "You tell him anything about us, do he know you know me?" I asked.

"No, I swear. I didn't even know yall was beefing. I don't talk about you around nobody anyway," she assured me. "I swear Tyrek."

Despite all the bullshit she had with her, I believe that she was loyal to me.

"I—ight, keep it like that. Imma holla at you later about this nigga," I walked off. Rell saw me coming through the crowd. We went back to the V.I.P.

I was given a 5 gallon bottle of Dom P. It was sent by Easy, with a note:

To my birthday girl, from the X.
Easy

I looked down towards Easy, who now had his eyes fixed on me. I knew he was trying to get me to start tripping with that note, he did. I didn't approach Shai with the bullshit, because I know that's what he wanted me to do. Instead, I went to go holla at him. Rell seen me bolt down the steps and headed out right behind me.

Easy followed me down the steps and watched as I moved through the crowd towards him. As I got closer he yelled.

"Tyrek, what's up boy?"

"T-Mac bitch, what's up?" I said, trying to get him to hop out there now. I was past talking and ready to deal with any consequences.

"You got that, you got that," Easy said, putting one hand up to stop his goons from moving. "Damn, Homie that's real disrespectful." Easy said, laughing. "You must have just found out about me fucking yo beeyatch."

Shai looked from the V.I.P. and saw me and Easy talking. She hurried down the stairs. Just as Easy made that comment, she was walking up. I was about to take off on him, but Shai stepped in between us.

"Tyrek, no!" she yelled.

I didn't even look at her. She grabbed my hands and held me. Karra walked up and saw Shai hugged on me and gritted her teeth. She went to stand behind Easy. She looked at Shai with a jealous expression. I could see she was getting angry. She didn't even look at me, her stare was fixed on Shai.

"What's up Baby, happy B-day," Easy said, looking at Shai with a smile.

"Nigga fuck you-" Shai said, spitting at his feet.

"N'all fuck him," Easy said, looking at me. "Enjoy yaself, cuz ain't no party on the other side," he added, then turned to leave.

Karra looked at me, she knew what I had on my mind, when Easy made that threat, she looked at Easy quickly breaking her fixed gaze from Shai. She had the same expression on her face as the one she wore when she beat that chick's ass for talking to me. I walked off. Shai tried to grab my arm, but I snatched it away.

"Bitch, you ain't tell me y'all were fucking around," I yelled. I didn't know what to think now. I didn't know who I could trust. Was everything a lie with her? Why was she even fucking with me?

"What?" she said, frowning. "Me and Easy ain't fucked around Tyrek. I only fucked with him one time and that was some years back, I swear." she added. "You know my line of work," she continued, but I walked off. I didn't want to hear anything she had to say right then. I needed to think this out quickly.

Easy left out smiling. He planned to shake things up and try to force Tyrek to make a move. He knew things would have went well if Shai wouldn't have been in the way. He also knew that was a death trap going in there like that, but he didn't give a fuck. To him, it was Live hard, die young.

As he headed to the car, he approached Karra and smacked her on the ass. "Go get in the ride, I'll be right over in a minute," Easy walked off. Karra looked at him with a deadly stare. She didn't take likely to anyone threatening Ty, and she wanted to prove that she wasn't disloyal. She wished she wouldn't have ever fucked with Easy now, because it may just ruin her chances of being with Ty. She knew she had to do something to regain Ty's trust again.

Easy walked up to the Bentley GT that was parked up the street from the club. A van full of niggas in all black sat behind it. Easy threw up a peace sign to the guys sitting in the van as he turned and leaned down to the window of the Bentley to talk to T-Mac.

"I got'em heated," Easy said.

"Yeah, that bitch ass nigga a sucka foe that hoe, huh. Man I'm ready to knock that nigga top back, straight up," T-Mac said, gripping his steering wheel tightly. It was hard for him to hold off the fight, knowing the man who had something to do with his nephew's death was just feet away from him.

"Oh, he gon hop out there, and when he does, we can just sit back and let them deal with him," Easy said.

"My nigga. What's up with that bad ass bitch you got, where she at?" T-Mac asked, referring to Karra.

"You know she in the ride. I'm bout to take her to the telly and knock her off real quick," Easy said, giving T-Mac some dap.

"I—ight be cool," T-Mac rolled up the window to the car. He turned on the lights to the Bentley and the van did the same. As he drove off, the van tailed behind.

Easy watched as T-Mac drove off. He looked at the van full of niggas. He warned T-Mac plenty of times to make sure he stayed strap. But T-Mac was too cautious as a result of the police and not these niggas, so he didn't ride with a pistol. Instead, he rode with a van load of niggas with pistols. Easy just shook his head as he walked over to his ride. He tapped his waist, feeling the .45 caliber while quietly mumbling "All I need in this life of sin, is me and my girlfriend."

***

"No, Ty you ain't gon trip off this little shit that happened a while ago, are you," Shai said, grabbing my chin to get me to look her in the face.

"Bitch, get ya hands off me!" I smacked her hands away from my face. Shai looked at Moni. They had just talked about this and she knew this would come back and bite her in the ass, just not this quickly.

"I ain't gon be too many more bitches, Tyrek," Shai warned, pointing her finger in my face. "How the fuck would I know all this shit would happen between me and you?" she paused. "I didn't know you and T-Mac would start beefing like that. I chose a side, I'm with you!"

"Look enjoy ya party and gifts, I'm out. I'll see you when you get home tonight."

"Where you finna go? Shai stepped in front of me. I pushed her to the side. We were beginning to make a big scene. "Don't worry about it, just enjoy yaself."

Shai realized that she couldn't stop me so she called for Rell to try and get me to stay.

"Rell get Ty, he trippin."

Rell look at her with a puzzled look. He knew how I felt and it was no one he would roll with good or bad but me. He also didn't want me going out there alone after what went down. So he followed me out of the club.

On my way out, I got a text from Karra, "What u want me 2 do n who wuz dat bitch!!"

I didn't feel like dealing with that jealous shit right then, but I needed her though; so I texted her back. Since she was with Easy that wouldn't look like I had anything to do with his death, especially if she was right about not telling Easy about us. I wanted so bad to tell her to kill that nigga, but I know she wasn't cut like that.

"Rob dat nigga make sure u get his keys."

"You alright Nigga?" Rell asked, stepping up to the ride. I could see the worry on his face. This is one of the rare moments of weakness when dealing with a female. We hardly ever witness this in eachother.

"Dog, I'm about to roll. Make sure she gets home safely." I closed the door and started the truck up.

"N'all nigga, I can't let you roll like that. Let Chad or somebody roll with you. What you on?" He added.

"I'm cool, just need to think this shit out real quick. Just make sure she gets home. Imma holla in a minute," I said, putting the ride in drive. I held my foot on the brake as Rell put his hand on my shoulder stopping me from pulling off.

"Nigga, I know that was a blow, but I don't think Shai's fucking over you at all. I ain't just about the connect, it's about everything she been doing. She loves you too much Homie. Don't fuck this one up."

Rell stood back, allowing me to make my decision to stay or go. I looked down at my phone to read the message Karra had just sent back.

Text: OK.

147

I threw a peace sign up at him and pulled off.

While on the Highway, I noticed a Black SUV behind me. It had been behind me for some time. I sped up to see if it would also, and it did. Quickly reaching for the heat, I prepared myself for whatever. Just when I looked again the SUV got off on an exit.

***

"You must be infatuated with my ass by the way you keep smacking it and shit," Karra said, leaning up against Easy in the elevator. Easy looked at her phone as it vibrated again. He thought it was her nigga texting her all night.

"That nigga missing you. Only if he knew the real, he would probably kill yo ass," he chuckled. "That's why I ain't gon never wife a bitch. That ain't some shit I can deal with, and most bitches ain't shit."

Karra told him that she bumped into her boyfriend's homie while they were in the club tonight. She quickly glanced at the text, then put the phone back into her purse, after texting back.

"Girl fuck that nigga, shit I'm ready to hit that," Easy said, hopping off the elevator. They entered the suite. "Call ya girl you was telling me about in the ride. Let's get this shit poppin," he said as he checked his phone.

Karra had promised Easy a threesome, which she didn't mind on occasions. She went bothways sometimes, but this time she had a hidden agenda. Instead of calling the friend she usually called for threesomes, she called Sasha. This was the one she worked scams and setups on niggas with.

"Girl what's up. Wanna come up to the Drury Inn Plaza downtown and bring some turners and knockouts," Karra said, hoping Easy didn't pick up on the code.

"What the fuck you just say, turners and knockouts?" Easy laughed. "What the fuck is that?"

"That's some X. What, am I suppose to tell her to bring some X and weed," Karra said. "Give me some X and I'm good to go." She added.

She walked to the full length mirror and looked at herself. She was glad he bought the script on the X and weed, really turners and knockouts was a code for chocolate covered strawberries. Usually they would use pills, but she knew that Easy wasn't that stupid to take a pill. So she had to go another route. She walked into the Jacuzzi area and started to run the water. She took out some scented oil she had in her purse and poured it into the Jacuzzi. She got undressed and stepped over into the tub, easing her way down into the hot water then laying her head back against the padded rim of the tub.

Easy was still in the living room talking on the phone. She got up and wiped off to go see what he was up to, forgetting that she'd left her phone on the table, she didn't want him peeking in it to see who may have been texting her. Although she never put in real names to the stored numbers, it was still the possibility that he would check a number and find out about Ty. Karra tip toed into the hallway and peeked around the wall to see him putting his gun under the couch, along with his billfold. She figured his jewelry and keys were still in his pockets.

She went to hop back in the Jacuzzi, trying to plot her plan on how she would get the keys from him. Minutes later her thinking was interrupted when Easy walked in.

"Damn, that shit smell good, what's that?" Easy asked, smelling the fragrance in the air.

"That's strawberry scented oil," Karra said, rubbing her arms. "I love strawberries. I ordered some chocolate covered strawberries too, shit that's my favorite food."

"You just a strawberry bitch, huh?" Easy laughed.

He pulled off his pants and got in. He didn't sit down, he stood over Karra and grabbed the back of her head and forced his dick in her mouth. He started to pump hard, making Karra gag and cough. Easy thought every femaled was money hungry, so he treated them with the least amount of respect as often as he possibly could.

"Ooh shit that's what I like. I like when bitches start gagging on this dick. Choke on that mafucka," Easy said, ramming even harder down her throat.

Karra pushed his hands off her head, but he just grabbed it again. She was getting pissed. She thought about the gun under the couch, and considered going to get it and using it on him. She would shoot his ass dead, but Ty didn't want that. If he would have told her to do it, she would have. She was relieved when her girl knocked on the door. Easy got out to answer and Karra followed behind, wrapping a towel around her head. She quickly wiped away the tears from her eyes that came from her choking and gagging as Easy opened the door.

"Damn," Easy said, looking at Sasha as she walked pass him into the suite. He smacked her on the ass hard. "Get naked beeyatch."

Sasha looked at him with an uninvited smirk. "Who he talking to like that?" Karra paid her no mind and grabbed the box of strawberries. "Girl is it half and half?" Karra asked.

"Yeah," Sasha answered. Sasha had been rolling with Karra for a while. They met at a party one night when Karra caught Sasha slipping something in a dudes drink. When Sasha noticed Karra watching her, she smiled and replied.

"Fuck'em all, that's all they want to do to us right." And from then on they were cool.

Karra looked to the back to make sure Easy was out of earshot. "Good let's get this nigga and get out of here," she added. Karra noticed the look on Sasha face as she was talking to her. "What's wrong with you?" she asked.

"Girl, is his name Easy?" Sasha asked.

"Yeah, why."

"Girl, that nigga will kill us if he finds out we trying to do this to him." Sasha said nervously. Karra looked at her hands as she grabbed the box because Sasha was shaking.

"Bitch, that nigga ain't gon find out and fuck him, we will kill his ass first." Karra looked around again. "You better get ya shit together, because we in this shit now, get naked."

Karra opened the box of strawberries and looked at them. She looked at the white paper that were folded on one side of the box. She took the box into the back bedroom where Easy lay waiting on them both. Sasha got naked and joined her. Easy watched Sasha's every move, which made her even more nervous. He wasn't suspicious of her at all, Sasha was beautiful. She was brown skin, with micro braids and some big ass titties and a cute round ass. Being half Italian and Indian, made her complexion flawlessly beautiful.

Easy laid on the bed as Karra went to work on him. Sasha sat down next to Easy and started to kiss him on his chess and neck. They tag teamed Easy while eating the strawberries, letting the juices drip down his dick then licking it up. Easy got so into it that he asked to have some strawberries too. Karra and Sasha threw a quick glance in eachother's direction. They knew it wouldn't be long before he wanted to indulge in the chocolate covered fruit. Every nigga that they got wanted to taste the strawberries, the forbidden fruit. Karra reached over into the box and gave him a strawberry. She anticipated this moment. It wasn't right unless they wanted to have one on their own, as they always did. She knew it would kick in moments later. While Karra sucked Easy off, Sasha prepared the drinks.

She took out the mickey and sat it next to the cup she would pour it in. She was still nervous and became more shakey once she saw Easy eat the strawberries. She knew that if he had any suspicion that they gave him something, he would kill them both. She poured the vile into one of the drinks and sat it to the left of her. As she quickly tried to hide the vile in her purse, she knocked over a drink.

"Damn," she jumped back from the spill. She grabbed the glasses and sat all of them together on the end table, then turned around to clean up the spill. "Shit!" she cursed under her breath again.

When she finished she turned around to grab the drinks. She looked at them and placed them one by one on the table. She grabbed the one she thought the poison was in and placed it to the side. She grabbed the other two and brought them in the room. Sasha knew if Karra found out she didn't pour the drinks or start over, that she would be in for it. But she only had one vile on her, she forgot to grab two just incase. She vowed not to smoke weed anymore if the night turned out in their favor, it made her forget shit.

Easy sat his drink on the dresser, he did not touch it. Karra sipped hers and Sasha watched as she drank. For a moment she wanted to tell Karra, but when a few minutes passed, she was sure it wasn't her drink, so she started to take sips of hers also. Easy reached over to take a few sips of his drink, he felt a sickness in his stomach and needed something to calm it down. He then walked over to Sasha and grabbed her glass, sat it down then bent her over and began fucking her hard.

Sasha screamed loud. She really couldn't take him in, she only liked women.

Easy pumped away, then stopped and tightened up his ass cheeks. Karra knew what was taking place. The ex—lax covered strawberries had kicked in. Easy tried to run to the bathroom, holding his hand over his ass before something slipped out.

"Mu—tha—fucka, oh shit!" He screamed as he sat down on the toilet. Karra scurried up her clothes and put them on.

"Come on bitch let's go!" Karra said, tapping Sasha. Karra ran and looked under the couch and grabbed the billfold and gun. Then she ran and got his pants to grab the keys.

"Got'em." she said to herself. She ran back into the room to get Sasha. "Bitch come—," Karra stopped, noticing Sasha was lying on the bed with her eyes open, yet she was unconscious. "Sasha, I know you ain't drink that shit! Damn." she added, looking into her eyes.

Sasha couldn't respond at all. Karra knew she couldn't try to lift her ass, she had to go. Some bitches were built for this shit and some weren't. Obviously Sasha wasn't built for it. Karra could still hear Easy in the bathroom yelling.

"Oh, Imma kill- what the fuck yall give me!" he yelled, as Karra ran by holding her nose.

"Damn," she whispered and ran out the door to the elevator. She was too nervous to wait on it, so she took the stairs. Soon as she got away from the hotel and safely in her car, she texted me:

"Got'em where u at?"

When the text came in, I was riding on the Eastside. I was on 25th and State, at the Gas Station. The lot was bumper to bumper on the weekends. You had hustlers moving through to serve weed, and females cruising through to see what and who was on the lot. Fiens hanging around and jack boys looking for a easy lick. Shai was blowing my phone up. It hadn't stopped ringing since I'd left her party. So I didn't look at my phone immediately when Karra first texted me. A half hour went by, by the time I checked it. It was a few text, letting me know that she had the keys and also telling me that she was down the street at the liquor store that I use to take her to on 25th and St. Clair. I texted her back ok and told her I would be there in a minute.

She was parked on the lot, when I pulled up. She immediately got out looking worried. She walked up to me.

"That bitch Sasha fucked around and drank a mickey that was supposed to be his." she said.

"What! Where she at now?" I asked. I knew where she was for real.

Something was telling me that she would not be ok, I didn't know who she was, but I would soon find out how she died.

"She is still there with him," Karra said, leaning up against the car with her hands folded.

"How you get out?" I asked.

"He ate the strawberries."

"Strawberries?" I asked, looking at her curiously.

"Yeah, strawberries, they were chocolate covered, and the chocolate was ex—lax." she giggled a little. I started to laugh with her.

"You crazy as a muthafucka, you hit him with some ex—lax."

Karra and I laughed. The thought of it all was hilarious as she described to me how it went down.

"It ain't funny though, what if that bitch Sasha tells him something about me." she said.

"Girl, you said she was knocked the fuck out. You think she gon be able to say anything about anybody," I assured. "Shit, she won't even remember her own name after tonight. That bitch drank a mickey, she gon have seven new identities," I added. "And believe me she gon be talking to all of them at the same time." I laughed.

Karra started to giggle. I walked her inside of the store and into the back. Mike was leaving out as we came in.

"Damn! Nigga, who's that?" he asked, looking at Karra.

"You don't remember me?" Karra said, waving her hand in his face. She then turned around and walked away.

"You don't remember her, the girl that was getting her ass whipped that night on the strip club parking lot," I said. "Nigga we went there after the store closed that night."

"Hell naw, that ain't her is it?" Mike said, recalling the night. "Damn, she done got right boy. I know you hitting that now. What that head like?" he added, laughing.

"Nigga, you know I ain't doing shit to her."

"What you scared?" Mike asked. "She got something," he joked.

"N'all, she like a sister to me, that's all."

"Nigga you scared, cuz I'd be fucking the shit out of my sister tonight if I was you," Mike smiled, walking back up front to maintain the register. Minutes later Mamun came in the back.

"What up Fool," he said as he came in the door. He moved around a few crates that sat on the floor to sit on. We were sitting in the back storage room behind the cooler. "Mike told me that's the little chick you rescued that night. Acting like you was a super hero and shit," Mamun jokingly said.

"Watch out Nigga. She was too young to let a nigga whip her ass like that."

He passed me the blunt. Usually I didn't smoke, but tonight I needed it.

"What you finna do? Or should I say, what's on the agenda for tonight?" he asked.

"Shit, bout to roll out and go lay it down, ya know." I passed him the blunt back. After just a few hits, I was buzzing quickly.

"I—ight, holla at us tomorrow or something."

We shook up, then I headed out the back. I went into the office where Karra awaited and told her to follow me. I knew after tonight she couldn't go home. So I thought to put her up somewhere until things clear up.

Chapter 18

I had a little Condo in O'Fallon, Il. It was one of the spots where I had some money stashed. I never kept large amounts of money at the house. Most of the spots were in my alias names and were Condos. It was free security and neighborhood watch for protection of thieves trying to break in.

We pulled up to the Condo, and got out. Karra grabbed her things and once we got in, she went straight to the couch to lay down. She seemed exhausted from the recent events. I let her know she could stay for as long as she liked to, or until she got another spot to move into of her own. Just incase Sasha did remember something. We got rid of her ride, also. She didn't want to do that at all, because she had fallen in love with the car, and begged me to take the rims off before I decided to sell it.

After assuring her that I would, and promising to get her into something nicer, I left to secure the money I had in the house. I couldn't keep the money here with her staying there. I just didn't trust her around that much money. I walked into the master bath, where the money was hidden. I lifted the tub by pulling out on the knobs on the shower head. Once I pulled the knob, it lifted the locks that held the tub in place, which I had secretly put in by a trusted mechanic, who specialized in creating stash compartments.

When I lifted the tub and unlocked the metal box, 600 thousand was there for the taking. It was wrapped in plastic to prevent the moisture from in the bathroom from mildewing the money. I had it neatly stacked along the floor neatly, and began to place it in a duffel bag. I placed the tub back in place and cleaned up some excess debris that fell from the cracks of the walls and seals. Then I took the money out to the truck, and came back into the house for a while. I wasn't worried about the money sitting out in the truck in O'Fallon, it was a very secure neighborhood.

Karra looked like she was about to doze off into a deep sleep. Before she fell asleep I took some money out of my pockets and gave it to her. I put it on the table in front of her.

"You can take this and go shopping tomorrow," I expressed, getting up to walk to the kitchen. I opened the refrigerator and noticed nothing was in there to eat at all. Karra got up and walked in the kitchen. She stood behind me staring at me while I was looking in the refrigerator.

"You might have to go to the grocery store also, because it ain't shit here—" I stopped in mid-sentence once I turned around to see her standing there behind me with nothing but a t-shirt on.

"Stay here with me tonight, please," she begged, reaching out to hug me. I slid her arms away from me.

"N'all, I can't. I gotta go do something."

"What you gotta do?" she asked with a higher tone. She grabbed my hand and slid it in under her shirt, and then between her legs. For a moment I found myself feeling how soft and wet she felt. My fingers moved as if they had a mind of their own, until I realized what I was doing then snatched them away. She grabbed my dick through my jeans. By that time it was rock hard. The liquor from tonight held me at attention, she tried to unbutton my jeans and belt.

"Stop!" I said, moving her hands and heading towards the door. She ran in front of the door and squatted down, pulling on my jeans as she dropped. They easily came down to my knees, and before I could stop her, she had her mouth locked on my dick, sucking it hard. "Aw, shit, hold on. Stop!" I said with little conviction. I tried to push her face back off of me. She just kept on, I couldn't stop her. I didn't want to either, it felt good.

Karra had skills that were undeniable. I was buckling at the knees. I had to place a hand on the wall to hold myself up so I wouldn't fall. She looked up at me, then stood up and pushed me back until I fell down on the couch. She slowly pulled off her shirt and sat down on top of me, slowly guiding me into her. She must have cumm already, because her juices slid down me quickly. She moaned loud. Then she started to bounce on it like a trampoline.

She couldn't take it all the way down, so she would stand up and shake her ass whenever I hit the bottom of her pussy. It was like she had to shake the pain off. Then she would put it back in and start bouncing again. I got into it and began grabbing her ass and pulling her down on me more. I began fucking her hard as hell, trying to take out on her all the anger I had built up from tonight.

"Aww! Awwwww shit! Baby... Damn!" she yelled loudly. I pushed her off, then turned her over, throwing her legs up on my shoulders as she laid on her back. "No Tyrek!" she begged, realizing the pain I was about to place on her.

"Shut up and take this dick, you been wanting it all this time, huh?" I said, gritting my teeth. I started to thrust hard. "Take this dick!" I said, pounding her harder.

She couldn't even scream, she was just looking at me like I was tearing her apart. She put the pillow that was on the couch over her mouth and sighed. I was about to cumm, so I pulled the pillow from off her face and hopped up and let it go in her mouth. She swallowed and started to suck the rest out. Shocked, I watched as she went crazy.

I thought she would get angry at me doing that, but she wanted it. She rubbed her hands along my legs and my stomach as she continued to suck me dry. She then leaned up and hugged me at the waist, resting her head on my stomach. She was breathing hard and looking up hoping that this would prove her love for me. She was hoping that this would last all night. I removed her hands, then got up and put my pants on.

"So you gon stay with me tonight?" she asked.

"N'all, I can't. I told you I gotta do something," I said, brushing my jeans.

"Why, you gotta get back to that bitch you was with at the club tonight!" she said with anger. She picked up the pillow and threw it at me.

"What?" I asked, looking at her. "You tripping," I shook my head at her then walked out the door. Before I slammed it shut, she made an attempt to stop me.

"Ty, wait!" she screamed, but I was already gone.

Karra sat on the couch, crying. She hated being alone. She had been alone all her life. She didn't understand why the only man who cared for her always left her alone. She thought sex would be the way to get him to be with her. She didn't understand why I didn't love her like she loved me. All night she thought about what she was doing wrong, why she couldn't have him. Determine to find out, she rushed to put her clothes on, grabbed her keys and headed out the door.

***

Shai had been blowing my phone up. She couldn't sleep, she was pacing the entire house. She had finally sat down at the kitchen table, waiting on me to come home. When she heard the garage door open and saw the headlights pull into the driveway, she came out the front door.

"Where the fuck you been! I been worried like hell!" she yelled.

"Shh, calm the fuck down before you wake the neighbors. You know they will call the cops on us in a heartbeat," I said, popping the hatch and grabbing the bags of money.

"Fuck these neighbors," she said in a lower tone.

I got the bags out the back and hurried into the house. Shai open one of the bags when I sat it on the floor.

"Why you riding around with all this money? You tripping over nothing and it's causing you to do stupid shit!" she said, putting her finger in my face, then walking off.

I laid down on the couch to get some rest. I knew I was tripping over nothing, but no man in his right mind would have been cool with the thought of his girl fucking with the enemy. This would be the last time I let my pride get in the way.

***

Karra parked on the corner behind another car. She sat crying, staring from behind the window tint at the sight of Shai walking out of the front door. She had followed me, by leaving her phone GPS locator on in his truck. She almost lost him a few times by getting out of range, but tracked it down. She was mad and furious with tears in her eyes. She knew now who was standing in the way of her and me, Shai.

I slept almost until 5 in the evening. When I awoke, Rell was sitting over on the other couch. My head was throbbing.

"What's up, bout time you woke yo ass up," he said.

"What up," I said, clinching the canal of my nose, trying to gain complete vision.

"Shit, Shai called me and told me to come over and get that doe out the crib. What happened last night?" Rell asked.

"Nigga, you don't even want to know. Where's she at?" I asked, looking around to make sure she was out of earshot.

"She gone with Moni. They getting something for the trip," Rell said. "You still going right, you ain't have a nigga get them tickets for nothing," he added.

I got up and stumbled into the kitchen. I reached and got a glass. out of the cabinet to fix a glass of orange juice. I felt in my pockets and pulled out the X pills Chad gave me last night. I needed something to take care of this headache and didn't feel like going upstairs to fish around for some pain medication. I took one out and popped it in my mouth, then sipped some juice.

"Nigga, did you just take a pill, what the fuck is wrong with you?" Rell asked, shocked to see me take a pill. I hardly fucked around like that with the pills, so for him to see me pop one was kind of unusual.

"Yeah, I gotta headache. I'm feeling real fucked up. Man, I ended up knocking down Karra last night. I got up with her after the club. And guess what?" I said, reaching in my pockets to grab Easy's keys.

"What?" he asked.

"I got that nigga Easy's keys." I said, dangling them in the air. Rell looked at me with a puzzled expression.

"What the fuck we gon do with that niggas keys?" he asked.

"Nigga, you gon see. Where Chad and Boo; we still hitting the club tonight?" I asked, grabbing my things off the living room table.

"Yeah, they chilling at the crib. Everybody came over after the party last night. I bout to hit them up now."

We were going out to the Strip clubs tonight before leaving the country. I wanted to spend some more time with them before leaving them in control.

"Guess who I bumped into last night?" Rell said while texting on his phone.

"That nigga C, he came through after you left."

Chris was one of our old childhood friends who we hung out tough with for a long time, until his family moved to Atlanta. He was a funny ass nigga, straight comical.

"Get the fuck out of here, C. What that nigga up to?" I asked, surprised to hear that he saw him, and disappointed that I wasn't there.

"Shit, you know he suppose to be doing stand up for some clubs in the ATL,"Rell said. "I invited him to come with us to the club tonight. He staying at the Adams Mark Hotel, we can pick him up when we leave."

"Cool, I'm bout to get ready. Imma be back down in a sec." I headed upstairs, eager to see Chris. I showered and put on some fresh clothes. The last time I saw him was a long time ago, way before we were sitting on money like we are now. I wanted to show out for him and at the same time let him know he ain't gotta worry bout shit no more.

I threw on a pair of Artful Dodgers jeans and a shirt to match. Put on some Prada boots, my Cartier Roadster watch, and a blue 3 carat diamond earring. I kept the safe in the closet stashed with a hundred or so, so I reached in and took out about 20 to fuck off tonight then shot back down stairs.

"Let's roll Nigga."

I hadn't pulled the Maserati out in a while, so I decided to drive it tonight. We pulled into the Adams Mark. C was suppose to be waiting on us in the lobby. He didn't know what we were riding in, so when we pulled up, he just looked at the car. Rell rolled down the window and waved for him.

"Nigga what's up!"

He came out of the Lobby and took a step back to look at the car. "Oh shit, we riding like this? Damn Nigga! I thought you was Rick Ross pulling up in this bitch. I see I need to come back home more often," he teased. I got out the car and greeted him.

"My Nigga, what up."

"What up boy!" C said excited.

"Chad and Boo bout to meet us down here," Rell said as he got off the phone. I looked around and they were pulling in the hotel entrance. Boo was driving his 2012 Cadillac Ent. on 26's.

"Oh, these lil niggas rolling too," C said, getting in the back of the Maserati. "Lil young ass rich niggas; damn! This muthafucka feel like a first class seat," C added,, feeling the leather.

"That's what you flew out in?" I asked, peeking through the rearview mirror at him.

"Hell n'all, Nigga. I wasn't even riding coach, I was riding in the new seating area. I flew out in poverty Nigga. Shit y'all niggas came a long way Homie."

"So what that stand up comedy do for you?" I asked.

"Man, it's a fucked up industry, but it's cool ya know. I get my chance to knock off a few every now and then," C said. "But I know you got the hoes on lock if you rollin like this." C leaned up to the front.

"This nigga on lock, he ain't doing shit no mo." Rell said jokingly.

"Who!" I grinned. "Nigga I'm good, you the one on lock. Moni will—" at that moment my phone rang. Rell looked and laughed.

"Yeah, locked like I said nigga, that's her right there," he pointed to the phone.

"You too Nigga, Moni with her," I added.

"Aw, y'all niggas ain't got no hoes," C sighed.

I picked up the phone, it was Shai. She wanted me to come over to the Loft apartment real quick. We were leaving the hotel and wasn't that far away. I prepared myself for a good argument. We pulled up, Shai came out waving to Chad and Boo who followed us. Then she made her way over to me.

"Good God, who's dis?" C asked, as he watched Shai walk up to the ride. "That's who got you stuck, shit I'll be stuck to Nigga, you tripping," C added. "Damn, that money a muthafucka."

I got out of the car. Shai and I walked across the street to talk. I looked back to see Chris shaking his head in approval to me. Rell tapped him to hand him some weed. C looked at the blunt.

"Nigga I can't smoke that shit. I'll be done hopped out this bitch while it's in motion. Let me get some drank," C said. "Damn, look at that bitch," C said, watching a female walk out of the building. She walked up towards the Maserati.

"Nigga chill! That's my girl right there." Rell said, rolling down the window.

"What's up," Rell hollered to Moni as she walked closer. She waved at C, in the back. She remembered him from the night before.

"Where y'all finna go?" she asked, leaning in the window.

"You know, boys night out." Rell smiled.

"Yeah, whateva, just don't let the boys get you fucked up." Moni said, looking real seriously at Rell.

"What, I ain't coming home tonight. I'm staying out. Me and my dude right here gon fuck bout four strippers with no rubbers," Rell said, trying to hold a serious look on his face. Moni reached in the window to hit him, forcing him to lean back and laugh. She knew he was playing, they played like that all the time.

"So you through trippin?" Shai asked.

"Yeah, I'm cool, I don't know if I trust you the same though."

"What, you better nigga, I love yo ass too much and I respect you way to highly to do something with someone else," Shai pled. At that response I felt a sense of guilt about fucking with Karra.

"I love you too." I kissed her softly, holding her hands. "I'm bout to roll thou, I'll be home late."

"You ain't come home last night," She paused to see my expression. I smirked at the comment. "I ain't saying nothing about it though, go ahead, I know ya boy in town. If you would've stayed at the party last night you could have kicked it with him already," she said. "You owe me a night," she added.

I was relieved that she let that go and didn't question me of my whereabouts.

"I got you. I promise." I said. We walked back across the street. Chad and Boo, pulled up along side of the ride. They were hanging out of the window laughing as Moni and Rell joked around with eachother. Moni looked over at Shai as she walked up.

"A Shai, you tell'em what we bought them to wear on the beach?" Moni said, giving a quick wink to Shai so she could play along with her.

"What, what y'all get us?" both me and Rell asked.

"We got yall some man thongs." Moni, Shai and everyone else, but Rell and I laughed.

"Y'all got us fucked up," I said.

"We ain't rocking no shit like that," Rell replied, as C leaned his head out of the window.

"Shit, I'll rock'em if y'all let me roll with y'all."

Shai and Moni gave him an odd look. Shai then leaned into my arm and whispered.

"Watch ya homie, baby watch ya homie."

"He does stand up comedy, he just playing." I smiled, getting in the car. "Imma call you later."

I slowly pulled off. We rolled up in front of Bottoms Up, a strip club in Brooklyn, IL. We decided to go inside the Pink Slip first though. So we walked down the alley behind the two clubs that sat adjacent to eachother. The Pink Slip, the most popular club on the East Side, had all the bitches you could imagine stripping inside. The clubs didn't have the no touch laws, unlike most out of town clubs I went to, you could reach out and touch them if you wanted to. We planned on hitting a few clubs tonight, and on our list were the Slip, Bottoms Up, and the Soft Touch. The Pink Slip and Bottoms Up were in Brooklyn, so we hit them first. Brooklyn, held most of the strip clubs in the East Side, besides Washington Park. Brooklyn was a small area about 10 blocks long, and three of the blocks were all strip clubs.

We had a few guys positioned outside, due to the situation that happen with Boo not to long ago. Brooklyn was grimey, and we had to be prepared.

"Nigga, y'all might have to sit in the ride, if y'all to young to get in," C said, joking with Chad and Boo. "Y'all ain't gon fuck up my night, and it ain't no milk in here unless it's a pregnant stripper, then y'all might get lucky."

We all laughed. Chad and Boo wasn't tripping off C, they got familiar with him the night before, too. He was crazy as hell. After throwing a couple hundreds at the door, we slid inside without a pat down. We headed straight to the bar to get some drinks. C went crazy after a few sips.

"Yeah, it smells like bootyhole in this bitch~" he yelled out. He looked around. "Damn, look at that bitch on the pole, she got some monkey in her ass." C watched as she worked the pole. When she turned around, he tripped. "Damn, and she look like a monkey too."

We copped a seat in the corner by the second stage. We knocked off a bottle of Patron, threw a few dollars out to the stage, talked shit, and once it was too packed, we headed over to Bottoms Up. A group of bad bitches flocked soon as we entered the door. We tipped big in there. C had his face in every bitch's booty in there. He got into it with security, but they didn't do nothing because we knew the owner.

One time C got to close to a girl and she pulled his head on her pussy and started gyrating on his face. She held his head there for a minute, rubbing her pussy all over it. He pushed her, trying to get free, and when he did, he was pissed. She ran to the back and he tried to give chase, but the security stopped him. We was laughing all night long at this nigga.

After that, he started talking about every bitch in the club. A chick came over to try to give him a lap dance, but she had some stretch marks on her booty. C looked at her and started laughing.

"Bitch, it looks like a midget been hanging on yo booty for dear life," he said.

"Fuck you Nigga!" she said, getting all up in his face, then she walked off.

He got up to follow her, but I grabbed his arm.

"N'all I'm cool Dog, I'm bout to clown this hoe," he said, assuring me that he wasn't bout to cause anymore trouble. He talked about every stripper in the club. "Look at you Bitch, with the way them titties hanging and shit, it looks like you use to strip in Africa. I can grab the nipples and play jump rope with another bitch."

He kept it up until the owner appoached us and told us to take him home. The females wasn't tripping that much off of C, as long as we were throwing money in the air, they didn't care what he said. But as requested, we left. We didn't go home, but instead we headed over to the Soft Touch. The Soft Touch was in East Saint Louis, off St. Clair Ave.

It sat off in the cut and was off the chain. You can go hard in there and most of the bitches were prostitutes posing as strippers.

"Man, don't get up in here on that bullshit," I said to C as we got out the ride.

"Nigga that bitch was out of pocket, I wanted to fuck her ass up." he said. "I'm cool now," he said as Rell got out and looked at C.

"Look Nigga, pick any bitch in here, it's on me tonight." Rell said.

"Bet that, give me some rubbers though, cuz I ain't got none." C insisted.

"N'all, you got to go bare back."

"Bare? Nigga a gorilla won't go bare on these hoes?"

The Soft Touch had a nice crowd, but it wasn't too packed. We got some drinks and took a seat. C had already scoped out a bitch of choice for the night. She had a tongue that could touch her forehead.

"Damn, you see that bitch's tongue Nigga!" C said excitingly.

Chad and Boo was standing next to him. "Hell yeah," Chad said, throwing some money in the air. Boo watched as a lovely carmel tone stripper approached him, forcing him down into the chair. She danced in front of him for a while, then attempted to straddle on top of him. When she tried to sit down he yelled at her.

"Hold on, hold on bitch these pants cost 900 dollars, and you ain't bout to get no cum stains on these by rubbing yo pussy all over my shit to get you off."

The girl didn't argue, she stood up and bent over clapping her ass in his face. She grabbed his hand and guided it into her pussy. Boo sprinkled a couple of hundreds on her in twenties. When she picked up the bills, she noticed they were all dubs, and sat down next to him.

"What type of jeans you got on that you won't let me sit down and ride that dick." she asked.

Boo chuckled, "First of all you ain't riding this dick, you just dancing for me, and they Gucci's."

The dancer checked him out from head to toe, looking at his jewelry and clothes.

"Where you going after this, maybe I can ride that dick with the pants off," she added. Boo looked at her, taking in her curves and looks. She was fine and had an amazing body. He loved the attention that was now given to him being that he was now getting money. He knew, about a year ago, she would never have given him the time of day. He could tell she was eager to fuck him too, and not for money but just to see if he was one of the many trick ass niggas she would normally run into.

C overheard Boo and the Dancer talking and interrupted them, "Shit, I ain't doing nothing you can ride me right now."

She looked at him, noticing he had no jewelry on, she walked off giving Boo a wink.

"Fuck you then bitch, with all them dimples in yo ass. If you spray some pink body paint on ya booty it'll look like a baboon's ass." he yelled. Rell walked up and patted C on the shoulder.

"You pick one yet?" he asked.

"Hell n'all, I'm waiting on the bitch with the tongue to get off the stage." C pointed. "Where Ty at?" he asked.

Rell gave a look in Ty direction, "He over there fucking with his phone, I told you that nigga sprung," Rell added. C shook his head and started walking over in his direction.

"Nigga what's up!" he said, taking a seat. "Fuck with us tonight; what you gon fuck with that phone all night, you is sprung, huh." I looked up from the text.

"N'all I'm good, just taking care of something right now." I waved for Boo to come over. I reached in my pockets and gave him Easy's keys.

"Here take these outside. You gon see a chick in a Challenger, give them to her." I said to Boo.

Boo took the keys and went out the door. He came back in moments later. "She said she know you in here." Boo said, laughing. "Who is that, she tough." he added.

"Where she at?" I asked, looking over towards the door. I didn't want her ass coming in to make a scene. I knew she was a live wire now.

"She gone, she pulled off soon as I gave her the keys," Boo said.

"There she go!" C yelled, then started laughing when he saw me look up. "Nigga, not ya girl. I'm talking about the bitch with the tongue!" C pointed, tapping my arm. "Where's Rell, she off stage now Nigga!"

Rell walked over to the female and whispered something in her ear, then gave her some money. She held up one finger, signaling to C, that she would be over in a minute. She came over shortly after she changed clothes. Grabbing C by the hands, she led him into the back. The back of the Soft Touch, was full of private booths. She stopped in one of them and got undressed. She ordered C to sit down and unbutton his pants. C hurried and was just as excited as ever.

"Bout to see what that tongue like," he said, pulling down his jeans. She licked her tongue out and made it touch the top of her nose.

"Damn, you like a reptile." He waved his dick at her. "Here lizzard, lizzard, lizzard."

When she clamped down on his dick, she sucked it hard for a couple of minutes and he nutted quick. "Damn!" she leaned back, looking at him. "You're a Premi?" she laughed. C was embarrassed.

"N'all, that's just the first one. Shit, give me a minute, I've been waiting on you all night. See I wasn't ready for how you got down," he babbled.

"Well we ain't got a minute, so I'll holla at you Premi." She put her clothes on. "That was a quick 200 dollars," she laughed.

"A, you ain't gotta say it like that," he yelled. C looked to the side, hearing laughter from the booth next to him. He looked over into the booth. A guy getting some head, looked up.

"Damn, Dog! You done already, huh? Viagra Nigga – Viagra!" he chuckled. C just looked at him and walked off. He came out from the back, Rell was laughing already.

"Damn, Nigga you wasn't back there but for what, 2 minutes." Rell said, laughing along with me, Chad and Boo. "Nigga I gave that bitch 200 dollars, you should've went in on that bitch," he added.

"Man, I'm straight shit," C said, trying to forget the situation. The girl came over and looked at C, then shook her head. I looked at them both.

"What happen?" I asked.

"Nothing!" C answered, trying to signal for the girl not to mention anything to me. She just smiled.

"He happened in less then a minute. And all I did was suck his dick," she smirked.

"What!" Chad said, laughing at C. Everybody started in on him.

"Man, fuck y'all! Don't act like y'all ain't never bust quick. Nigga, I wasn't prepared, plus I was waiting on her all night," C explained.

We rode his ass all night long. Before we left I saw Monz at the bar with a couple of dudes. This was my opportunity to holla at him on that green. I heard he'd been moving a lot of it lately, and I wanted to tap into some of that money.

I approached the bar where he sat. Monz watched as I approached and for that moment, I recalled the time T-Mac approached me in the club. Monz had that look on his face, the same, 'what the fuck this nigga want' look I had.

"What's up Nigga." I said, reaching out my hand. Monz shook my hand.

"Ty, what's good boy," he said.

"Shit, been trying to hit ya up. You still fucking with that one demonstration you was telling me about?"

"Yeah," Monz said. "It's kinda fucked up right now though, what up." he added.

"You. Here take my info down, I might be able to show you something tomorrow," I said.

"I—ight bet that." Monz punched my number into his phone. He dapped me up and let me know to hit him up early tomorrow. I agreed, then went back over to the fellas, so we could head out.

Chapter 19

We split up after the club. Chad and Boo said they were about to go over a few chicks houses they fucked with. I dropped Rell and C off at his ride, because they said they were going out to Rell's crib, and I went to check on Karra.

I had given her Easy's keys earlier at the club. Hopefully it wasn't too late and Easy didn't raise suspicion. She was to go back to the Drury Inn Plaza, and holla at this female at the front desk by the name Keisha. She was to give her the keys, a couple of hundreds, and she would call Easy to tell him that the maintenance crew found them in the garage when working. She would also give her the address that was on the I.D. that he used to cop the room.

I pulled up at the Condo in O'Fallon. She was there, her car parked under the carport. I opened the door and heard the shower running, she came out of the back room with nothing on. It seemed to me, she was looking more seductive each time I saw her.

"Oh, shit you scared me," she said. "Why you ain't come out to bring me the keys?" she added.

"Did you do that?" I asked, avoiding her question.

"Yeah, it's on the dresser," she said. She bent over to feel the water in the tub. I took a quick glance at her. I didn't want her to know I was looking. She came back into the room. "I guess you can't stay tonight either, huh?" she asked. "It's all good, I know what's up," she smiled.

I grabbed the information and walked out into the living room. She followed behind me. She ran and stood in front of the door again, blocking me from leaving.

"So we ain't gon fuck?" she said.

"Not tonight, I'm on something," I pushed her to the side and left.

Karra watched as I left, then walked back in the bathroom and got in the tub. Her hatred was growing more eachday, but it wasn't for me. It was for the woman standing between us in her warped little mind.

I woke up to Shai hitting me, telling me that Chad and Boo got picked up last night by the police. We called to check for a bond, but it wasn't one. The officer on the phone said they were being held for questioning. I knew it was behind that situation with Steph. I just hoped they had all their shit together for this one.

***

Boo and Chad were placed in separate holding cells. Boo was lying down when the officer came in to get him. The electronic door slid back and Boo walked out. The officer frisked him then lead him down the hall into an interrogation room.

"Have a seat," the officer said. Another guy came in shortly and sat down across from Boo. He was dressed in plain clothes. Boo searched the guy visually for a badge, and noticed he was a federal agent.

"I'm Federal Agent Boon, how are you doing?" the agent said. "You know you are here for Stephen Smith, so let's cut the bullshit. How long have you known Steph, that's what you call him right?" he asked, looking up to Boo from a stack of papers. Boo just looked at him, then put his head on the table like he was going to sleep. The agent hit the table, Boo didn't move. "We know you and Chad were his suppliers and we know you know who killed him! We know who did it! Steph was wired that night, we got the voices on tape!" he said angrily. "And we are going to run them threw voice analysis to find out who they are," the agent continued. "You need to help yourself, because you know Chad will when we question him."

Boo and Chad practiced this and played it out in their mind. They would get high and watch First 48 every so often and laugh at how stupid them dudes were who told on themselves. They knew once they got in the position, not to ask for a lawyer, because that would raise suspicion. And to never say anything to them, at all. That's what Boo did, said nothing. When Agent Boone realized Boo was snoring, he yelled to the other cops.

"Get this asshole out of here!"

Chad was waiting in the room alone for about an hour. He figured they were watching him, trying to see if he was nervous or not. He just sat there stiff. When the agents came in, Chad took it as a chance to get something to eat. He acted like he was going to cooperate.

He asked them for some food and sodas, taking one sip out of the can then asked for another one. He smoked up all of their cigarettes, and he didn't even like smoking. He kept on until the agent got angry and smacked the chicken off the table, then stormed out of the room.

"We're not getting anywhere with this asshole either," the agent said to the other one standing in the hall. "What you want to do?" he added.

"There's nothing we can do," he replied, exhaling. "There's not enough to hold them on anything."

"What about the surveillance?" Agent Boone asked.

"We can try to keep them under the eye for a while, but most likely we don't have the time, if we can't get something on them," he sighed. "these two muthafuckas will fuck up soon. Every now and then, sick a uniform on them to see if we can catch them riding with something."

Chad and Boo were released. They smiled all the way out the door. They knew nothing could hold them as long as they didn't talk. They caught a cab to the tow yard and got the truck back out the impound. Soon as Chad got it out, he got his phone and threw it away. They swung by the Arabs spot and got another phone, then called Shai.

"Hey, we straight," Chad said, riding in the passenger seat. He was looking for the can of corn curls. He grabbed the can twisting the bottom of it off and grabbed the weed out of it. Then he started rolling a blunt.

"Where y'all at?" Shai asked. "Look meet us at Sweetie Pie's, over off Manchester and Tower Grove. I'll be there in bout 5 minutes."

"I—ight." Chad said then hung up. He passed the blunt to Boo. Boo inhaled and took in a deep breath, holding the weed in his lungs. He started coughing and choking, til he almost swerve and hit another car in passing. "Damn, oh shit, that's that fire right there."

Sweetie Pies, a soul food restaurant in St. Louis, has some of the best food in the city. I waited in the car along with Shai until everyone pulled up. Rell, Moni. and C pulled up shortly after we did. Then Chad and Boo pulled up. Shai noticed they were still in Boo truck.

"Ain't that the same truck they were in last night?" Shai asked.

"Yeah, why?" I asked. She didn't answer, she just got out. Shai walked up to them before they got completely out of the truck. "Why y'all still in this fucking truck?" she yelled at Chad as he tried to put the blunt out before she saw it.

"We just got it out of the pound," Boo explained.

"Yeah, Nigga and you was just in there for investigation. How y'all know they ain't wire this mafucka, get rid of the truck now! It could be a tracking device or anything in this ride," she said angrily. "Meet us later on."

Boo and Chad knew Shai was serious. She took the game just as serious as her old man and was a lot smarter then any nigga out there hustling. So they got back in the truck and pulled off.

"Where they going?" I asked, walking up to Shai.

"To get rid of that truck, let's go eat, we hungry." Shai said, rubbing her stomach. She wasn't showing yet, but she was gaining weight fast.

We sat down and ate good. I was full and could hardly move. My phone went off and I didn't recognize the number so I didn't answer it. Then it went off again.

"Who dis?" I answered in a disguising tone.

"This Monz Nigga, what's up?"

"What up?" I said. "I'm grabbing a bite to eat now."

"Shit, I'm trying to see what up with you."

"Bout to leave her in a minute, Imma hit you up soon as I do."

"I—ight, shit well do that." Monz hung up. I had forgotten about Monz. I didn't really feel like doing anything today, but I needed to at least get Monz on the team. And today might be my only time to.

***

Agent Boone knew it would be a good idea to follow them after the release. Usually all of their suspects would take him right to their source. He sat two blocks down on Tower Grove taking pictures of them all. He wondered who the woman was approaching their truck and who the male was that stood by her. He made sure he got close visual photos of their faces, so he could run a facial check on them both. He knew situations like this could have been a long shot, but it was worth the chance.

Chad and Boo pulled into Pookies spot, an addict they knew who taught them how to cook up dope.

"What up, what you on?" Chad asked Boo.

"Man, Shai tripping. This mafucka aint wired," Boo said. "I ain't trying to get rid of my shit." Boo got out and searched the truck for any signs of tampering. "Hand me that manual." he asked Chad. Boo opened the manual and looked at the overhead digital panel. He looked at the side of it and saw the cloth was sticking out a little. "What the fuck," he uttered under his breath. He pulled the panel and it popped open. He saw a lot of wires and a mini microphone hanging down with a red bulb connected to it. He snatched it out. The panel was still lit. "Damn, nigga look." he showed Chad. Boo put the panel back in and tossed the wires out of the truck.

"Glad we ain't drive my shit." Chad said. "You don't think that was that On—Star shit?" Chad asked.

"Man, you know that wasn't no On—Star shit." Boo answered. "Fuck."

He went to Auto Zone and grabbed a For Sale sign and stuck it in the window. He parked the truck over his girl's mother house, and they got dropped off to Chad's whip.

Chapter 20

Meno had been meeting with his boss in Sinaloa, Mexico. His boss, El Chapo, was head of the Sinaloa Cartel, the umbrella over the Mafia Mexicana. El Chapo's compound was huge and Meno was always nervous in his presence. El Chapo was a very dangerous man. Everytime he thought, someone died. It was rumored that he escaped from prison years back and has never been caught or seen since.

Meno had been approaching the situation with him and Elan delicately. He had been asking El Chapo for assistance and blessing to handle the situation. To take out Ramiero, Elan's bodyguard.

"Hola Meno." El Chapo said, entering the room with several armed men.

El Chapo was a short cocky man of bronze complexion. He always moved as if he had no care in the world, which was totally opposite. A drug war was constantly going on and he was the most wanted target.

"It is an honor, Senor Chapo." Meno said, bowing.

"What business do you bring?" El Chapo asked, signaling for a glass of water.

"I have a problem. First let me say, I am very loyal to my family, La Familia. And if it means me giving my life to get rid of anyone who isn't loyal to my family, then I must do that," Meno pleaded, he knew by bringing any type of situation to El Chapo it could mean his own death.

El Chapo leaned up in his chair at the mentioning of a problem and loyalty.

"What and who are you speaking of?" he asked.

"Elan, he has threatened my very existence." Meno explained.

El Chapo sat back in his seat and looked at one of the guys holding a gun.

"You know what you speak of isn't allowed. If there is a problem between you and him, then why not get rid of both," El Chapo was waiting on Meno's reaction. Meno did not show any signs of weakness.

"Like I said before, if it means giving my life for the familia, then so be it." Meno pleaded again.

174

"What is the problem?" El Chapo asked, as he sat and stared at Meno.

"Elan has become greedy and wants to climb with deceit." Meno explained.

El Chapo sat his water down, "How can you prove this? Elan does well for us, he has taken business from you, yes." he said, waving his hands in Meno's direction.

"So how do I know you're not trying to rid the competition," El Chapo said, growing louder as he spoke.

"Let me prove it. All I ask is to allow me to take Ramiero, he means nothing to the familia. Let me prove to you, Elan is not as loyal as you think he is." Meno begged. Meno did not break a sweat. He was willing to die today, to get revenge for Shai.

"You have a week, if this is not true Meno, then I will give you another week to pick out your attire to be buried in," El Chapo said, lifting a hand for Meno to leave.

El Chapo waved at one of the guards. A lean, long haired one stepped up to his side and bent down close to lend him his ear.

"I want you to keep an eye on Meno, and find out why him and Elan are such a problem for eachother." he whispered to the guard.

Meno was leaving the compound. He walked out the double doors, down the steps and out to his car to get inside. His guard opened the rear door and Meno got in. They pulled off. Once Meno was outside of the compound walls, he picked up his phone and called Shai. He leaned up to the guard in the front passenger seat.

"Juarez, I want you to find Ramiero, take him and bring him to me." Meno ordered. Juarez nodded his head, assuring the order would be taken care of quickly.

Meno waited on Shai to answer the phone. The guard he was riding with was the only one who knew that Shai was his daughter. Juarez was very loyal to him and would kill anyone, even El Chapo, if ordered.

"Shai?" Meno asked.

"Hey, Meno." Shai said into the phone.

"It's okay to talk now." Meno assured her that he was around trustworthy people at the time.

"Father, I have some news for you," Shai paused not knowing how Meno would take to her being pregnant.

"News, what kind of news?" She took a deep breath.

"I'm pregnant," she said.

"What!" Meno paused, trying not to get upset. He could sense she was happy and didn't want to ruin it. He didn't want her pregnant at all; although he wanted her to be happy and have a normal life, but in his business, nothing was normal. He shielded his anger the best he could. "That's good, but listen. I am in Sinaloa, and I have gotten approval. Shai I need to know if what you saw was true. Was it Ramiero?" Meno' asked. He knew he had to be sure, because the threat from El Chapo wasn't a warning.

Shai grew quiet because she knew that Meno would be killed if he was not right about Elan. She knew all about El Chapo.

"Yes, I would never steer you wrong."

"I know, I know, just be careful and wait for my call. I will need you to come out to see me and take care of something," Meno said. "I love you." he told her, then he hung up.

Meno didn't want to say much more. He was fuming from the thought of Shai being pregnant. His hatred was growing for Senor Ty eachday. He blamed him for everything that had happened thus far; especially for what happened to Shai.

Revenge would be hard, but when it happened it would be sweet. Shai just held the phone in her hand looking at it. She prayed that Meno would be able to prove this to El Chapo, because if he couldn't, then he would have to delivere himself to the Cartel and be willing to die. If not him, then anyone who was in his family. I watched as Shai sat worried after her phone call with Meno. That worried me. She had mentioned the pregnancy to him and I didn't know how he took it or what he said to her. By the look on her face, he may have wanted her to get rid of it.

"You alright?" I asked, taking a seat next to her. "What, he don't want you to have the baby?"

"No, it's not that. We might have to hold on the trip. I have something I must do soon." she said.

What?" I asked.

"I can't say."

What, what the fuck you mean, you can't say?" I wondered, annoyed by her secrecy.

"I just can't because I don't know yet!" she screamed. I stared at her for a moment, trying to sense a lie. I just couldn't sense anything with her. I grabbed our things.

"Let's go!" I said, walking past her.

We pulled up at home. We didn't speak at all on the ride home. She just looked out of the window. Once in the driveway, Shai got out and went inside. Our neighbor was over in his front yard messing around. He was an elderly man, about 6 ft., brownskin, looked to be in his 50's or 60's. He mostly stayed to himself and always waved whenever he saw us. He started to walk in my direction as I got the bags out of the car.

"Hey, how are you doing?" he asked, extending his hand to me. I was prepared to give him the 'I own real estate' script. I didn't know if he was being nosey for the other neighbors or what.

"I'm fine and you?" I said, shaking his hand.

"Fine, I was meaning to tell you, the other night I saw you come home a little late. I was in the kitchen at the time and I noticed a car that looked like it followed you. It was one of them new cars, that uh, Challenger, I think. Yeah, it also has been a black truck cruise threw here, but they never stop," he said, pointing towards the corner. "The Challenger was parked over there. I always try to keep an eye on the neighborhood, so I got my wife's dog and took him out for a walk. I started in that direction. Then the car pulled off, it looked like a young lady, a fine one too. I figure you got a fatal attraction on ya hands, if you don't mind me saying so. That's why I didn't mention it in front of ya misses," he added, smiling.

I was taken aback by what he said. I knew who the Challenger was, but the black truck drove me to anger. I thought about the other night after I left the party, the black Navigator on the highway. I studied the ole man for a minute. He meant no harm. He was quite cool after we chopped it up for a while. He said he was from the St. Louis city area, too. He told me how he ran with the Moors back in the day. And from his own admission, I had some suspicion that I was talking to an old gangster. We talked a little while longer before I went inside.

Rell picked me up shortly afterwards, so we could take care of some business. We rode in a F-250 pick up truck. We did most of the pick ups and drop offs in the truck being that it was considered lowkey. We looked like a few construction workers.

"Where the burna at?" I asked, referring to the phone we talked business on. "Let me call that nigga Monz real quick." I called Monz and he answered on the first ring. "What up Nigga, I'm out here in traffic where you at?" I asked.

"Um, meet me off Lucas and Hunt at the Gas Station right off 70," Monz said.

"I—ight." I hung up. "Let's roll to the gas station off Lucas and Hunt."

We pulled up to the gas station. Monz was already parked on the lot. I pulled in right besides him and got out.

"What up Derrty?" I said, dapping him up.

"What up, what's poppin?" he replied.

"Shit," I turned to Rell, "A, hand me that demo." Rell slid me the bag out the window. I tossed it inside of Monz ride.

"Damn, this some fruit, Nigga." Monz said as he sniffed the bag repeatedly and looked at the buds. It looked like popcorn kernels with orange and lime colors, hardly any seeds in it at all. "What you want for this?" he asked.

"A dollar." I answered, meaning a thousand.

"Yeah, what if a nigga wanna snatch about a hundred of them." Monz asked.

"I'll let you rock them for the seven fifty." I said.

"Bet, shit, I gotta patna on the East Side, he's gon wanna fuck with some of this fo sho. Imma hit you up in bout an hour after I get the change together. Can you meet me on the East Side?" Monz asked.

"Yeah, that's cool." I said.

"I—ight, Imma hit you in a minute." Then Monz pulled off.

I got back into the truck and informed Rell about the amount. Monz was all I needed to get this weed off quickly. If he can consistently cope a hundred on the regular, then knocking off a ton a month wouldn't be a problem.

Monz peeked through the rearview, watching me as I got into the truck. He had plotted on this moment every since I'd given him my number. At first, Monz had no knowledge of my beef with T-Mac, until T-Mac spoke of it. When Monz told T-Mac of the recent encounter with me, T-Mac promised Monz a generous come up to take him out, and Monz was with it.

Chapter 21

Rell backed in the driveway. We had a spot off 170 and Airport Rd. Some of the weed was stashed in the garage in some deep freezers, that was kept on low so the weed would stay fresh. I unlocked one of the freezers and pulled the bales out.

Rell went to the cabinet and took out the scale. I weighed each bale, 20 pounds. I tossed aside a certain amount for everyone I dealt with. Then placed them in the back of the truck and closed the lid to the bed.

When I first started messing with the weed, I use to break down pounds individually. I got tired of that shit quick. It took us hours to do, especially when you got over 6 to 700 of them. All together we had over 300 pounds in the truck. Pulling out of the garage, we honked the horn at the neighbors and others on the block as we drove by. My cousin stayed in the neighborhood, so he was often in the area and everyone knew him. Therefore security was tight.

I reached in the back seat and unlocked the compartment we had made into the truck. The entire backseat was only an inch of cushion, and the rest was a safe to stash money. The seats unfolded from the inside out. After a few stops we had over 90 grand in the seats. Riding and seeing cops in passing was nerve wrecking.

We had guns on our laps, and weed and cash in the back. After a couple of hours passed, Monz still hadn't hit me up. We had stopped riding and parked over Wayne house off Chambers. He copped from us also and was very low key. He worked for the cable company in the day and grinded at night. All I had left in the back was Monz hundred pounds. Rell ran through the change to see if it was all there. It was all good, and we had to stuff the money in the safe to close it.

"Monz still ain't hit?" Rell asked, pushing down the seats. He was thinking what I was thinking. We should go drop off this money before we go anywhere else. We were not about to keep riding around with 150 grand on us. Monz would call once he was ready.

Just as we pulled off in route to drop the money off, Monz hit me up. I picked up quickly.

"What up?" I answered.

"I'm ready for you, I'm over off 42nd in Charlie," Monz said. "My truck parked in the front, you'll see it," he added. I hesitated when he said where he wanted us to meet. Washington Park, called Charlie, wasn't a good place to be period. You either had to be from there or crazy to meet someone out in Charlie, jackboy central known for robberies and murders. I knew something wasn't right, but then again, I knew plenty of niggas who got money in that area.

"Hit off 42nd in Charlie," I said to Rell.

"What?" he said, immediately looking at me crazy. "Nigga you trippin! I'm not bout to roll through Charlie with all this shit on us." he added.

"N'all, shoot by the store first, then we gon see what this nigga on," I said. I knew it was risky going through Charlie period. The State Troopers could get us, Marshals, or those niggas out there. And trust me, you would rather them Troopers or Marshals get you, than them niggas.

Monz hung up the phone. "He's on his way," he said to the guy sitting across from him. He then left the room and came back with a S.K. He cocked it and stood by the window. Monz had been planning this for the last hour. He told me it was slow, but really he had fallen off due to fucking with a connect that went sour. So maybe I could help him speed it back up. This hundred along with what T-Mac had for him, definitely would help him bounce back.

"A Mike, put this in y'all's safe for me," I asked, handing him a duffel bag full of money.

"Damn, man this shit ain't gon fit. Imma have to put it in the office and lock the door. Ain't nobody going in there but my uncle to make salah." Mike said as he grabbed the bag.

"Where that A.R at?" I asked, following him to the back.

"Why, what's up, you straight, cuz I'm ready to use it on one of these muthafuckas," Mike said.

"N'all, I need it just in case I gotta do something. I ain't got mine in reach. So I need yours and if it go down Imma give you mine," I said as he reached in the bag to pull out the rifle. Mike lifted it and pointed it at my head. "It's loaded?" I asked.

"What you think Nigga." Mike smiled. I grabbed the barrel, moving it down, and then took the gun and tucked it in my pants leg.

"Good, I'll be right back." I said. I know mafuckas would notice me walking out the store with something in my pants. I walked as if my leg was broken all the way to the truck. I got in and put the rifle on the back seat.

"Let's roll Nigga." I said. Rell looked at the A.R.

"My nigga."

While riding up 42nd, I saw Monz's truck. We bent a few blocks around the corner before we parked at the house. I had to be sure it wasn't anyone waiting on the side of the house or on the other block for us to pull up. I noticed only his truck was parked at the house. The streets were narrow with no sidewalks. Some kids played bare footed outside up the street. It was the epitome of the ghetto. Most of the houses were rundown, vacant, and condemned. I parked behind his truck and called him.

"Come outside."

Monz opened the door, and minutes later he ran down the stairs to the truck. He tried to hop in the backseat, but we had the doors locked. I got out with my Beretta in hand. Rell popped the rear hatch to the truck bed.

"Where that doe at Homie?" I realized he didn't have a bag with him or anything.

"Shit, come in, Nigga we can't move like that out here."

Monz tried to convince me, "Nigga this Charlie, ain't no muthafuckas calling the cops out here."

"N'all go get that bread," I said pausing, before opening the truck bed up to grab the bag. I looked at the gun in my hands then back at him. He turned and went back inside. I saw someone in the curtains; they tried to close them back when I looked up. Something wasn't right.

Soon as Monz went inside, Rell crept out the truck to the blind side with the A.R. in hand. He squatted down so they wouldn't be able to see him. I moved to that side also, positioning myself on the side of the truck so that I could take cover just in case they came out blazing. When the door opened, a nigga came out with a choppa.

"Bitch ass niggas, don't move!" he yelled. I threw my hands in the air, but stayed standing behind the truck so he couldn't take a clean shot. I looked around, the kids stopped playing to watch the scene like they were taking notes. I pointed to the bag of weed.

"It's right there dog."

He came down the stairs and walked right in the path of Rell. I looked to the side of the house, anticipating Monz return. He was no where in sight. I could see Rell tracking his footsteps from the bottom of the truck. When he stopped, I ducked as

Rell rose up and pointed the A.R straight at him catching him completely off guard. He pumped four slugs into the guys chess, then came from around the truck, shooting at the house. I closed the back and hopped in the driver's seat. Then leaned over to open the passenger door for Rell.

"Fuck that nigga, come on," I yelled, trying to get his attention. Rell was on his way inside the house, when I called him back. He jumped off the stairs and pumped several more rounds into the house then into the body lying on the ground outside. I pulled out quickly and spun out of the driveway. Driving by the kids that played, I noticed them running along the truck imitating Rell shooting the gun. I punched the truck, bending the corner to get the fuck out of Charlie.

***

Monz ran into the back room to grab the AK. He checked the clip before he came back out, it was near empty. He couldn't go out there with a few bullets in the clip, and he didn't think to try to bluff me either, because that could have been fatal. He told his guy that he would be right out and not to go out without him. That's the problem when you deal with thirsty niggas, his guy was anxious to get the money. He sniffled and scratched all the time he waited looking out the window impatiently. When he looked out the window again, he felt he had the ups on us, so he bolted out the door with the choppa high.

Monz was putting another clip in when he heard the gunshots. He came out the room and almost got ripped apart from the bullets that flew into the living room. He dropped and crawled to the kitchen and out the back door.

"Shit!" he uttered under his breath. He ran through the backyard, hopping over the fence. He didn't know if they were giving chase or not. When he heard the tires screeching, he ducked under someone's car that was parked in a drive way. He prayed he wasn't being hunted down. He knew he had to get out of dodge. I had too much doe to be hanging around after this shit.

A door opened and the owner of the car Monz hid under came out of the house to the car.

"What the fuck!" the owner yelled. He then ran back into the house as if he was going to get something. Monz quickly got up from under the car and bolted. He would have to hide out now, because there was no way I would let him live after this.

Chapter 22

Juarez had been tracking Elan since Meno gave him the order. He studied Elan's every move, and learned Ramiero's schedule also. He stalked out Elan's place and had gotten numerous recordings of Elan talking with T-Mac and others about his plot on Meno and other Cartel leaders. Juarez took off the Sonic Ear headphones. He turned off the recorders and gave them to Meno for evidence for El Chapo.

Elan and Ramiero always met in the mornings on the veranda of his estate. Ramiero wouldn't part from Elan often, except on weekends when Elan would spend time with his family. Then Ramiero would drive down to Van Buren Boulevard, during the weekends to catch some prostitutes. That's when Juarez would decide Ramiero's fate.

I only did things like this once a year, usually on New Years or some holiday. But today we had to know the new worth. Since early this morning, we'd been running money threw the machines. I ran it so much the sound of the beep when it stopped got annoying to me. All I kept hearing was fl—fl—fl—fl—fl—fl—beep; even when I left out of the room for a second or two.

Rell estimated we were somewhere along the line of 4 mil and counting. That was a piece and entirely too much dirty money for us to have laying around. We had to do something quickly. Moni had a few people in her family that were good with laundering money, and we needed to move it through offshore bank accounts. It was perfect for getting the money back into the states without suspicion. So after we finish counting, we bagged it back up and started the process of funding the accounts.

Chad and Boo came over shortly afterwards with their bundles. I was surprised at them. They were well over a mil a piece. Shit, they were not too far from Rell and I. When we decided to take the weed and let them run the work, they used that to their advantage. They got everything they could out of it. They re-rocked the cocaine so that it would still be in brick form after they stepped on it. They said they were turning fifty bricks into sixty. They had the game and ran with it.

Shai sat peering out the window, rubbing her belly. She was getting plump. She didn't like the sensitivity that came along with pregnancy. She wasn't use to dealing with the emotions. When I walked up, she didn't turn to acknowledge me at all. She just started speaking while looking at me through the reflection in the window.

"You wanna raise a baby in this?" she asked.

"The baby ain't gon be part of this," I said, grabbing her from behind to put my hands on her belly.

"Ty, I'm scared for the baby. You can't feel what I feel," she turned around and looked me in my eyes. I never saw her so emotional, so afraid before. "All while those money machines chirped, the baby was excited. When I smell the weed in your clothes when you get home, the baby gets excited," she said.

"You tripping, they can't understand what's going on out here. Have you been to therapy?" I smiled, trying to bring a smile to her face. She gave me a light grin.

"Why, you think I'm crazy?" she asked.

"Yeah."

***

"Bitch look here, you gone get lose and produce out here! Or Imma smack yo ass to the back of the Lac!" A slim pimp sat in his Cadillac as he screamed at one of his prostitutes along Van Buren, in downtown Phoenix. "Now get the fuck out and move ya ass foe the cash!" The young hooker got out of the car, pulling her dress down. The blue CTS pulled off from the curb, leaving her in faint smoke. She walked down to another corner and noticed the CTS doubling back around the corner. It pulled up along side of her again. "And Bitch try to get missing and they gon find you when they fishing!" he yelled, then drove off once more. She wore nothing but a mini skirt, showing the bottom of her ass cheeks with a short halter top. She stood on the corner for a few minutes, waving at different cars that passed down Van Buren.

They passed by with little notice of her. Van Buren was a common stroll and the residents of Phoenix gave hookers little attention. She sat down on a bus bench with her legs slightly open. She was a beautiful Latino, very full in the chest with nice hips. She looked up when a Mercedes Benz slowly pulled up in front of the bus stop. The driver signaled for her. She looked around and noticed the other prostitutes making a run in her direction, so she hurried to the car and hopped inside.

186

Juarez dropped the gear in drive and followed them. He was waiting on Ramiero to surface. He tailed him to a cheap motel not far from the Boulevard. He thought Ramiero to be very stupid for coming on a hoe stroll in a Benz, then taking a prostitute to a cheap motel. He couldn't have had it any better.

Ramiero pulled up in front of the room. He ordered the girl out of the car, then they quickly entered the room.

"Get naked!" Ramiero ordered as soon as he closed the door.

"Hold on, first where's my money. Five hundred dollars," she said, jacking up the price because he was driving a Benz. She figured he was either a cheating spouse or a lonely business man with a little dick that couldn't satisfy anyone.

"Come here," Ramiero said. She smiled, walking seductively over to him. "Let me get that money for you." He reached in his pocket and pulled out his fist, smacking the girl into the dresser. "Five hundred dollars, huh bitch! You're not even worth fifty, Puta whore!" he yelled.

"Okay, I need a hundred please! Or Dallas will kill me!" she pleaded.

"Bitch, I will kill you, here!" he threw a hundred dollar bill on the floor. She crawled to it and grabbed it, cuffing it in her hands. She got up and took off her halter top and mini skirt, then relaxed on the bed. She started sucking his dick for a while, and then straddled on top of him as she stuck him inside of her. She rode him fast in hopes that it would be over quick. She bit her bottom lip, tasting the blood, while trying to fight back tears.

Juarez figured that Ramiero would be naked and fucking by now. He got out along with another guy and they screwed the silencers on their guns. They walked into the front office and asked for the key to Ramiero's room, 142. The clerk looked them up and down, then took one of the cards and slid it in the machine, pressing the code and programming the room number, then sat it on the counter.

"Can I see some I.D. please?" he mistakingly asked. Juarez reached into his coat, as if to grab his I.D.

"Sure." he said, pulling out the Smith & Wesson .40 caliber, hitting him two times in the chest. The clerk leaned against the counter, feeling the wound and in shock, then dropped to the floor. Juarez grabbed the cardkey then walked out of the office. They came up to the door and slid the cardkey in the slot, the light went green. They burst in the room quickly.

Ramiero slung the girl to the side of the bed. He slung her off like a rag doll and she hit the wall putting a hole in it. Before Ramiero could reach for his gun, he had a barrel pressed to his head.

"No te muevas!" Don't move, Juarez warned.

The girl laid on the floor shaking her head. She hit the wall hard and was semi conscious. She stood up slowly, wobbling to her feet. When she got on her own two, the guy looked at Juarez. Juarez nodded to him, then he shot her, too.

"Que chingaos es esto?!" What the fuck is this, "Ramiero yelled.

He knew this wasn't a robbery. Juarez threw him his clothes and gave his gun to the other guy. He then took out the chains and handcuffs and places them around Ramiero legs and hands. The other guy backed the car up to the room, and they threw him in the trunk. Ramiero didn't say anything, he figured if they wanted to kill him dead they would've done it already. He was sure that he didn't do anything that they could prove.

Meno sent the recordings that were given to him to El Chapo. El Chapo had confirmed receiving it and assured Meno that he would take care of Elan personally. He gave him the call on T-Mac, allowing Meno the pleasure of taking care of the problem. El Chapo also called for Chavez, and ordered the hit on Elan too.

Chapter 23

"Can I get your bags, Sir?" the concierge at the Drury Inn Plaza hotel asked. Easy got out of his car.

"Do it look like I got bags?" he yelled as he walked by the man headed into the lobby. He had finally made his way down to the hotel after getting several phone calls from the manager, stating that their maintenance staff had found his keys. He approached the front desk,

"Yeah, I'm here to pick up my keys."

"Your name please?" the lady at the desk asked. He gave her his name and she reached in a drawer, giving him the keys. He checked them to see if they were all there then hurried out of the hotel. He hated being inside that muthafucka after that night. He wished he could catch that bitch, Karra again. He would surely get the pleasure out of making her pay for that night.

***

Elan paced the Veranda. "Where the fuck it Ramiero, I've been calling him all day?" he yelled at the other guards. They stood there shaking their head, they didn't have a clue. He walked over to the bar and fixed him a drink. "Somebody find that fucker!" he yelled as he slam the shot glass down on the counter. Elan was pissed and called T-Mac. He was leery of Ramiero's disappearance. He felt he needed to move fast and put his plan into motion. Elan spoke with the nephew of El Chapo, whom promised him a vast amount of territory once he took over the empire. All he needed to do was persuade the other leaders to move against the familia. He had half that were willing, and the rest he knew would have to perish along with El Chapo.

"Thank you for the money Uncle T." the little girl said, giving T-Mac a huge and kiss.

"It's all good babygirl." he stood up. It was his niece's birthday and he stopped over to drop off his gifts for her. He looked up and saw a truck parked down the street. When he looked up again the truck had pulled off. He reached for his phone as it buzzed in his pocket. He knew it had to be Easy checking in on him. He hadn't heard from him all day.

"Where you at?" he asked without looking at the screen to see who it was calling.

"What do you mean?" Elan answered.

"Elan?" T-Mac asked, "What's up?" he said as he started to walk to his car.

"Time can wait any longer, I promised you this and now it is time." Elan said then hung up. T-Mac smiled as he put the phone back into his pocket. He sat in his car and texted Easy.

text: get'em

He waited to get his revenge for so long. It made him angry to even visit his family and see Jeremy's little sister on her birthday, without Jeremy being present. He felt it was all his fault, now it was time to pay it back the best way he could.

***

Several of El Chapo's guards were sent to find out what was going on. Six of them were in St. Louis and had been tailing me and T-Mac around lately. They were equipped with the latest technology for surveillance. They listened in on our conversations and recorded what they thought would be threatening to the familia.

The one they just received from T-Mac and Elan, was all they needed. They called El Chapo to inform him of the recent events. Chavez, the head guard, phoned Chapo.

"Boss it seems what Meno said is true." he said, peering at T-Mac driving off. "Elan has staged a silent war. He has gone against your wishes, and T-Mac is with him," Chavez added.

"And senor Ty?" El Chapo asked.

"Nothing, except his girl Shai has some wondering ties to Meno." Chavez said.

"Take care of this T-Mac and his family, and I will deal with Elan myself." El Chapo ordered.

Chavez looked at the others and nodded his head. They got out of the truck and headed in the direction of T-Mac sisters house where the party was taking place.

***

Shai didn't pack anything. She knew it wouldn't take long at all, Meno had called for her and she had to go. I rushed her to the Airport and watched her board the flight. I wanted to know what was going on. She looked so worried, but I had a feeling she was truthful about not knowing why she had to go. For a moment, it crossed my mind that I may never see her again. I didn't know what to think. To me it seemed like all this came right after she said she was pregnant.

I got back in the car and went home. I got in the door and laid on the couch. Someone knocked on the door. I thought it was the old man from next door. No one stopped through without notice, so when I open the door, and it was Karra. I was pissed.

"What the fuck is you doing here?" I yelled. "Bitch you got it fucked up now, coming to my mafuckin crib and shit!" I added. She was crying and looking scared, shaking and shit. "What the fuck is wrong with you?" I asked.

"They found Sasha." she said. "They found her body along the river by Alton."

If we were anywhere else, I would feel sympathetic, but she had crossed the line by coming to my house and I had to let her know that.

"Yeah, that's fucked up but you gotta get the fuck outta here!" I said. She looked up at the cold reaction I gave to hearing about her friend Sasha being found.

"Why, yo bitch here!" she screamed, placing a hand on the door, as if she was blocking me from closing it.

"N'all, but the ambulance gon be here if you don't get yo ass outta here!" I warned. I open the door and pushed her from the porch. I looked around to make sure there were no neighbors looking.

"So you love her more than me Tyrek! She means more to you than I do!" Karra yelled. She was getting louder, and I didn't want the neighbors calling the cops. I walked up on her and grabbed her by the arm.

"Love, Bitch, I don't love you! I told yo ass I care for your ass. What happened was a mistake. We cool, so now you need to quit tripping and take your ass to the crib. I'll be over there later and then we can talk," I said in a low tone, trying to keep the neighbors from hearing us arguing. She cried so hard, it looked like her eyes were melting into her cheeks. She walked off and got into her car. Before she closed the door, she looked at me.

"You gon love me," she said then pulled off. I looked around, mumbling to myself.

"Crazy muthafucka." I noticed the old man looking at me from his porch.

"Yeah, you better watch yo ass," he said then walked back inside.

***

"Here boy! Stop all that god damn whining!" T-Mac's sister yelled. She was serving the food at her daughter party. "Okay, now y'all drive safe." she said to the guests who were leaving. Her daughter ran up to her and almost knocked her over. "Girl what?"

"Mama, can I go over Tasha house tonight?" she begged. "Please!"

"Did her mother say it was okay?" she asked. The little girl shook her head yes. "Alright then, go ahead," T-Mac's neice ran into the house and got her things, then she quickly ran back and jumped into the car along with her friend.

"Now I gotta cleanup all this mess alone," her mom mumbled to herself.

She picked up the leftovers and took them inside. She was tired and dying to lay down. She paused for a minute; glancing around at all she had to clean.

"Damn," she mumbled, thinking *kitchen first*. Suddenly, she turned around and gasped at the sight of two men holding guns in their hands standing on the patio. "God, no please~" she yelled as she turned to run. The bullets ripped through her abdomen, and she fell to the floor. "God no ~" she pleaded as she watched the gunman walk up to her. He raised the gun to her head, and fired.

***

The flight to Phoenix was restless for Shai. She wondered why she had to visit in such short notice. Meno didn't pick her up from the Airport, he sent his guards. She was taken to an abandoned warehouse, and as she pulled up on the property, chills quickly shot through her body. Any abandoned meeting area for the Cartels meant someone was about to die. Being that Meno called her to come, she had no clue as to

192

what was going on. Meno greeted her as she got out of the vehicle. He hugged her tightly then escorted her inside. They walked down a long hallway into a boarded up room. Meno turned to Shai before entering the room. He waited until some of the guards were out of earshot, and then he spoke.

"You know I am not happy with your pregnancy." He said as he looked down to her stomach. Shai tensed up at his expression of disappointment. She had no clue as to what that would have to do with this meeting. She knew Meno was the one man she trusted not to ever harm her. She started to say something, but Meno cut her off. "How was the trip?" he asked softly, calming the tension.

Shai looked down and noticed specks of blood on his shirt. "It was okay," she said.

"Good, good, come with me."

She followed him into the room. Several men stood surrounding someone cuffed to a chair. He had black clothes covering his head. Blood dripped down the side of his neck, traveling along the chest cavity. He was bleeding badly.

"You may or may not remember him," Meno said, then nodded to one of the men.

He walked over to the guy and snatched the clothe off his head. Ramiero's head moved limply, jerking backwards as he sat there. The guard pushed his head up then forward. That's when it all came to Shai, she was looking at the man who shot her. Ramiero open his eyes. The light was blinding. He had been in total darkness for days. He fought to gain sight as he looked around the room. The images were blurry and he couldn't make them out. The guard behind him grabbed him by the hair, lifting his head up.

"What, what is this!" he yelled. The images began to clear. He noticed Meno. "Meno, what is this? I did nothing!" he shouted.

"Shut up!" Meno said, grabbing the gun from one of the armed guards. "Now you told me Elan is the one responsible, right." Meno asked. He looked at the two guys in the corner. They sat watching, witnesses for El Chapo.

"Yes, yes, he ordered the hit and he is planning your demise as well. He is plotting a rise in the familia." Ramiero explained. He begged

Meno not to take it out on his family. He promised to tell him everything if he would spare is son. He couldn't bare the pain anymore. Juarez had broken every finger and busted his knees. He finally agreed to tell after Meno threatened to visit his son's soccer team.

The two guys witnessing for El Chapo, nodded in approval and left the room. Meno open the door and let them exit.

"Shai you can have the pleasure." Meno said, handing her the gun. She looked at the gun. As she reached out and took it she felt the same excitement from the baby as the other day when they were counting the money. Although she waited for this revenge, she wanted her baby to have no pleasure in killing. She couldn't pass up this moment, so she raised the gun slowly, savoring every minute before pulling the trigger. She felt the baby moving inside of her. The baby was just as excited as she was.

She placed one hand on her stomach, she could feel the baby pressing against her hand. As she squeezed the trigger releasing several more shots into Ramiero's body, the baby jump to the sound of the gunshots. She exhaled, pleased with her revenge.

Meno looked at Shai with a wondering look. He knew that feeling, he saw it in her mother. She did it plenty of times when she was pregnant with Shai. He approached her and lowered the gun down out of her hand. Come with me now. Meno walked her out of the room.

"Why did you hold your belly?" Meno asked, "Was the baby bothering you, was it startled?"

"No, I'm okay," Shai assured. She didn't want to tell him her theory, she didn't want him to think she needed more therapy. Yet, no real answer, Meno felt compelled to tell her about her mother.

"You know your mother use to do the same thing when she was pregnant with you. I use to take her to the shooting range and you would get excited," Meno smiled. Shai stopped and looked up at him. She was relieved to know that she was carrying some of the same traits as her mother. She wanted to have a piece of her mother with her so bad, and she was happy that their habits were similar. Meno continued, "But that was only because she was excited, so the baby was also."

"Is that the reason why I'm like that?" she asked.

"Like what?" Meno wondered.

"A killer." Shai said in a low tone.

"You're not a killer Shai, you are very lovable and caring. A killer is Juarez, he doesn't have a family, no wife, nothing, just him and his skills. Luckily I am the only one he cares for, well besides you." Meno chuckled.

Shai wanted to know more about her mother during her pregnancy. She wanted to know what she ate and how she acted. She grew happier as she realized that her and her mother like similar things when they were pregnant. Meno and Shai got a bite to eat as they continued to talk. Meno grew proud at her choice of keeping the child. Though he didn't approve of me being the father, simply because I was in the business, Meno thought about the growing situation.

"It will only get worst now, so stay out of sight," Meno advised. "I have some business to finish, so Juarez will be taking you to the Airport." Meno explained. He leaned over to kiss her cheek. "I love you." Then he got up from the table. Shai watched as Meno left.

She wanted to have a normal family with him being there for holiday dinners and birthdays so badly, but that would never be an option. She grew worried about me, because she knew Meno would never feel comfortable around us together. As long as I was involved in the business, him and I would never be able to have a normal life.

Chapter 24

"Nigga, you gotta move." Rell insisted after I told him Karra popped up at the house. "That bitch is crazy."

"Hell yeah," I agreed, staring out of the passenger rearview.

It felt like someone was following us. I seen the same truck many times through out the week. Everytime I tried to see who was driving, but couldn't because of the heavily tinted windows. Maybe I was too paranoid. After counting that money, I knew I had to switch. Cooly warned me that soon a good run would only end in a hail of bullets or a sentence of life. Either way, your life was gonna end. I stayed staring at the world through my rearview, then Rell interrupted my thoughts.

"Chad and Boo said they rolling whenever we decide to take the trip." he said.

"Shit that's cool." I said without looking up from the mirror. I saw a car speed up behind us. I tensed up, realizing that it wasn't slowing down as it got closer. I reached for my gun. Rell noticed.

"Nigga what's up?" he said, watching my reaction. He reached for his gun also and began looking out the rearview.

I kept looking at the car. I didn't say anything until it swerved again over to the side of us. We were driving up Marybelle, a two lane road on the East side. It got closer, pulling up along side of the vehicle, then sped up. I tapped Rell and we both leaned the seat back, preparing to shoot. When I looked up once more before firing, I noticed a lady and her kids. She started blowing the horn and holding her middle finger up at me. I guess we were driving too slow.

"Dumb ass bitch, almost got her ass lit up with that stupid shit." Rell warned as we watched her swerve in front of another car. We kept looking at her for a while not noticing the real threat coming up from the rear of us until the gunshots erupted through the window, shattering the rear glass. Rell ducked and punched the gas. We swerved around the curves of Marybelle and was coming up on 59th Street. I reached down and picked up my gun that dropped to the floor and leaned out, to shoot back at the dark blue Yukon. I didn't have time to see who was driving or who was inside. They swerved back and forth behind us, ducking the bullets, so I tried to hit the windshield of the truck, but couldn't as they swerved out of view over to Rell's side and started to shoot through the back window.

  Rell hit the brakes, fishtailing and turning onto 59th. If we could get to State we can have Dirty or Fats come out and lite they asses up. The truck tried to turn onto 59th, swerving into a spin. The weight of the truck lifted two wheels off the pavement and slid straight into a pole, wrapping itself around it. We stopped at the sight of the accident. Rell threw the car in reverse, backing up quickly. I leaned out the window just incase someone got out and tried to run.

  We got out of the car and ran up on the truck to look inside. I didn't recognize anyone of the passengers that were in the backseat. The front passenger was in the windshield. It was hard for me to see who he was until I pushed him over. The body fell back limply as his face came into vision. \

  "Easy," I mumbled. His phone started to buzz and chirp. Rell yelled for me to hurry. I quickly searched his body for the phone.

  "What the fuck you doing? Ngga come on!" Rell yelled again. I tried to hurry before the distant sirens caught up to us. I grabbed the phone and looked at the screen. I saw a text.

  "That muthafucka got sis, bag that nigga and bring him to me."

  I ran and got into the ride, we pulled off. There were people taking cameraphone picks of the accident and us pulling off from the scene. We had to move quickly and get out of that vehicle we were in. After my heart stopped racing, I read the text again.

  "What the fuck is this nigga talking about?" I wondered.

  Shai had been blowing my phone up. I looked at all the missed calls. I didn't feel like calling her back right then, I wanted to take care of that nigga T-Mac. I didn't give a fuck about the peace treaty or the Cartels. This nigga had to die tonight. I used Easy's phone to my advantage and sent a text to him:

  "Meet me at the RiverFront on the south by the barges."

He bought into the text quickly. We punched it over to the Riverfront, so we would arrive before he did. I kept thinking about the text he sent accusing me of killing his sister. We parked in the shadow of the bridge and turned out the lights. Me and Rell puzzled over the thought of someone killing T-Mac's sister and only could come up with one conclusion, the Cartels. I remember Elan and Shai warning me of how they would target families. If they are targeting his family then why haven't they targeted mine? Or will I be next?

I saw headlights coming over the railroad tracks. All I could think about was being set up by someone. More headlights were coming, but they turned off onto another street. Another car came driving quickly, I knew that was T-Mac. We both leaned back into the seats, guns in hand and ready to kill. T-Mac pulled up along side of the ride and got out, unarmed. When he walked up on the car, he couldn't have looked inside first, he must have been too anxious. He just opened the passenger door. I hopped out with the gun pointed at him. He backed away surprisingly.

"What the fuck you thought, Easy was gon rock me Nigga!" I yelled. Rell got out and came around to the other side with his gun in hand also. T-Mac leaned his head closer as if to get better look at who was talking to him. He noticed it was me and lost it.

"Bitch ass nigga, you touched my family!" he screamed as he tried to charge me. I side stepped the charge and smacked him with the gun.

"Recognize who got the burna muthafucka," I said, watching as he fell to his knees. "I ain't have shit to do with that!" I aimed the gun at him. Feeling no reason to explain to him anymore. Before I could finish him off, two black Navigators drove up out of nowhere and came to a screeching halt. Rell backed up, waving his gun back and forth, waiting for a target to emerge from one of the trucks. I grabbed T-Mac from behind.

"Get yo ass up!" I fussed, placing the gun to the back of his head. It was the same Navigators I had been seeing around. I thought we were surrounded by cops.

The doors open and armed gunmen ran out aiming their assault rifles at all of us. Chavez walked from the passenger side of the truck,

"Put yout guns down." he ordered as he looked at Rell and Me. Rell looked at me, I gave him a quick glance also. They were 6 deep with assault rifles; we were good as dead if we didn't follow their demands. I didn't understand what was going on. We lowered the guns and I stepped away from T-Mac. Chavez looked at me.

"You can leave Senor Ty." I looked at T-Mac, whom was looking at me curiously.

"What, what's up!" T-Mac yelled. "What's up with this shit, you can call Elan," T-Mac was cut off.

"Elan is dead," Chavez said, assuringly. He walked over to our car and opened the door, "Good bye Senor Ty." he said, signaling for me to leave. "El Chapo sends you his blessings," he concluded as I got in then he closed the door. He turned to T-Mac. "Now for you Senor T-Mac. El Chapo sends you his wrath." As if on cue the other gunmen lifted their automatic guns and fired into T-Mac, ripping him open like paper. T-Mac fell slumped over his car and to the ground.

We pulled off quickly. I watched the gunfire through the rearview. I couldn't believe that a Cartel hit was placed on T-Mac and Elan. All I could answer to Rell was the trip that Shai took. Shai had to be the reason behind it all. Shai had just gotten home. Moni had picked her up from the airport. They walked in the house and sat the bags down in the kitchen. She looked around and noticed some of the things out of place. She called me, but I didn't answer. Moni followed her through the house as she pointed out more things in the house that were out of place.

"Girl, somebody been in here." Shai cautioned.

"What, you think somebody broke in?" Moni asked.

"N'all, it's something else." Shai said, picking up the vase that was knocked to the floor. She went inside of her room and found clothes on the floor. She went in the closet to find more torn down off the hangers. Moni went to search throughout the house for anything missing. Shai didn't feel right and went to get her gun.

Moni walked down into the basement. She went to check on her and Shai personal little stash they had hidden. She entered the area by the theater when she heard the noise from a movie playing. When she walked inside to look for the remote to turn it off, she was smacked across the back of her head with a gun. She fell to the floor, holding her head and squirming from the pain. She was smacked once more with the gun, knocking her unconscious. The intruder stared at her, then crept up the stairs. Shai searched for her gun, but it was gone. She grabbed her phone to call me again. My phone buzzed, causing me to jump. I quickly answered it when I noticed it was Shai calling.

"Hey." I answered.

"You alright?" she asked.

"Yeah, I need to talk to you ASAP." I said.

"Well I just got home, have you been here?" she asked. She was looking at the dresser and back at the closet. It looked like someone was looking for something.

"No why!"

"I think someone's been here."

"N'all, I been gone all day, what you mean someone has been there?" I asked. I looked over at Rell as he was concentrating on driving.

"Because it's shit that's been thrown around and I think somebody was here."

At the second mention of someone being there, it dawned on me. T-Mac thought I killed his family, what if he or the Cartels were after my spot.

"Who's there with you?" I asked.

"Moni, why?" she asked cautionly.

"Get out of the house, you and Moni leave and go downtown." I said then looked over at Rell, "Punch this muthafucka!" I looked back out the rearview, no one was behind us.

"What's going on Ty?" she asked.

Shai walked through the house to look for Moni. She peeked inside every room, turning the lights on. She continued walking slowly, creeping to silence her footsteps. She wanted to call out to Moni, but she didn't want to alert anyone if they were still in the house. I listened as she stayed on the line. "Oh, shit Moni!" She yelled, seeing Moni layed out on the floor. "Moni!" she yelled in a low tone again, trying get her conscious.

I looked at Rell. He was focused and still driving. I didn't want to tell him that Moni was hurt.

"Oh shit, here comes them boys!" Rell yelled. We had to highspeed it. I had to make it home.

"Nigga we bout a few exits from the crib, pull over and let me out!" I said determined to get home before something else happened. "Moni and Shai in trouble. Moni hurt Homie," I said sincerely. Rell gritted his teeth. He looked in the rearview, then to the road. Without looking at me he replied.

"Make it there and get'em nigga, I got this cop," he said, giving one glance then immediately bringing the car to a stop so I could get out.

I tried to grab everything, then got out running. The officer had jumped out his cruiser at the sight of me getting out and bolting from the scene. He drew his gun and ran to the back of his patrol car to take cover, pointing the gun at the car.

"Driver! Get out of the vehicle and put your hands on your head now!"

I could hear him screaming at Rell as I ran through the bushes along the side of the highway. Rell got out with his hands on his head. The officer slowly approached him and grabbed one arm, placing the cuffs on him. Rell thought about running also, but that would only have the cops pursuing us both. He wanted me to make it home. So he surrendered. The officer placed him in back of the patrol car. He then went to search the car and found a gun that was left behind. He came back and grabbed a camera, taking pictures of the gun then read Rell his rights.

I ran through the bushes quick as I could. All I was thinking about was getting to Shai. I was several blocks away, in an upscale community, black and running with a gun in hand. I didn't think I was going to make it at all.

Shai didn't want to leave Moni's side. She ran back up stairs and looked in the kitchen for a knife. She opened the drawer to grab one. When she turned around, she caught a blow to the head. She fell to the floor, the knife slid out of her hands and across the floor. She quickly looked up and ran out of the kitchen. As she ran, she heard a gunshot.

BONG.

Shai slammed into the wall, dodging the gun blast as the case shattered in front of her. She kept running as the intruder kept firing.

Bong-Bong.

Shai ran down the hall, hitting the banister as she tried to duck another bullet. She fell through the banister down the steps to the basement. She looked for Moni, but she was gone. Another shot went off, so she dove on the couch then rolled onto the floor. She looked up to see if they were coming, but she saw no one.

Moni got up at the sound of gunshots. She staggered to the theater seat in the front and reached under the seat to grab Rell's gun. She caught a quick glance of the intruder walking by and ducked behind a seat. She followed behind to see how many were there and it was only one.

Shai got up slowly and ran to the garage. She was hurting really bad and limping. Her stomach felt like it was one hundred pounds. She held her stomach, trying to feel for the baby. She couldn't feel the excitement she would normally felt when the baby heard the gunshots. She started to cry. She was sure she'd lost it.

BONG.

Shai ducked again from the gunshot, blasting the glass right in front of her, sending pieces flying into her arm. She turned around preparing to see the intruder and meet her end. She rolled over and seen Moni standing behind the intruder, aiming her next shot correctly at the intruder.

BONG! Moni shot again, this time she didn't miss. The intruder flew back onto the floor. Blood filled the carpet instantly. Moni reached down to see who it was, lifting up the mask. She did not recognize the person at all. Shai looked down, staring at the female. Her face was familiar, she realized it was Easy's girlfriend that was with him at the club that night.

A patrolman responding to the shots fired in the area, ran into the house at the sound of another gunshot going off.

"Police, drop the gun maam!" he yelled as he saw Moni standing there with the gun in hand. Moni dropped the gun, then she fell on the floor. Shai slumped down also. She was bleeding heavily from her vaginal area. The officer lowered his weapon and called for paramedics. After a series of questions to Moni and Shai, the paramedics wheeled them on the ambulance and took them to the Hospital. She asked one of the medics for her phone, she needed it so she could call me. She worried that I may be in trouble. She feared she would never see me again. The medic ran inside and got her phone. She instantly tried to call, but got no answer. She thought the worst. The medics warned her to calm down, she became irate. They had no choice but to sedate her.

I sat in the hedges of a neighbor's house watching as police cruisers and ambulance surrounded my home. I tried to convince myself that they were okay. I needed to get to a phone fast, so I could find out for sure. I didn't have anywhere to go. I needed a ride, so I started to run back the way I came. I got out to the main street and a car pulled up along side of me. The window rolled down.

"Youngster!" the old man from next door yelled. "What's going on?" he asked, unlocking the doors. I looked in the car, then got inside. I was breathing heavily,

"The cops and shit all over the house, what's going on, you know." I said trying to catch my breath.

"Shit, I don't know. I been out for a while and I came back to see sirens every fucking where. You need to go somewhere?" he asked.

"Let me use your phone." I asked. He gave me his phone and I tried calling Moni, then Shai. Both of the phones went straight to voicemail. I kept trying and still got no answer. "Fuck!" I yelled. "Just chill until they leave." I said, leaning the seat back to watch the house.

We parked up the street until they cleared the scene. Before going into the house, the old man looked around to make sure it was clear. We pulled up in his driveway, then walked over into the house. It was fucked up. I could see the holes in the walls from gunshots and the upstairs banister broken like someone had fallen through it. I closed my eyes imagining what happened. I tried to hold back tears but couldn't. I walked over and observed the blood on the floor. It was two seperate spots next to eachother. I thought one was Moni's and the other was Shai's. I clinched my teeth in anger.

I went upstairs to the bedroom to look around and get some of my things. When I came back down the old man was gone and a Mexican stood in the doorway. I froze up, feeling for my pistol. I was caught empty handed, I held my hands to the side. I saw the old man creep from behind the door putting a dillinger to the Mexican head.

"You know this muthafucka Youngster?" he said, looking at the Mexican like he was hoping he would make a move. The Mexican looked at the old man. Then several infer red lasers came shining through the house, pointing right at the old man chest and head. "God damn!" the old man said, dropping the gun. The Mexican stepped forward towards me.

"If so much wouldn't have taken place already, your old friend here would be dead." he said. I recognized him from the riverfront.

"What you do to my people?" I asked angrily. He grinned at my expression.

"We had nothing to do here." he answered. "The Boss would like for you to come with us to meet him." he ordered. "There's no need to pack." he added, walking out the door. I followed him out to the truck. Two guys got out and opened the door for me and I got in. The last thing I saw was the old man standing in the doorway of my home, staring at me as we drove off.

-The End-

Insert from Affiliated Pt. 2
'Black Pablo'

Silence, that's all it was during the flight. We were on a private jet. The guys walked around silently packing the guns up inside of luggage. They looked like machines, seals or army men waiting to be given an order. I didn't want to say anything to them, although I wanted to know where I was going. After hours in the air, I heard a voice from the radio, saying that we were approaching Mexico air.

"Mexico?" I said to myself. All the while I thought about Shai, Moni, and Rell. I had time to go over everything, to try and figure it all out. I thought hard about who could have been at the house. Karra crossed my mind. I thought about T—Mac hit, it must've been a result of Elan placing a hit on Shai. Shai had to inform Meno. The peace was broken and that was a violation of the Cartels, but why would he want me. I was sure I was on my way to a grave in Mexico. Then again, like Chavez said if El Chapo wanted me dead, I would be.

The plane was landing and fear shot through my mind. I tried to prepare myself for what was to come. So many stories of the Boss, so many men died in his presence. Why would a small level nigga like me be in the presence of a real life Kingpin.

"Get up," one of the men said to me. He waved me towards the door. We landed in Mazatlan, Sinaloa, Mexico. Where El Chapo lived. I exited the plane and walked down the steps. Two G55 Benz trucks awaited on the tarmac. The drivers got out and open the doors and we all got inside. I sat in the back as the tow guards in front spoke spanish. They were talking about me.

They were saying, "The american looks dangerous, I wonder is he as deadly as he looks." They laughed.

We traveled through hills and valleys until we reached the compound. It looked like we were in the middle of a jungle. The gates open and we drove pass a crew of armed gunmen, along a dirt road passing two buildings before reaching the main house. It was huge and one would have to have an army to try and come in here.

"Hello, Senor Ty," a slim man greeted me, "The Boss is waiting for you." he waved for me to follow him. He whistled to the other men to stop standing around.

They walked off quickly to secure their areas. I was still unable to speak. I didn't know what was about to happen. Every turn I prepared myself for the worst. I never witnessed this type of shit, first hand, you only seen this in the movies. To be a regular street hustler is one thang, but to be a druglord is a whole other part of the game.

I wasn't rehearsing nothing in my mind, whatever happen was going to happen. We walked through the courtyard outside of the house over to a building that sat at the bottom of a hill. A couple of guards stood out front. They open the door as we approached. The slim guy walked behind me as Chavez stepped in first.

I hesitated, "After you," he said holding out his hand. I stepped in slowly, then was pushed by one of the guards. The guard gave a stern look, then close the door.

"Keep walking," the slim guy insisted. I was ready for my fate. If it was going to happen, there was no escaping anyway. I had a nice run, no regrets. As I entered the room, I noticed a tall muscular fellow and another short stocky guy standing by a big hole in the wall. The hole in the wall was dark and about the size of a basketball.

"Tyrek?" the short stocky guy asked, while extending his hand. I shook his hand. He held a menacing look on his face, with a mean demeanor, he looked dangerous. "You have created a problem for me, and within my organization. A problem that I must exterminate." he paused looking at me. "See, I hate problems. I have too many of them and when a person creates more for me, then that is another problem in itself." He stepped close to me, "You have given me problems and I hate problems, I hate rats also." He paused again to search my face for a expression of guilt. I wasn't giving any sign. He walked off and picked up a machete from the corner. I heard a door slam nearby. It sounded like it came from the other side of the wall.

"With rats, I wait patiently." he clutched the machete with two hands as if he was getting ready to chop down on a branch. "Patiently until the rat sticks his head out of the hole." he said. I heard scuffling and screaming on the other side of the wall, then a man head was forced threw the hole. El Chapo lifted the machete and swung down chopping through the man neck, like butter. His head rolled down to my feet. I looked down at the familiar face. He was one of Elan's guards.

"I am still exterminating because of you." El Chapo said flipping the machete out of his hands like it was just a table knife. He kicked the head out of his way into the corner as he walked up to me. "You created this problem, so why should I take care of your mess. I got rid of your problem so you will get rid of mine." he said walking pass me, heading out the door. The big dude pointed for me to follow.

We walked back up the hill into the house. A guard brought a towel to El Chapo and pulled a chair out from the table allowing him to take a seat. He wiped his face and hands then sat down.

"I have a nephew in Chicago, he is a pain. Cost me millions. So since he is my sister child, no one in the familia can harm him. So you will." he said while firing up a cigar. I nodded my head. I could tell this was a order, not a option. It was nothing I could say. "In return you will no longer deal with Meno, you will deal with me, though not directly, but through Chavez. Kilos of Cocaine, herion, or tons of mota, it's your choice." he looked up at me after dumping his ashes. "Well?" he asked impatiently.

I thought about the deal, which will put me in this shit for life. I was fed up with being forced into situations with them and wanted to let him know how I felt. I knew saying the wrong thing would get me a trip down to the hole in the wall, so I was careful with my words.

"Look, El Chapo, I'm saying this with the upmost respect. I'm not trying to get tied up in something I can't get out of." I said.

He looked at me for a moment, then burst out in laughter. The others began laughing also.

"Senor, that is too late." he said, his face then grew serious. "You will not and cannot leave, except through death. That is out!" he hissed as he leaned across the table. I looked at the other guards, then back at him. "Believe me Senor Ty, there are many benefits to this. We have to much money and political influence to go to jail, the rats die, and the judges get paid well. You are among the elite of the underworld. And plus if you fuck up, you don't die, just your family." he laughed. I thought to myself, this muthafucka is crazy.

I smiled, "That's funny?"

"No, it's not funny," he grew serious again, "What is funny is you, thinking this is a game. This is a business, and you have just

become an executive, deal with your position. Now I will arrange two tons of mota, two hundred kilos, one hundred cocaine and one hundred herion. Every month. Chavez will notify you for the money and the shipments will be delivered by plane and 18—wheeler. I have
a warehouse in the Midwest, you will be responsible for unloading the trailer and securing the product." he said, "Payments will be two point five million a month, non—negotiable. By the time you get home the first shipment will be there already." he added.

"And when will I be going home?" I asked while trying to figure out the numbers in my head. The deal was too sweet, nobody could fuck that up. He waved at one of the guards.

"Soon." he said to me then turning to the guard. "Take Senor Ty to Chavez and see to it he has a good time."

Chavez walked me through the mansion. He gave me a brief tour, then escorted me to a room that I would be staying in. "If you need anything, just ask?" Chavez said.

"Where's the phone?" I asked.

"Anything but that, no calls from here." Chavez said while leaving the room.

I laid down and put my hands behind my head. Looking around the room, it was elegantly decorated with a balcony. The silk drapes hung to the floor. The ceilings were high and had murals painted on them. I watched the drapes blow from side to side as the wind blew in. I got up and stood on the balcony. From my room I could see the building with the hole in the wall. I watched for a while and listened to the gunshots.

Shortly afterwards two men emerged from the building dragging bodies and tossing them aside. They looked like construction workers throwing trash out a building. I walked back into the room and layed back down. I listened to the shooting for another minute or so before it stopped, then I drifted off to sleep.

I awoke to a cart being rolled into the room. An elder woman sat the trays down on the table out on the balcony. She nodded her head then left the room. I got up and walked out to the table to get a peek at the food she brought. I lifted the stainless covers from off the plates and looked at the dish. It was a Mexican steak dish, Chuleton. A T—bone steak with Mexican sauce, along with a bottle of champagne and pitcher of water. I sat down and tried to eat, it was delicious but I couldn't enjoy it. I had no appetite. I kept thinking about Rell, Shai, and Moni. I wondered what about Chad and Boo, and how they must be going crazy right now. Chavez entered the room and walked over to the balcony, where I sat.

"Senor, get ready, we go to have a drink." he said sitting down at the table. He noticed I didn't touch the food, "Not much of an appetite?" he added.

"I'm cool." I said. He just looked at me with a curious look.

"Let's take a ride." he said, getting up from the table.

***

Rell had been in the County Jail for 2 days. He was charged with possession of a firearm, and aiding and abetting a criminal. It took him a while to get in touch with his lawyer. He wondered why Ty didn't come and get him, he thought he didn't make it, it was too late. Rell had the feeling that he lost every one, but he would have to find out if it's true, and if he did, whoever was responsible, would definitely pay. Moni didn't answer her phone, he was on edge. He got into several fights while he was inside the dorms. Others in the blocks kept bitching about him using the phones so much. The first day, a guy tried him and end up getting beat with the phone. Rell snatched the receiver from the wall and almost beat him to death. If the dude wasn't such a asshole to the cops, they would have charged Rell with assault. They threw him in segregation for the time being. He tried calling his lawyer again, until he finally got in touch with him. By that time he was pissed. The lawyer was paid fifty thousand on a retainer up front for any trouble they might come across. So when Rell contacted him, he came quickly.

The lawyer bonded him out. Rell waited till they were outside of the police station, then hit the lawyer in the stomach. The lawyer bent over holding his stomach, trying not to throw up the lunch he had earlier. Rell bent down to his ear. "Listen mafucka, I didn't pay you to fuck off while I sit in jail," Rell warned, pushing him in the face and walked to the car, "hurry up and take me to get a rental." he ordered.

Shai got up from the bed. She hated the smell of Hospitals. She had been running to the bathroom all day, vomitting. She came back in the room and sat down on the bed. Moni sat in a chair in the corner. She had stitches on the side of her head, from the blow the intruder landed with the gun. "You hear anything yet?"

Shai asked, hoping that Ty would have called. She leaned over the bed to grab the phone.

"N'all, the phone been dead, I just got a charger." Moni said, turning over to her side. She had been thinking about Rell and trying to call him. She ruled out death and prayed that he was okay. She never realized how much she cared for him until now. Shai dialed Meno, she needed to know what was going on. Meno picked up,

"Hello?" he answered. Shai could hear some speaking in the background. She tried to make out what they were talking about but couldn't.

"Meno?" she said, wondering was he on the phone talking to her or others.

"Shai, what, I mean how are you doing?" Meno said surprisingly.

"What is going on? Ty is missing and we can't find him at all," she sighed.

Meno paused to think of what to say. He knew this was his chance to save his daughter and make her forget about Tyrek. He knew where Ty was and knew that if Ty and her got back together that she would be in grave danger and it would be nothing he could do about it.

"Shai, listen, you must listen to me carefully. You are in danger, after I get off the phone you must throw it away. Stay off this phone, get another one."

Meno paused, he started to act out his sorrow for her, "Everything you know of Ty is dead." Meno added.

"No!" Shai yelled into the phone. She gripped the sheets tightly, anger ran threw her blood like a jolt of electricity.

"Yes," Meno said, "You must not surface like before, you are in danger, you and Moni." Meno stopped to catch Shai attention. "Are you listening?" he asked.

"You and Moni will disappear. When you get another phone call me and we will keep in touch." Meno waited for her to speak. Shai held the phone quietly. "I'm sorry my Shai." Meno added.

"Shai tears flowed enough to tell Moni what happen without speaking. Moni just bowed her head in her legs and cried. By the time Rell reached his lawyer to make bond and get to a phone. Shai had soaked up her tears with the sheets, put her clothes on turned the phone off and dumped it in the Hospital trashcan, then left.

About the Author

Ra Tem Jones Sr., was born in St. Louis, Missouri, but raised in East St. Louis, Illinois. He was very curious at a young age about his environment and the things that were going on. As he got older, he explored many different areas of his talents trying to find his way in society. His artistic nature has led him to win contest and awards in drawing and painting. He was also drafted into a summer art course in his adolescent years. Becoming an artist of music shortly thereafter, he wrote and performed music on stage. Living in the inner city he became familiar with the environment and his curiosity led him to become a product of his environment. Fighting against the culture of East St. Louis, he began to write literary novels realizing he had another talent available for him to explore. He began to study the skill and used his imagination to write numerous novels.

We Help You Self-Publish Your Book
The Big Flex Teaser $799.00
70 page books or less ONLY
NO Exceptions!
1 free proof of novel before print, 1 Book Cover, 1 Year Free Subscription to Mink Magazine,100 Books, 2 month Ad in Mink / 1 CD with novel set in word & PDF format. **Order our Self-Publishing Guide On a Value Meal Budget Today for $11.95**

Best Wishes,

Crystal Perkins-Stell, MHR
Essence Magazine Bestseller
CEO/ Founder Crystell Publications
 No One Can Beat Our Prices!
PO BOX 8044 / Edmond – OK 73083
(405) 414-3991

Our competitor's Cheapest Plans- AuthorHouse Legacy Plan $899.00-10 books Xilibris Professional Plan $1099.00 11 books ,   iUniverse Premier Plan $1099.00 – 10 books

Big Flex E-Book – 695.00
Scan Typeset, Proof, Bk Cover, Masters, ISBN, E-Book Upload, Ad in Mink,

Option A $1399.00	Option B $1299.00	Option C $1199.00
2 Proofs –CP & Printer	2 Proofs –CP & Printer	2 Proofs –CP & Printer
Book Cover/	Book Cover	Book Cover
ISBN #	ISBN #	ISBN #
100 Books	100 Books	100 Books
Regenerate E-File Typeset/ 8 hrs Consultation	Regenerate E-File Typeset/ 8hrs Consultation	Regenerate E-File Typeset / 8hrs Consultation
1 CD with novel in Word & PDF format	1 CD with novel in Word & PDF format	1 CD with novel in Word & PDF format
Correspondence	Correspondence	Correspondence
1 Year Subscription to Mink Magazine	1 Year Subscription to Mink Magazine	1 Year Subscription to Mink Magazine

We Offer Affordable Assistance & Payment Plans
No more paying Vanity Presses $8 to $10 per book! We Give You Books @ Cost. **We Offer Editing For An Extra Fee- If Waved, We Print What You Submit!** These titles are done by self-published authors. They are not published by nor signed to Crystell Publications.

Quick Order Form

Please send the following book(s):

StreetLink Publishing
PO Box 24270
Belleville, Il. 62223

____ AFFILIATED MAFIA MEXICANA $12.99 plus 3.99 Shipping

Shipping To:

Name:_____

Address:_____

City:_____State:_____Zip:_____